SAVING HER SHADOW

SAVING HER SHADOW

LUTISHIA LOVELY

THORNDIKE PRESS
A part of Gale, a Cengage Company

Copyright © 2020 by Lutishia Lovely.
Thorndike Press, a part of Gale, a Cengage Company.

Thorndike Press® Large Print African-American.
The text of this Large Print edition is unabridged.
Other aspects of the book may vary from the original edition.
Set in 16 pt. Plantin.

LIBRARY OF CONGRESS CIP DATA ON FILE.
CATALOGUING IN PUBLICATION FOR THIS BOOK
IS AVAILABLE FROM THE LIBRARY OF CONGRESS

ISBN-13: 978-1-4328-7988-4 (hardcover alk. paper)

Published in 2020 by arrangement with Dafina Books, an imprint of Kensington Publishing Corp.

Printed in Mexico
Print Number: 02   Print Year: 2020

Hey Lovelies!

I'm so excited to bring you *Saving Her Shadow*, the first Lutishia Lovely standalone *ever*! Yep, more than a decade and twenty books since debuting with *Sex in the Sanctuary*, I have written *Shadow* to stand all by her lonesome. Can you believe?

There were several points of inspiration for this story line, mostly television shows I've watched and found fascinating. At the top of the list was *Leah Remini: Scientology and the Aftermath*, found while idly scrolling through the channels for something interesting to watch. What she reveals in this docuseries is incredible. On one hand I found it hard to believe that anyone could be so completely brainwashed. On the other, as a preacher's kid who spent a large part of my life in church, I knew exactly how it could happen — had witnessed it firsthand. The instructions that were followed, the rules they believed. The punishments accepted when a member was found to have done "wrong." I could go on. One of her shows veered from Scientology and dealt with another religion whose followers had sent dozens of letters asking her to report on their denomination, Jehovah's Witnesses. While slightly more familiar with this religion, I was still taken aback by the stories. I sympathized with the family members who'd been shunned, and cried for the children who'd died rather than seek medical treatment and were later touted during a national meeting as martyrs for God! Watching that episode reminded me of the phone call I'd received last year from a close friend, who'd just left the hospital after visiting a relative whose religion didn't allow blood transfusions. The relative had had surgery and was rapidly losing blood. If they lost another pint, my friend was told, the patient would die. They chose to leave the hospital rather than witness that outcome. Unlike those child "martyrs," the bleeding stopped. My friend's relative lived. Somewhere between Leah and stories on Warren Jeffs, hit shows like *Escaping Polygamy* and my overactive imagination, this story was born.

Lest someone from these faiths read this and are offended, I mean no disrespect. Everyone is free to follow who/what they choose. There are several sides to every story. This one reveals the workings of a fictitious family, and highlights the power of love, the biggest and best religion of all!

Combined with my alter egos, this is my thirty-third book for Kensington Publishing, thirty-two of which have been edited by the incomparable Selena James, who I consider a sister-in-write. She is the midwife to my book babies and also doubles as a therapist, cheerleader, and EST (emergency scribe technician)! Thank you, Selena, for everything! This journey is made more amazing with you along for the ride. Rebecca Cremonese is a master production editor who dresses many of my book babies on their way to the shelf, including this one. Thank you for not blowing a gasket when minor changes and typo corrections were, well, not so minor. I still owe you dinner . . . and drinks! Barbara Brown, I have two words for this cover. Stun. Ning. It quickly became one of my all-time favorites and made me work to ensure that the content inside equaled its brilliance. Thank you for such great work. There are more noteworthy members of the Kensington village helping to raise my literary children, but in trying to name them all I might leave someone out so . . . THANKS EVERYBODY!!! I do want to give a shout-out to Steven (Zacharius) the Great, who pretends (or actually) can't tell me from Zuri. It's all in the shades.

Lovelies, most of you already know you're the wind beneath my writer wings. From those who've been with me since my first book, to the ones for whom this is their first

7

Lovely novel, THANK. YOU. Your support means more than those two words can convey or this writer can say. If I begin to name names, again, I will leave someone out, but those long-time loyal lovelies know who they are, and know they are truly appreciated. LOVE YOU BUNCHES!

At some numerology chart positions, thirty-three is considered a master number. It is a number representing family, harmony, idealism, and creative self-expression. In that way, *Saving Her Shadow* is the perfect thirty-third offering in my Kensington partnership, as these qualities are highlighted throughout Raina's story. Ironically, or not, they also very much embody who I am and what I represent, a creative artist and light worker, using my gift to educate, enlighten, inspire and entertain, and to make the world a brighter place. Thank you for reading. I hope you enjoy. Until next time . . . keep shining!

CHAPTER 1

It was early afternoon in Lucent Rising. The sun was bright, the music was loud, and Raina Reed danced like moves were money and she was set on getting rich. Her body, lithe and compact, twisted and turned to the beat of the hip-hop magic pouring out of the Bluetooth Jam speaker, one of several pieces of contraband not allowed in the home, stuff she kept tucked away and hidden from view until rare moments like this when she was alone, could take off the mask, and let the real Raina come out and play.

This is how we do it!

Raina pointed to her reflection in the mirror while trying to twerk, an attempt she'd be the first to admit was pitiful at best. She continued, undaunted. Arms flailed. Shoulders popped. Booty moved to the beat — pushed on the one, pulled on the two. Clapping her hands, she changed the rhythm.

Her head went one way, hips another —
Bam! Pow! — from side to side, paying
respectable homage to the first dance her
mother, Jennifer, taught her, the classic cab-
bage patch. Shoulder-length curls freed
from the band that usually held them tame
now bounced to the beat, shaken into a sort
of drunken afro, a halo of black hair around
her shoulders. Energetic, wild, fully defiant
— just like her.

Leaving the space in front of the mirror,
she danced around the room with abandon.
The Montell Jordan anthem gave way to
Destiny's Child, Will got jiggy with it, and
the Fugees' Lauryn Hill talked about "that
thang." The music made her happy, trans-
porting Raina back to a time when it was
just her and Jennifer living in Kansas City
with a variety of music a constant backdrop
to their lives. Mornings, hip-hop or R & B.
Evenings, jazz or pop. Saturday cleaning,
definitely old-school, the stuff Raina's
grandmother had played when Jennifer was
little — Motown, Stax, the sounds of Philly.
On Sunday a little food for the soul, courtesy of Kirk or Fred or a sister named Clark.
They had a small, two-bedroom apartment
near the historic Eighteenth and Vine dis-
trict where sometimes on sultry summer
nights, when the windows were up and

10

nearby club doors were open, and her mother was supplementing her income as an administrative assistant by waiting tables at the Riff, jazz notes pierced the air, poured into Raina's small bedroom and bounced on the sheets. On those nights she imagined the musician to be her father, a sax man who'd left when she was five years old and whom she barely remembered, the one who, until Jennifer married her stepdad, Raina hoped would swoop in as swiftly as he flew out, and rescue them from a humdrum life, take her and Jennifer to live in California, where she'd heard he resided, next door to the prince of Bel Air. There was little extra money but lots of love and even more laughter, when the only light she thought about came from a bulb or the sun. Back then, the word *illumination* meant lighting up a room or gaining a new understanding, not being a part of an insular organization with conservative, even controversial views that made most of that which used to bring joy to her life, stuff she should no longer do. Like watching certain TV shows. Wearing jewelry, makeup, and fly clothes. Letting her hair hang loose and free. And, of course, dancing. Secular music was forbidden not only in the Reed home, but in the entire subdivision, hundreds of acres owned by the church. To Raina's benefit, the cultlike religious organization, of which her parents were staunch members and supporters, had a private school that only went up to the sixth grade. Those older were either home-schooled or went to the town's public school, Chippewa High. An angel in the form of her grandmother Lorraine, for whom she was named, made sure Raina was a part of the latter crowd. Going to a regular school allowed Raina the chance to hear and enjoy today's contemporary music and be more like a "normal" teen. She liked the new sounds well enough. Had a few favorites. But her mother's old-school? That stuff from the nineties? It was the total feel-good formula to brighten any mood, including the one Raina had felt just before coming home. She bopped over to the stereo, increased the volume, danced in front of a full-length mirror, and imagined herself a video queen.

"Sister!"

Raina jumped. Not a dance move, but the kind that preceded having her epidermis appear on the floor, which, if jumping out of one's skin was literally possible, would have just occurred. A layer of cocoa cuteness would be on the carpet, next to the heart that threatened to jump from Raina's chest.

In one fluid movement she crossed the room and tapped a key on the laptop. The music stopped, replaced by a silence that reverberated around the room.

"Shadow! You scared the crap out of me!"

To almost everyone else Abigail Denise Reed was Abby, but to Raina, when the two were alone, she was Shadow, the baby who'd followed her every movement since learning to crawl. The day she was born, then ten-year-old Raina dumped her favorite career Barbie for a live, half-sister doll. Two years later for Raina, and occasionally Jennifer, Abby became Shadow. Despite the ten-year age difference between the siblings, the love ran deep and created a close, impenetrable bond.

"Stop cursing, sister."

"*Crap* isn't cursing," Raina patiently explained. "Now if I'd said shi . . ."

Abby gasped. Raina laughed.

"What do you mean sneaking up on me like that?"

"I knocked, but . . ." Abby's eyes slid pointedly from Raina to the now silent laptop and back, wordlessly conveying why her taps hadn't been heard.

Raina missed the message. Her eyes weren't fixed on Abby but on the hallway behind her, even as she strained to listen for an opening door. Her parents had a knack for smelling trouble long after the aroma of action had happened. For more than one reason, seeing either her mom or stepdad right now would not be good.

"Are they here?" Raina mouthed, while knowing that if they were her stepdad would have already barged into the room, made like a thundercloud and rained on her private party of one.

Abby shook her head. "Why are you dancing? You know it's forbidden. Where are your clothes? And look at your hair!"

"Um, where is my mama because you aren't her?" Raina offered up major attitude but, knowing one or both of her parents would be home soon, walked into the closet and retrieved the more Illumination-appropriate baby-blue maxi dress she'd worn to school. She slipped it over the renegade tee and booty shorts. "How'd you get home?"

"Ms. Stone brought me."

At the mention of Abby's third grade teacher, Raina's brow furrowed of its own accord. At twenty-five, Lucy was only seven years older than Raina but lived and breathed the organization's teachings with the judgment and fervor of someone three times her age. She'd snitched on Raina

14

three years ago when Raina had seen her at the high school, mistaken her as "one of the girls" and showed her a social media post about the Kardashians. Reality TV was considered unsanctioned viewing, and muted — not allowed — as was much of popular culture phenomena. Lucy snitched. Raina got grounded and was made to "go deep," a multi-week deprogramming process that had cost her parents almost two thousand dollars. During those sessions the religion's rules, tenets, and values were reinforced. Anyone suspected of being "dimmed" by exposure to negative influences outside their church culture — unsanctioned music, television, movies, video games, books, and the like — was moved into a property owned by the church and run by licensed clergy, isolated from family and friends, and reilluminated. There were dozens of common activities that were forbidden, against the rules. Raina had broken half a dozen in less than ten minutes, just by being herself.

"Mother and Father aren't here, Shadow. Why are you over there looking terrified?" Raina walked over to the window, tilted the blinds to take in the driveway and the street beyond it, then hit a set of keys on the computer. The room felt happy once again, this time courtesy of a guy named Pharell. "Come on, Shadow! Let's move!"

Raina began to dance again while Abby stayed glued to the doorjamb. Her thick blondish-brown braids waved stoically with each adamant shake of her head. "We're not supposed to do that, sister. Dancing makes us dim. Jamie got caught watching TV and has to go deep for a month."

Raina took in her sister's worried expression and turned off the music once again. There was no easy winning-over that level of fear, the kind instilled in organization members, especially younger ones like Abby and her grade-school classmates, who'd been taught privately at the local organization's Illumination Academy since their preschool years. In the past, listening and dancing to their mother's music was one of many secrets the two sisters had shared. Raina sadly realized that as her sister got older, there would probably be fewer secrets between them.

After turning off the music, Raina returned the forbidden Bluetooth to its shoebox hiding place in the closet. She retrieved a brush and hair tie from their Jack and Jill bathroom, plopped onto her bed, and began subduing her wild mane, returning it to the coiled ponytail the world saw.

"Come here, kiddo, and tell me about your day."

Abby pushed off the doorjamb to join her on the bed. Only then did Raina notice her sluggish movements and slightly flushed skin. She reached out and placed a hand on her forehead.

"Shadow, you're burning up!"

"Ms. Stone says I'm hot because I got mad at Jamie for getting his parents in trouble. She said that glow children controlled their emotions and that I'd feel better after appealing for healing."

As far as Raina was concerned, Lucy Stone could take her prescription for feeling better and go straight to hell. Abby had claimed being tired the night before and had gone to bed early. And now on top of being tired she felt warm to the touch? Raina wasn't buying what Lucy was selling. Something else was going on. Raina doubted reciting mantras would fix it.

"I don't think you're hot because you're angry, Shadow. I think you have a fever because you're sick."

"Glows don't get that way, Raina. Stop saying that word!"

Raina fought back a side-eye. Like if one didn't say the word *sick* then it would never happen. It was just another ice cube of

17

bullshit that she increasingly found floating in the organization's philosophical Kool-Aid. It wasn't Abby's fault that she drank from the only cup of knowledge she'd ever been offered. But after four years of interacting with people taught to be dim, germy, and unsanctioned, Raina no longer sipped out of that glass.

"Teacher gave me some vitamin juice."

"Did it help?"

"A little."

"Are you really feeling better? Seriously, Shadow, you can tell me the truth."

"I'm getting better," Abby repeated, though the opposite message came through her eyes. "In knowing, I'm glowing, like the sun."

Raina maintained a look that belied the chagrin she often felt toward her family's religion. Along with their conservative views on personal appearance, the arts, and roles in marriage, the church required upwards of thirty percent of a member's income through tithes and mandatory, ongoing illumination and enlightenment courses. They believed anyone outside of the religion was obscure, literally a dimwit, and that interacting with such would lessen one's own light. They considered stars to be angels, communicated with extraterrestrials, and held to the teachings that after an end-time explosion they'd be the foundation for a new earth. For this reason, they kept to themselves as much as possible and forbade personal relationships or marriage, intermixing, with the outside. Only after Raina's mother Jennifer joined the Nation did her stepfather Ken ask her out. They shunned modern medicine and its procedures, believing all sickness was mental and could be cured through their trained specialists with herbs, vitamins, stardust, mantras, or an energy machine designed by the church's founder. Raina was all for positive thinking and believed in the power of words. But she also trusted the power of Advil and remembered how quickly she and her mom used to get better before joining a group where even over-the-counter cures were banned.

Turning onto her stomach, Raina looked at her sister, then reached out for the person she loved more than her own life.

"Come here, sister," she whispered, enveloping Abby into a giant bear hug. "Let's glow together, okay?"

Raina began reciting the healing-mind mantra. "I see you better."

"I see me better," Abby repeated.

"Good health you know."

"Good health I know."

19

"Mind over matter. My body glows."

Abby repeated the words after her sister half a dozen times. Raina checked Abby's forehead again and was sure she had a fever of at least a hundred degrees. Hoping to will some life into her sister's lethargic presence, she began the mantra again, this time with a snap of her fingers and in a funky, singsong style.

"Raina!" Abby's giggle lit up Raina's heart. "We can't say it like that!"

"Why not? Music isn't bad, Shadow. Only the words placed in rhythms that are not what we believe."

Abby looked doubtful.

"Okay, I've got an idea. What about to the tune of . . . hmm, I dunno . . . 'Old McDonald,' maybe?"

Abby laughed again. "No! It'll sound stupid!"

"I agree. But it's a melody that's sanctioned. Plus, it will be fun. Come on."

Raina began the chant again, drumming on the bedspread as their voices grew louder.

"Mind over matter. My body G-L-Ohs!"

Soon they were both off the bed and on the floor, clapping, foot-tapping, and half singing, half rapping to the beat. Within minutes anyone watching wouldn't have known whether Abby actually began to feel better or was having so much fun she forgot to be sick. Either way, when they heard the sound of a car pulling into the driveway, Raina ran to turn off the music. Abby's shoulders fell, along with her smile. There was no written rule that happiness was forbidden. But most times when their father, Ken, was present, it was not allowed.

CHAPTER 2

By the time the sound of a closing garage door drifted upstairs, the Reed girls presented the perfect glow tableau. Abby was in her bedroom indulging in an approved children's pastime, putting together a jigsaw puzzle. Raina was seated at her study desk, working on a science assignment. Jennifer greeted each of them as she passed their rooms on her way to the master suite. Raina's stepfather and Abby's father, Ken, had gone directly into his study, as usual, leaving communication for the dining room, where forty-five minutes later they were called down to dinner.

"Good evening again, Mother," Raina said, using the formal language encouraged by the religion. "May I help?"

"You may bring in the salad," Jennifer replied. "There are two types of dressing in matching carafes. Abby, did you wash your hands?"

"Yes, Mother," Abby replied.

She coughed into circled fingers and earned a stern look from her dad, who walked in at that moment.

"Sorry, Father," Abby said softly.

"Hello, Father," Raina said on her way to the kitchen. Even eight years later she was struck with the difference in households she'd occupied, the pre- and post–Ken Reed eras. Reaching for the colorful salad in a crystal bowl, she recalled the good old days when it was okay, natural even, to cough, sneeze, belch, fart, without apology. They excused themselves. There were manners in place after all. But Raina would never get used to the appeasing silence, the formal existence that Ken preferred, or the deference this new mother, the one Jennifer had become over the past eight years, chose to pay him.

Conversation was limited as plates were filled and drinks were poured. Once done, and only after Ken had taken the first bite of a medium-rare steak being served with a baker and fresh green beans, did the rest of the table begin eating.

"I saw you working on the puzzle, Abby," Jennifer said. "How is it coming along?"

"I almost have the whole frame put together," Abby responded. "Now I'm separating the pieces for the rainbow, fish, and flowers. The water is going to be the hardest part. So much blue."

"What is the name of this puzzle, honey?" Ken asked.

The question had been posed to Abby, but Jennifer answered. "Amazing nature, and it truly is. It was one of several new puzzles being sold in the bookstore. This one has five hundred pieces. Abby's most challenging yet!"

"What are you working on, Raina?"

"A science project for school."

A slight frown creased Ken's handsome brow. At fifty years old his looks had matured like a fine wine. Hints of silver now painted his chestnut temples, making his uniquely gray eyes even more outstanding. He reached for the cloth napkin before him, then sat back as he patted his mouth.

"What rubbish theory are they teaching you now, that we'll have to deprogram."

It was what Raina's friend's mother Valarie would call a soapbox set up. Her answer would give her father the chance to rail against the obscure, the unsanctioned, something he did as often as he could.

"You don't want to know," she answered, buying a few extra seconds.

"Let me guess, climate change."

24

As they'd been studying its effects for most of the semester, this was an easy get. Raina nodded.

"I didn't hear that."

"Yes, Father."

He snorted. "Thank the Light that the plans for an expanded educational building were approved." He looked warmly at Jennifer. "The middle school will be finished in two years, the high school a year later. We won't have to worry about Abby being dimmed by those lies."

Jennifer returned a warm smile. "The education received at Lucent Rising Elementary Institute is absolutely top-notch. Abby is testing out two grades above those of the same age in public school. While it is a more challenging environment, and she must sometimes submit materials against her personal beliefs, I am proud that Raina has maintained a near perfect grade average at Chippewa High."

She looked at Raina. "It can't be easy, having to constantly shield yourself and your mind, to keep glowing in such a place."

"I agree," Ken said. He resumed eating. "Which is even more of a reason she should consider forgoing college, get claimed by an upstanding Beam of Light and join one of the women's ministries. We've got an aggressive agenda for bringing in more members, more funding, spreading more radiance. I don't see where four more years in a blind educational system will benefit either her or the Nation."

"It's necessary for her to be a teacher, darling," Jennifer said, discussing Raina as though she were not in the room.

It was just as well, because any plans they discussed were theirs, not Raina's. She played the role of the dutiful daughter and had even switched the degree she planned to pursue from business to English when her father had balked at her studying a curriculum "more suited for men." But Raina didn't see herself teaching, especially within the Illumination educational system. More and more, she didn't see herself in the religion at all. But those who chose to leave lost their families, too. So Raina hadn't shared those feelings with anyone. She hadn't even fully admitted them to herself.

"Raina, did you hear me?"

Jennifer's question brought Raina out of her own thoughts. "Sorry, Mother, my mind wandered."

"Your father has some exciting news."

In spite of his stoic nature, Raina watched her dad's face color a bit. A gleam came into his eyes. Add the aquiline nose, full lips, and tall, lean frame and anyone seeing him would have no questions as to why, when he'd popped the question, Jennifer had said yes.

"It's not yet official," he said, reaching for his napkin once again.

"Mere formalities remain," Jennifer said, with a wave of her hand. She looked adoringly at her husband. With her shoulder-length black hair pulled back into a sleek ponytail, emphasizing deeply bronzed skin, a long sleek neck, high cheekbones, big doe eyes and a dazzling smile, she was Ken's exact opposite and perfect complement at once. His real-life Barbie, and second chance at love.

"What is it?" Raina asked. "She speared a piece of broccoli from the casserole and shoved it into her mouth. At Jennifer's frown, she took the next bite more daintily.

"Babe?" Jennifer looked at Ken.

"I've been selected to become a Supreme Master."

Raina's jaw dropped. Abby, who'd quietly pushed around the salad on her plate, looked up in surprise. Becoming a Supreme Master Seer was the highest position in the Illumination organization. It required thousands of hours of volunteer work, hundreds of sessions, years if not decades of loyalty, and a recommendation by five members of that rank. While not discussed much, it often cost hundreds of thousands of dollars as well. After more than a quarter of a century with the organization, a stellar reputation within the ministry and a lineage through his father, Ken could check all of those boxes.

"Congratulations, Father," Raina said, and meant it. Knowing how much he treasured the ministry is why most times she tried to behave. Not to mention how happy he made her mother. Raina didn't get it, would probably never understand it, but Jennifer had been able to leave a party life behind and never look back.

"Thank you, daughter," Ken responded, adding an endearment that whether consciously or no he rarely used with his step. His eyes narrowed. He used his fork as a pointer. "You know what this means?"

"What?" Raina asked.

"You have to behave."

Raina physically recoiled. "Father!"

"Ken!" Jennifer exclaimed.

He crossed his arms. "Seriously? You two are going to sit here and act as though we've not had to reprimand Raina on numerous occasions for infractions against the rules? Do you want me to run down the list?"

"No," Raina said. "I get it."

Ken ignored her and began a countdown on his fingers. "Forbidden music. Unsanctioned smart phone apps. Wearing jewelry, makeup, perfume."

"That was in the privacy of my bedroom!" Raina defensively replied. "And we were kids!"

She shook her head, not wanting to believe her father had brought up the makeup story, which happened to also be one of Raina's fondest memories. Her cousin Trinity came to Chippewa for her and her aunt's first and only visit. The girls had been left home alone while her parents and aunt had gone to dinner. Trinity had pulled out a treasure trove of contraband — foundation, blush, eye shadow, lipstick — and turned eleven-year-old Raina into a femme fatale. She'd found an R & B station on the stereo and turned the upstairs hallway into a runway. They pranced and danced, waiting to hear the garage door open, the sign that law and order of the Illumination kind must be returned. It was one of the few times her dad parked in the driveway. They got busted, big-time. Seems her father intended to never let Raina forget it.

"This is all so new," Jennifer had said at the time, defending her daughter's actions.

Tonight she said nothing at all.

"I mean it," Ken continued. "A higher level in the ministry means a much higher degree of visibility. You all will be judged as an extension of myself, your actions my actions, the family as one. After the formal ceremony, there is a ninety-day probation period in which every area of my illumination must be blemish-free."

"In that case," Raina began, feeling her heartrate increase, "I need to tell you something."

The room stilled. Ken sat back and crossed his arms. "I'm listening."

"It's about school, a project we're doing for English class. It requires extra work outside of the classroom." She paused, swallowed. "I'm with a team of unsanctioned."

Ken's shoulders heaved. "Great."

Jennifer's face showed concern. "Can you get out of it, honey? Perhaps take a test instead or find another way to earn extra credit?" She looked at Ken. "I'll speak with the teacher. See if there is a way to get her participation waived on religious grounds."

"The work will still be done on school grounds," Raina explained. "We'll be doing research in the library and may need to take a brief road trip out of town."

"That won't happen," Ken said.

"I already told them I couldn't do that part," Raina said, working to keep desperation out of her voice. If her parents knew how badly she wanted to be on this project with these specific unsanctioned, they'd definitely make doing so impossible. If they knew all six-foot-one of the reasons why, she'd spend the last five months of her high school years being homeschooled. Raina was certain of that.

"But this project is ongoing and a third of our grade. With all of my other classes, college-prep courses and studying for finals in a few months, I'm not sure how I could fit additional assignments or testing into my studies and maintain my 3.8, a requirement for getting the scholarship. If we keep going the way we are, though, my guidance counselor thinks I've got a great chance."

Jennifer placed a hand on Ken's arm. "Honey?"

"There are dozens of Nation members at your school. Why can't you work with them?"

"I tried," Raina lied, asking the Light to cover with mercy. "The teacher selected the teams and told us we couldn't switch."

"These students you're working with. Boys or girls?" Ken asked.

"Girls."

"Then given the circumstances you described, I'll allow it. But only with other girls, no exception. I will not have you keeping company with an unsanctioned male."

"Then it's settled," Jennifer said, obviously relieved. "We'll shine like the brightest star in heaven for your father. After his probation is lifted, and the license is officially given, we've got quite the surprise to help us celebrate."

Jennifer looked at her youngest daughter, watched her moving food around on her plate. "What do you think about that, Abby?"

"It's very good," she dutifully responded. "Congratulations."

"You've not eaten much, honey. Are you . . . is everything glowing?"

"I'm fine, Mother," Abby said.

"Her forehead was warm earlier," Raina added. "Hot, actually."

"I'll get her some vitamin juice," Jennifer said to Ken, placing her napkin on the table and leaving the room.

"Have you appealed for healing?" Ken asked.

"Yes, Father."

"How many times?"

Abby shrugged. "Maybe twenty."

"Then do fifty, or a hundred," Ken responded, dispassionate. "You are a radiant, healthy being of light. Make yourself glow."

Raina stood to clear the table and to keep from saying something about the religion's stand on health, which could get her in trouble and have Ken change his mind about her project. She reminded herself that for the most part their methods seemed to work, that the ILLUX energy machine had added years to her grandmother's life. That's how Jennifer viewed the matter, and how Raina chose to see it, too. She decided to focus on her victory, having more time with her unsanctioned besties. And more chances to see the unsanctioned boy that made her heart go boom.

CHAPTER 3

The next day, Raina was extra careful making her after-school transition from a glow girl to a you-go girl. Changing out of what Jackie and Monica called her Amish attire to rock the outfits that for the past two months she'd hidden underneath. She was uberobservant while heading down to the gym to change in the locker room, a place that with the exception of physical education classes, Illuminated students rarely went. Glowers were encouraged to shine the light on each other whenever necessary. Translated, snitch to the elders if something was perceived to be wrong and receive praise for not minding their business.

For the most part, she was on good terms with the church members who attended the high school. She sat next to them in class, ate with them at lunch, and socialized with them at church. The one thing she'd refused to do was end the friendship with Monica, whom Raina had known in Kansas City, or with Jackie, the only one who'd stood up for her while she was being bullied years ago.

It was weeks into their move to Chippewa. Raina had been only nine years old. A group of local girls had threatened to beat her up after school. Never one to back down, Raina said they could try. She'd hoped they were bluffing. They were not. She'd come around the corner to find a gaggle of mad preteens ready to pounce. She swallowed a mouthful of fear and looked around her, wondering if she could channel some Usain Bolt and break a track record home. One of the girls followed her eyes and moved over. Soon, there was a line of beat-up-the-new-girl she'd have to burst through. She wasn't much of a fighter anyway but could handle one-on-one. Just as she saw visions of cat scratching, hair pulling, windmills, and dirty clothing, the girl's eyes shifted to over her shoulder. The instigator took a step back.

A complete stranger came up beside her, arms crossed, legs wide, looking like Okoye from Wakanda. "Whoever fights her is going to have to fight me. Who's got next?"

One by one the girls turned and left. "My name is Jackie," the Okoye clone said.

"Raina," she'd replied.

"It's obvious you're new in town," Jackie had joked. "About to get your butt whipped cause you don't know the rules."

Raina checked the large clock on the gymnasium wall as she slipped between the double doors. Working hard to not be noticed had cost precious time. Her ride to meet Jackie and Monica would be there in less than five minutes. Their last class was study hall. As happened today, they often skipped it. She eased into a bathroom in the hallway and took the last stall. There she pulled the wool maxi over her head, revealing a tight gold sweater and black skinny jeans. She pulled a multicolored scarf out of her backpack, stuffed her dress inside, then artfully draped it around her neck. The earth tones made her brown leather boots seem less plain, especially after she pulled out a pair of wooden hoop earrings and bangles to match from the side pocket, along with a pouch holding mascara and gloss. A hard pull on the hair band freed her curls. Always a shake away from an afro, she tossed her hair forward and back, then slid the band on to keep the hair out of her face while it did its thing behind her. Easing into her coat, she glanced around to make sure nothing remained, swiped her lips with the gloss, donned a pair of sunglasses, and left the building from a side door. She hurried across the lawn, down the alley, and to the shiny black Mustang that idled two buildings down. She slid into the back seat, lay down, and exhaled. She always felt better once hidden by steel, sure she'd escaped the school grounds without anyone seeing her.

The only thing is . . . someone had.

"What's up, Rainbow!"

She loved the nickname Bryce had given her the day they'd seen one together while sneaking around in his car. But at times, like right now, instead of making her feel all gushy it grinded on her nerves.

"Just drive, okay!"

"What, no hug, no kiss or nothing for your boyfriend?"

"Bryce!"

He laughed and put the car in gear. "Okay, girl. Keep your head down, there's someone walking in our direction."

Raina slid from the seat to the floor, surrounded by packages and boxes Bryce was set to deliver in his independent contracting job as a Big Box driver.

"Dang! You're acting like we just hit a lick. Or if your parents find out about us, they'll kill you."

"There's worse things than death," Raina harshly whispered.

She closed her eyes and didn't open them again until Bryce said they were blocks from the school. She pulled herself from the floor, and once in the McFadden driveway rose out of her slouched position, pulled off her shades, and opened the door.

"Get over here," Bryce demanded, looking like an ad for Hip-Hop Hunks as he leaned against the car.

Raina made to walk past him. He grabbed her and pulled her close.

"Stop!" She wriggled out of his grasp and bounded up the stairs. Bryce's laughter trailed her, a slow, deep chuckle of confidence dipped in swagger. Despite being frustrated by his PDA, a smile crept onto her face and refused to move. Traitor. Just as the sound of Timberlands echoed on the concrete steps, the front door opened.

"It's about time," Jackie said, an iridescent crystal glistening from between her eyes.

Raina's comment about that was forgotten with one step inside their home. "You've already got Christmas!"

Jackie delivered a dramatic eye roll. "Crazy thing, that Christmas. It comes every year."

"I know, but we don't celebrate it. Lucent

Rising looks the way it did in July." She walked into the living room and stared up at the expertly decorated Douglas fir, with shiny ornaments and blinking bulbs. "It's always so exciting to see a tree in somebody's home."

She leaned forward and smelled it. "Um, just like Christmas."

"Yeah." Bryce came up and hugged her from behind. "And I'm going to be your Santa Claus."

"Don't make me retch," Jackie said, heading toward the hall. "Come on, Raina. Monica's already back here. Let's make your stolen hour count."

"Half hour," Bryce said as they both left the living room. "Those last thirty minutes are mine."

When it came to last night's creative communication, Raina hadn't been totally dishonest. There was an English project. But she'd chosen Jackie and Monica to make up her team. Extra work was required. Extra hours would be required to complete it. But they wouldn't happen in a library, unless you counted all of the urban, YA, and romance books in Jackie's room. The project would officially begin after the holidays. But she'd snuck over to Jackie's several times, ever since she'd struck up a deal with the phys ed teacher who was also the basketball coach. An off-handed conversation about low grades and college eligibility for two of his best athletes led to an agreement to secretly tutor them via the internet in exchange for an A in physical education. That's how her last class of the day sometimes moved from Chippewa High to Jackie's house, and allowed her to spend more time with her heartthrob, Bryce Clark. After weeks of flirting during car rides, quick conversations with others around them, and innocent kisses, she'd agreed that sometime during the holiday, they could spend time alone.

"What took you so long?" Monica asked, when Raina entered.

Raina shimmied out of her backpack and pulled off her big down coat.

Monica loudly reacted, then answered her own question. "That's what took you so long," she said, admiring Raina's outfit.

"This your first time seeing the transformation?" Jackie asked. "Her going from *Escaping Polygamy* to *America's Next Top Model*?"

Jackie high-fived Monica. They both guffawed.

"Whatever," Raina said, jumping on the bed and scooting between them.

40

"You look so different," Monica said, patting Raina's hair. "Ooh, it's soft, thick, too. That's all you, huh?"

"Yep."

"Why don't you wear it down all the time?"

Raina explained her religion's dress code, and modesty about hair.

Monica listened, shaking her head. "All that good hair and can't even show it off. Might as well be wearing a bonnet."

Jackie reached for her tablet. "Don't give her mama no ideas."

"Shut up!" Raina said with a laugh. Oh, how she loved her girls.

"So, you changed your clothes before coming over, that's the transformation Jackie talked about?" Raina nodded. "Why? Wait . . . you're trying to look cute for Bryce?"

"You're slow, girl," Jackie said.

"She likes Bryce and you didn't tell me?"

Jackie shrugged. "Not my secret, not my place."

"How can there be a secret when there's nothing to tell?" Raina looked pointedly at Jackie.

"Uh-huh."

"There's not! Bryce and I are just friends."

Monica's eyes slid from Raina's hair to

41

her boots. "That's why you're over here looking like a cross between Beyoncé and Tracee Ross's mama? Somebody's liking somebody over here. How long have y'all been dating?"

"I could never date him, Monica. He's an unsanctioned."

Monica held up her hand, cutting off further comment. "Pull up that assignment, Jackie. Let's get some work done. This girl is on my nerves."

While she couldn't always get away, Raina saw Bryce as often as possible. Which meant spending more time with Jackie, with Monica often over, too. She'd met Jackie's mom, Valarie, and her grandmother Christine, whom Jackie called Nanny. She'd met Bryce's cousin Larry, and the third musketeer, Steve. Every moment spent away from members of the Nation brought Raina further back into who she really was. It became harder to maintain the mask of Illumination and easier to realize that when it came to religion, her heart was not with that Light. It was something she'd noticed but hadn't actually acknowledged until one night not long ago at the Illumination Center when she had been approached by Dennis Patterson, a Beam who for the past year had been trying to claim her.

"Good evening, Light Vessel," he'd said.

"Good evening, Dennis," she responded.

He feigned being affronted as he sat down beside her, close, but not near enough to touch. "I believe the correct title is Elder."

"Even though I've known you since you played with toy trains and had a founding fathers lunch box?"

"Hey! I still play with trains and loved that lunch box."

They laughed together.

Raina decided to play along. "Good evening, Elder."

"How are you, Raina?"

"Busy. You?"

"Busy, doing what? I haven't seen you on the nights they conduct Vessels-In-Training."

"I applied for and was able to get accepted into an accelerated program that starts in January and lasts twelve weeks."

The Vessels-In-Training program was a required course for all women in the Nation once they turned seventeen. Ostensibly, it was conducted to prepare girls for womanhood, to become healers, specialists, or other approved positions available to the "weaker sex." Along with classes on spiritual health, spiritual humility, nutrition, and budgeting, a focus was placed on the home

— home cleansing, energy healing, cooking, and childcare. Everyone knew the real reason behind the classes was to prepare Vessels for marriage. To get girls who were barely women ready to be claimed.

"It's interesting that you were given the fast track, given that you weren't born into the religion. Your father is high level, though. He's almost a master."

Raina almost forgot that the news shared over dinner was not yet official. She remained silent instead of spilling the beans.

"Then again, we're almost out of high school. After that there will be plenty of time for you to do the three-, six-, or even twelve-month course."

"After high school I'm headed straight for college."

Dennis's head whipped around. "You're still on that kick?"

"Absolutely," Raina replied, tamping down her annoyance. "After graduating I'll be on that kick for the next four years."

Dennis stood and began pacing in front of her. "Why, Raina? That's just a waste of time that could better be used here, at the Center. We have plans to grow exponentially in the next five years. Your father is one of the leaders in this expansion, and your gifts would be greatly beneficial as well."

Raina listened, taken aback at Dennis's comments. She had no idea he'd been so observant, or that he held her in this point of view. In her mind they were still the same kids that had competed against each other in noodle-eating contests, or gone camping during conferences at Tulsa Central, calling out to the angel-stars. She still remembered him playfully as Dennis the Menace. Who was this dude? His next words brought her back to the present.

". . . you're a being of Light, a blessing to the Nation. You're smart, beautiful . . ."

Everything stopped for a minute at this declaration. It obviously took both by surprise.

"What I mean is . . . you're an attractive Vessel who'd make an above-adequate container for future glows. It is important that the Nation's seed bears the mark of beauty, which is a sign of Light."

Had he really referred to her body with the same term used for a bottle, bucket, or jar? Yes, technically a vessel was a container, but the latter sounded crass. Raina could barely contain herself; how offensive she found his ignorant, backward, condescending comment. Was she listening to a fellow classmate, a teenager? Or was she listening to Daniel Best, the Illumination founder, who'd written the *Book of Light*? Dennis sat abruptly, seeming suddenly a bit at odds with himself.

"Will you sit with me this Saturday, at the concert of gifts?"

It was as much a request for a date as if he'd suggested dinner and a movie. For them, though, in the dating world there was no such thing as casual. Saying yes would have significant consequences. She would have set herself up to be claimed.

"I like you, Dennis. You're a good guy and a great elder for the church. But in May, I'm going away for four years. There's no guarantee I'll come back here. It's not fair to say yes to a sitting on Saturday when it would be so meaningful."

"Then perhaps we could take up letters?"

He was asking that they be pen pals, another precursor to being claimed. Basically, if you started anything within the ministry with the opposite sex, it was with the expectation that it led to claiming.

"I'll be so busy," she said with a sigh, even as she felt his mood shift beside her. "It's difficult handling my high school class load. I can't imagine it not being harder in college." Trying to get back to the casual camaraderie of friendship, she continued.

46

"How are you feeling about this last semester?"

"Fine."

He was hurt. Raina understood. Rejection was never fun. "Will you go to Tulsa this summer for advanced elder classes?"

"I like your hair."

She wasn't sure what part of her question prompted his comment, but answered, "Thanks."

"Have you ever worn it down?" The question came from left field, asked as he peered straight ahead.

"Every night before going to bed," she joked. Fear tried to creep into her belly but she willed it away. There was no way Dennis knew about her traipses deep into the town of Chippewa. The path was always clear before she ran to the Mustang, and once inside she made sure no one saw her during the ride. Granted, they lived in a small town, with less than four thousand people, almost a fourth of those being members of the Nation. Eyes were everywhere and gossip spread like spilled milk on linoleum. Still, she felt sure that her secret was safe. No one in the Nation lived on the McFaddens' side of town, which meant none of them ever had a reason to be over there.

"Only at home, never outside?"

"What are you asking me, Dennis? You know that's not allowed."

He turned to her then, his hand inching forward, millimeters from hers. "I'd be honored if you'd sit with me Saturday night. Yes, I have plans to claim you. But we can go slow. There are online college classes. All education is not bad. It can help the Nation, help me, once I become —"

"Dennis."

Without thinking, she placed a hand on his arm. He jerked away as if scorched. She pulled back, equally shaken, not believing she'd forgotten the church's stance against touching between members of the opposite sex.

"Forgive me, for touching you and hurting you, too. I can't accept your invitation to claim me. I can't promise you marriage. It wouldn't be right."

"We don't always do what's right, though, do we?"

Okay, this dude is tripping. Raina held on to major 'tude by a thread. "We strive to be perfect," she said, reverting to sayings from their founder's teaching, all found in the *Book of Light.* "We strive to shine, to glow. But no, we are not always successful."

"My invitation will remain on the table, both to the concert and to being claimed. I don't mean to sound boastful, but your dad and mine are both in the elite. I have a bright future in the Nation, pun intended. You can be my brightest star. I hope that you change your mind." He managed his familiar lopsided smile, his demeanor back to that of the neighbor she'd known half her life.

"You know where to find me."

Raina smiled, relieved. "Just over the fence and around the bushes," she said playfully. He left then, and Raina rose, too, and went in search of Sara and Roslyn, her Nation friends. She wanted to discuss what had just happened with someone, wanted an outlet for her jumbled feelings, one side of her clinging to the religion's familiarity, the other screaming to get out.

"Hello, Raina," Sara said, her eyes shining.

"Saw you talking to Dennis," Roslyn said. "He's so cute."

"And an Elder," Sara added. "Oh my gosh, Raina. I think you're about to get claimed!"

Raina smiled, but inside any thought of talking to her friends dissipated. Sharing the conversation with her mother was out as well, and heaven forbid his interest got to her father. Ken might renege on paying her tuition for school. No, when it came to her increasingly mixed feelings about the Illumination situation, Raina would have to keep her own counsel. As for the matter of her heart currently in the hands of an unsanctioned, that was definitely something the Vessel would have to keep to herself.

CHAPTER 4

Over the next couple weeks, Raina spent more time at the Center than she did with her unsanctioned best friends, and only saw Bryce once. While the Nation did not observe Christmas, there was a holiday during this time that they recognized. The winter solstice, in the third week of December, was a very big deal. That night, there would be a huge outdoor celebration in a field near where the religion was founded — in the Kansas City, Kansas, countryside. The women were busy creating objects to be used in a variety of rituals and preparing food to feed the upwards of six thousand Midwesterners from all over Kansas who would descend on the site. But on the Wednesday before school let out for the rest of the year, Raina managed to get a couple hours away from the group. The weather had turned cold. The promise of snow hung in the air. She wore the bulky patchwork sweater that she'd left home in but had traded her maxi denim skirt for a pair of suede leggings, and released her hair from its banded jail. Instead of Bryce, it was Jackie who waited for her in the alley. She slipped into the car's front seat and kept herself low.

"Go!" she hissed, peeking over the rim of the window.

"Girl, nobody from the school is hanging out in this alley."

"You wouldn't think so, logically," Raina said, easing up to a sitting position as they traveled farther north. "But bright eyes are everywhere."

"Bright eyes?"

"Called snitches in your world."

Jackie tsked and teased. "In my world there's only love and light."

"As long as a body don't cross you," Raina countered.

"I wish a muthafucka would," Jackie replied.

Jackie explained that what she'd said was an imitation of Cedric the Entertainer. Raina had no knowledge of this comedy king, but the way Jackie said it cracked her up.

"How do you do that, have all of these spiritual qualities but still keep it real?"

52

Jackie glanced over. "Have you met my mama, Valarie?"

"Ha!" Raina had met her, and liked her. "Enough said. Where's Bryce?"

"Waiting for you. I think you have my cousin a little bit sprung."

"Huh?"

"Look, I told you when y'all first locked eyes that he was a player. I told him that whenever he messed up I'd let you know. But the two of you are just friends to hear him tell it."

"That's right," Raina said.

"Which just means you haven't let him hit it . . . yet."

Raina fixed her with a look. "That's not going to happen."

"Bryce is the cousin that I love like a brother. But he also loves the ladies. Hold on to your heart. Hold on to your panties. That's all I'm going to say."

Conversation faded after that, organically, without tension. Jackie turned up the radio. Raina stared out the window, thinking about the first time she and Bryce locked eyes.

It was just past the start of their sophomore year. Raina and Jackie had just exited the school's main entrance when Raina saw a sporty black Mustang charge into the circular drive. The windows were tinted, the tires were fat, and the music shook the sidewalk.

Raina's eyes followed the cool car. "Who's that?"

Jackie rolled her eyes. "My ride."

"You know them?"

"Yeah, it's my cousin."

The car stopped in front of them. The passenger window came down and Raina looked into the most gorgeous pair of eyes she'd ever seen on a man, even better than the heartthrob she secretly watched on YouTube, before her parents found out and added a so far unbreakable parental control code.

"See you later," Jackie said, before turning and walking toward the car.

The guy with the eyes looked past her at Raina. "Aren't you going to introduce me to your friend?"

"No." Jackie opened the back door and slid inside.

Raina watched the young man put the car in park, open the door, and stroll around to where she stood. He held out a hand. "Hi, I'm Bryce."

"Raina," she replied, her voice soft and tentative, her handshake as weak as her knees.

"You need a ride, too?"

She'd almost said yes, but just then she'd looked over and noticed one of the Vessels, Roslyn, staring straight at her. She shook her head. Bryce noticed the nonverbal exchange and looked back at Raina. "That your boyfriend's sister?"

"No!"

"What, you can't talk to boys or something?"

"I'm talking to you."

"Yeah, but I'm a man, baby girl."

"How old are you?" Raina asked, knowing she shouldn't, understanding that with Roslyn looking on she'd already spent too much time with this stranger.

"Nineteen. What about you?"

"Sixteen."

"Damn," he'd said with a long whistle. "That's jailbait, baby." He began to back away. "When you turn seventeen, I'll hollah at you."

The easy banter ended, but true to his word, he asked for her number the following year. He also asked for a date. She told him that couldn't happen. But they continued to talk over the phone and Facetime, followed each other on social media and then, after that fateful day two months ago when she gave in to her desire to embrace the outside world and went over to Jackie's house, they talked face-to-face. She learned Bryce was staying there temporarily, and while his close proximity challenged her willpower, she stayed true to her faith and to herself. There was hugging, a little touching, and chaste kisses. But she remained a virgin. The fear of being found out and permanently obscured was enough to hold on to her panties, as Jackie had wisely suggested.

Raina's mind returned to the present and her surroundings, reminded that everywhere but in Lucent Rising the holidays were in full swing. She took in the decorated homes, storefronts, and blinking Christmas lights as a young Michael Jackson announced that Santa Claus was coming to town.

I'm going to be your Santa Claus.

Raina's face grew warm at the implication in Bryce's voice when delivering the innocent comment.

Hold on to your heart. Hold on to your panties. Jackie hadn't said nothing but a word.

They pulled on to the block where Jackie lived. In the short time she'd been away, the whole community mood had changed. Almost every house was lit up. Raina took it all in, amazed that Lucent Rising was mere minutes outside of this small town but seemed a whole world away. In their subdivision, owned by the church and inhabited by more than seventy-five percent of its seven hundred and fifty members, there was no hint of yuletide cheer, not even a peppermint candy. The Illumination worshipped the Sun, not the Son, and would celebrate the winter solstice in less than a week, one of only six recognized holidays.

Jackie pulled into the McFaddens' two-car driveway, turned off the engine, and reached for her purse.

"Uh-oh."

"What."

"Mama's home."

Raina's eyes widened. "Is that a problem? Am I not supposed to be here?"

"It's all good," Jackie casually said. "Just wasn't expecting her." She pulled out her phone and sent a text.

"You're texting your mother?"

"No, Bryce." A couple minutes later, Jackie's phone pinged. "Okay, come on."

The times Raina had met Jackie's mom before had been in public, once at the school and once at the local grocer. Harrowing experiences. Very intimidating. Not that Valarie McFadden was a monster. In fact, parts of her reminded Raina of how her own mother, Jennifer, used to be before marrying Ken — direct, intense, a straight-up boss. Raina tried not to be nervous, but as they stepped into the home's foyer and she took off her hat and mittens and unzipped her coat, she second-guessed all she'd been doing of late. Lying to her parents. Sneaking into unsanctioned territory. Forgetting to shield herself and risking the dim. Taking a shaky breath, she followed Jackie's lead and hung her coat in the closet, then followed her friend down a hall that spilled into an open-concept area with vaulted ceilings, a kitchen straight ahead and hallways on either side.

Raina gave her black curls a quick shake, hoping she looked presentable. They reached Valarie's office.

"Hey, Mama."

"Hey," Valarie said, her eyes glued to the computer screen.

"Hello, Mrs. McFadden." Raina spoke from the doorway, as Jackie had done.

"It's Ms. McFadden," Valarie replied. "Mine is the only name on the mortgage and I'm the only one paying the bill. Which means I'm paying the cost to be my own boss," she continued, her eyes still glued to the computer in front of her. She finished typing and spun the chocolate-brown office chair around. "Do you get what I'm saying?"

Raina looked into inky black eyes gazing from behind big, tortoiseshell glasses. Valarie's attractive face was devoid of emotion and makeup, one brow raised as she awaited an answer.

"Well, do you?"

Jackie intervened. "Mom, please. Stop prosecuting."

"Prosecuting is what I do in the courtroom, to criminals worthy of interrogation and more. Here, I'm asking a simple question to get a simple answer."

Her eyes returned to Raina, who simply said, "Yes, ma'am."

"Oh, Lord! Do I look like my mama?"

"Ma'am?"

"My mama is ma'am. I'm just yes or no." A hint of a smile dented Valarie's sharp exterior. "But I appreciate the manners. It shows somebody raised you right."

Raina smiled, too. "Thank you."

Valarie turned back to the computer. "So what project are you guys working on tonight?"

"We're just going to chill for a little bit. We're all going to be so busy during the holidays, it's one of the last chances we'll have to get together until next year."

"All right, girls." She returned her attention to the computer. "Have fun."

"Nice seeing you again, Ms. McFadden."

"You, too, sweetheart." Valarie turned back around. "Merry Christmas."

"Mama, they don't —"

Raina interrupted. "And a very merry to you."

Jackie led the way to her bedroom. She stopped just outside of her closed door and turned to look at Raina.

"What?"

"Nothing. Just making sure you look presentable."

"To who?" Raina lowered her voice. "I'm not seeing Bryce. Your mother's home. There's no way I'm going anywhere near his room."

"Not a problem." Jackie opened the door. Raina entered behind her. Someone flipped a switch. The room lit up. A chorus of voices yelled out. "Surprise!"

Raina stood dumbfounded, her jaw dropped as she looked around. The first thing she noticed was something as miraculous as the birth of Christ. Jackie's cleaned room. White lights had been strung across the ceiling. Balloons were everywhere. Bryce stood in the center of the room, looking like a Christmas gift that needed unwrapping.

Monica, Larry, and Steve were there, too, beaming.

"What is this?" she finally managed.

Bryce walked toward her. "We know you don't celebrate birthdays," he said. "But if you did, Jackie said that today you'd be eighteen, officially grown. It's a special moment. We wanted to mark it with you. I . . . wanted to make sure to be a part of the celebration."

He gave her a hug, and a kiss on the forehead. "Happy birthday, or whatever you want to call it."

Raina. Was. Floored. She hardly remembered mentioning the date to Jackie, had said it in passing during a conversation at school about going to college. It had come up as they talked about transitioning out of their parents' homes, handling responsibilities, like bills in their names. She'd explained then about the Nation's belief that the time the world recognized was not the true time at all. So birthdays and most holidays were not celebrated. In the minds of the Illumination, the meanings were no more than fairy tales and all the dates were wrong.

She stood silent, her mind empty of something to say.

Jackie walked up and placed a hand on

her shoulder. "Don't be mad at us, Raina. We just wanted to do something nice."

"I'm not angry. It's just . . . been a long time since I had a birthday party." Tears sprang up unbidden. Her inner child leaped. "I can't celebrate it. I mean, I can't party —"

Bryce's cousin Larry came to the rescue. "Who said anything about a party? I just saw some cupcakes at the store and realized I was hungry. Found out you were coming over and thought you might be hungry, too."

"I remembered you like stars," Jackie said, waving her hand across the inflated wonders. "Nothing up there about a birthday. Just stars, love, and light."

They'd gone to such trouble and were trying so hard to accommodate her religion's unusual rules.

"I do have a bit of a sweet tooth," she said. "And the angels are our stars."

There was no singing "Happy Birthday," no cards to open, no colorfully wrapped gifts. Valarie heard the noise and added her congrats.

"Do anything crazy now and you'll be tried as an adult."

Raina hadn't felt this free in years. The moment was too good, the fun too much. She became paranoid.

Less than an hour later she turned to Bryce. "I think I should go. Can you give me a ride?"

"Jackie said you had two hours," he said.

"I know, and I don't want to leave. It's just . . . I should go."

He reached for her hand. "Okay. But first, you've got to come with me."

She pulled out of his grasp. "I'm not coming to your room."

He looked at her for a long moment. "All right then. Be right back."

He was gone for less than a minute. When he returned he said, "All right, everybody. I'ma need y'all to get out."

Jackie took exception to the order. "This is my room, fool."

"I need to borrow it for a minute." He tilted his head toward Raina.

"Oh," Jackie said. "Come on, y'all, party's over. You don't have to go home, but you've got to get out of here!"

After a series of hugs and goodbyes, Jackie closed the door with a wink. Raina's heart immediately flip-flopped. The temperature in the room rose, now that her and Bryce were alone.

"This isn't for your birthday," he said, holding up a gift bag with HAPPY BIRTHDAY blazoned across the front. "Just a little something from me to you. Okay?"

Raina raised a hand to her throat and wondered when she'd swallowed the butterflies that now fluttered in her stomach.

"You don't have to take it," he added.

"I want to," she said, feeling that she was talking about more than the gift. His phone pinged, bringing her out of the fog. Needing to go, now, she reached for the bag.

Inside was a velvet box that held a crystal-covered star hanging from a delicate chain. It was beautiful and perfect and totally inappropriate. In the Illumination, jewelry wasn't allowed. But it was a star! An angel! How could she deny it? She ran a finger over the sparkling jewels.

"It's beautiful," she whispered, near tears again. For someone who didn't cry often she was suddenly Niagara Falls.

"Here, let me put it on you."

It would have to come off on the ride home, but she allowed it. He walked behind her to gently clasp it around her neck. When he returned to face her, everything shifted.

"You're a woman now," he whispered.

"I know," she said.

"Which means we can do what grown folk do."

No, it didn't. But her mind was curious, and her body wanted more. "Okay."

He put an arm around her and led her to the bed. They sat, knees touching, looking into each other's eyes.

"You're beautiful," he whispered.

"I'm not," she coyly answered, watching the distance lessen between them.

He kissed her, softly at first and then with more urgency. She felt his tongue swipe her lips. Not unusual, he'd done that before. They parted slightly in welcome, as a hand rested on and then under her blouse. That had never happened. He laid them down as he deepened the kiss, his hand continuing its journey from her waist to other places. Then he touched her. There.

Someone should have warned her about that first precoital caress. But they hadn't, so Raina got gobsmacked. Startled. The world as she knew it instantly and utterly upended. The couple had kissed before, but this intimate caress was foreign. She wasn't prepared for the jolt of energy that shot through her insides, sending tingles from her head to her toes. Was this what love felt like? she mused, caught up in the wonder of his soft, plump lips brushing against hers, of the strength in the arms now around her.

Or was it because he was an outsider? An unsanctioned.

A mixed touch while unclaimed is a mixed

touch unclean. A quote from the *Book of Light,* drifted into her conscience.

Startled and sobered, she broke contact.

Bryce's eyes flew open. "What?"

Raina pushed him away and sat up.

"What's the matter?"

"I shouldn't have done that."

"It was just a kiss."

"It was more than that." Raina jumped off the bed.

Bryce's confused expression gave way to smug swagger, his smile wide and bright. "That's the first time you've been touched like that? Ten seconds is all it took to rock your world, girl?"

Actually, the rocking had begun the first second, but Raina thought that was a fact he didn't need to know.

"Wait, church girl. Don't tell me."

"Tell you what?"

"That was the first time."

"No." Technically true. That private paradise was touched each time she showered. But it had never felt like that.

"Oh. I gotcha." Bryce read his own message into the silence. "First time from a brother who knew what he was doing, huh?"

Raina crossed her arms, hiding goose bumps that had nothing to do with winter's chill.

"You're really a virgin, like you told me that first day?"

Raina was offended. "Of course. Come on. I've got to go."

Once her denim skirt was back in place, and hair tightly secured, Raina and Bryce left the McFaddens' residence. The ride home was quiet. Raina's mind was a mess. Memories played. Voices ping-ponged around her head. The church's teachings. Old-school music. Her father. Mother. Grand. Jackie, and her warnings about hanging on to her heart and other things. Raina felt that she may have already lost whatever was hers to hang on to and knew it would be harder than ever for the real Raina, who for all intents and purposes had just been claimed by an unsanctioned, to masquerade as one still untouched.

CHAPTER 5

That thing she most feared happened sooner than expected. The Dennis Dilemma. The Patterson Proposal. Her family finding out about their glowing neighbor's interest in marrying a young woman who did not want to be claimed. Yesterday, the family packed up and headed out of Chippewa for the winter solstice celebration, a two-day event out in the country, under the stars. Despite her mixed feelings regarding the Illumination, her concern over maintaining her scholarship chances via a high GPA, or the focus needed to keep the heart beating that someone else held, she was excited to make the familiar, annual trek. Abby was excited, too, sharing the very back seat of the van and playing road games with her best friend, Naomi. The healing techniques of the Nation had worked. A few days after Raina felt her little sister's warm forehead, the fever broke. No other symptoms of illness followed. Abby's mind had overcome matter. Her body glowed.

Raina sat next to Roslyn in the seat behind her parents. They played a card game, from a deck that the Nation had designed and approved. As with many other amusements glow children enjoyed, it was greatly inspired by an unsanctioned counterpart. They listened to lively music produced by the church, while Jennifer passed out tasty treats from the trip basket and Ken plied them with stories about life in the heartland, growing up on a farm in the seventies and eighties, before computers, cell phones, or social media.

The conversation wound around to the church and its members. When the subject of Dennis came up, it was Jennifer who mentioned him, not Ken, as Raina had imagined would be the case.

"When describing your teen years, you know who it reminds me of?"

"Who?" Ken asked her.

"Graham's son, Dennis."

Raina became super preoccupied with her card game. If possible, she would have crawled into the box.

"Fine young man," Ken responded.

"Nice looking, too," Jennifer added.

Raina was mortified. Except within the

context of a church matter, she hadn't heard her mother give an opinion on another man's looks in ten years.

"What do you think, honey?" Jennifer asked.

"About what?" Raina asked, as if she weren't less than two feet away from her mother's mouth.

"Dennis Patterson."

"Our neighbor? What about him?"

"He's a nice-looking young man, don't you think?"

"He's okay," Raina said, while thinking that compared to Bryce, he was seriously lacking.

"Looks aren't everything," Ken said.

"They help," Jennifer replied. "It's what first drew me to you."

A deep shade of red crept from Ken's neck to his cheeks. Other than *thank you,* he didn't have a comeback. Yet the way he reached for Jennifer's hand and the depth of love in the glance that he gave her was proof her comment had touched his heart.

"He's going to advanced elder classes this summer," Roslyn said, sounding impressed. "I think his goal is to become a Supreme Master Seer."

"I'm sure he's seeking the perfect Vessel," Ken said, watching Raina in the rearview mirror. "With such a bright future in the Nation, any woman would be fortunate to have him."

The girls got loud in the back and thankfully the conversation shifted. But Raina's calm had been disturbed, the night with Dennis remembered. Had he shared his intentions to claim her with her parents? Is that why they'd given their approval unsolicited, trying to write a page of her life before she'd turned it there? Any peace in the situation came from the fact that Dennis knew how Raina felt. She'd not sat with him at the concert, nor spoken anything much, other than *hi,* after that. She hadn't led him on. Hadn't made promises. And although they lived just yards away from each other, he hadn't sought her out again.

They reached the campsite just before noon. It was a beehive of activity. Tents were being erected, tables set. Church-sanctioned vendors were setting up shop to hock everything from candles to star water, from blankets to shawls. The church had erected a sturdier construct, a mini market containing everything needed for the solstice celebration that a member may have forgotten. There were books, cleansing wands, incense, and small musical instruments. Horns to blow and drums to bang. There were elaborately decorated muumuu dresses for women and loose shirts for men, most boasting white fabric covered with beads, crystals, and symbols of the faith. Pictures of the godlike founder, Daniel Best, were on sale in a variety of models and frames. Even though most families brought coolers of drinks and baskets of food, the market also had a variety of drinks, food items, and vitamin juice. In the center was a table laden with stars of various sizes and in every medium — wood, crystal, glass, paper, aluminum, plastic, and more.

The group piled out of the SUV, grabbed their gear, and headed toward registration, where they would be assigned work duties and told where they would be housed. Because of Ken's status in the organization, theirs would be a sturdier tent with electrical outlets, shower hookup, and a private toilet. Attendants, as ministry volunteers were called, came over to help the family with their luggage and other belongings. Soon after dropping off their things, the family was swallowed up in the goings-on of celebration preparation. Ken was whisked off to meet with the elites. Jennifer joined the elders' wives in the main hall, where several aspects of tonight's more casual meeting and tomorrow's celebration were being organized. Raina and Roslyn joined other Vessels who were handling the tent decorations, program folding, and tending to the beams doing physical labor in basically erecting a church in less than four hours. Abby and other kids her age did whatever they were told. Mostly they enjoyed themselves and the wide outdoors, free from the constraints often placed on them when inside the more formal Chippewa sanctuary.

"Shadow!" Raina called out, seeing her little sister racing across the grass. "Catch!"

She threw Abby a foam ball covered with stars.

Abby caught it and threw it back, adding, "Tag! You're it!"

That's all it took for a play break as several Vessels and Beams joined in the fun. Soon foam balls were flying everywhere. Someone suggested a game of dodge ball, boys versus girls. It was a rare time when other than setting up sides, no distinction was made between the sexes. No subservient behavior was required from female to male.

"Good job, Shadow!"

"That was pretty good," agreed a girl from a center in a neighboring city. "That your sister?" she asked as play resumed.

Raina nodded.

"What'd you call her?"

"Shadow. That's a nickname. Her real name's Abby."

"Hmm. Why do you call her Shadow?"

"Because she's followed me around like one from the time she could crawl."

"Ha! That's a little sister for you. I've got one of those. My name's Kathy."

"Raina."

"Watch out!"

Raina ducked just as Dennis's ball whizzed past her. She wriggled her index finger. *Not today.* Everyone cracked up. The teens played the game for another hour. As they strolled away from the open space, headed in different directions, one of Raina's frenemies, Elizabeth, fell into step beside her.

"Hey, Raina."

"Hey."

"I heard you talking earlier, about why you call your little sister Shadow."

Raina kept walking. She was as sure that she didn't want to hear what Elizabeth had to say as she was that Debby Downer would tell her.

"That really isn't a good word, you know."

"It's a word, Elizabeth. Good or bad is how you use it."

"Not really, not for us. I looked it up."

She pulled out her cell phone and clicked

the face. "Ominous. Oppressive. Sadness. Gloom. Is that really how you want to describe your sister?"

"Those words don't describe my sister. They describe you!"

Raina stomped off and left her sister-Vessel to talk to the wind. Elizabeth had always acted jealous of Raina, had been critical of her from the time the Turners had moved to town. She was homeschooled, and to hear her tell it, was dipped in daylight and wrapped in sunshine. She acted superior to all of her peers. When Raina had said as much to Jennifer, she had replied, "That's because she feels like less than all of you."

Raina was sorry the girl had low self-esteem, but it was the wrong day to use her for a come up. She purposely avoided her for the rest of the day, and while it was probably petty and not a very high wattage, after sharing what happened with Sara and Roslyn, they ignored her, too.

By evening, everyone was ready for downtime. Dress was casual, the agenda light. A dinner boasting a variety of chilies and soups was set up on dozens of rectangular tables, along with huge vats of salad, crackers, and bread. Songs were sung. Music was played. The church bent the rules to allow "shine" dancing, which would resemble square and line dancing to an outsider looking on. Just after eight, over a thousand members gathered inside the massive tent, most sitting on folding chairs, others on blankets spread out on the hard ground. Heaters placed strategically throughout the structure warded off the cold from dropping temperatures, and rousing numbers from the musicians and singers got the crowd moving, creating more warmth. Ken and other elite members of the clergy gave short talks on the meaning of the winter solstice and its value to the Illumination. The night ended with s'mores and stories told around a smattering of campfires, and later with Ken and Jennifer sleeping inside their tent while Raina and Abby snuggled together in a down-filled sleeping bag outside. They lay on their backs, side by side, looking at a profusion of stars brilliantly shining against an inky black sky.

"They're so pretty," Abby whispered.

"And so far away," Raina said.

"How many do you think are up there?"

Raina pulled an arm outside of the bag's warmth, pointed toward the sky, and began counting. "One, two, three . . ."

Abby joined her.

"Wait, did you count that one?" Raina asked, when pointing at a dense cluster.

Abby giggled. "I don't know."

They'd reached a hundred stars in a small segment of the sky just above them. Raina imagined that trying to cover the limited amount of sky that they could see would make for a very long night.

"I give up," she said at last.

"There's too many to count," Abby replied. "It would probably take several lifetimes to count them all."

Instead they focused on constellations, quickly identifying ones Abby had recently learned in class and adding those that Raina remembered. Soon the air grew colder and their lids heavy. Abby wriggled deeper into the bag and cuddled up against her sister. Raina pulled the bag over their heads and zipped it almost closed.

"Goodnight, sister," Abby said, amid a yawn.

"Night, night, Shadow," Raina said. She hugged her and added, "I love you."

Abby patted the arm that was around her. "Love you more."

It was a beautiful ending to a wonderful day that left Raina feeling happy and optimistic. Everyone she cared about seemed in such a good place. Dennis appeared to have gotten over his hurt. They'd laughed and joked during shine dancing, but she'd caught him and Roslyn exchanging long smiles. She'd gotten texts from Jackie and Monica, both travelling to hometowns and extended families for the holidays. Her last text had been from Bryce, with the message that he was thinking about her. In a spontaneous move she turned on her camera, adjusted the flash, and took a pic of her buried inside the sleeping bag, wearing the star gift he'd given.

Thinking of you, under the stars, her caption read.

To which he responded, "You're my star. Twinkle, twinkle."

She fell asleep fingering the necklace and thinking that life was pretty good right now. She was experiencing the outside world she desired, yet retained her family's bond and love. It was indeed the best of both worlds. What could go wrong?

CHAPTER 6

What could go wrong? Plenty.

The first blip on Raina's happiness horizon began the very next morning, when she felt a spray of small fingers pushing into her back.

"Sister."

Raina shifted but didn't respond.

"Raina."

"What?" she croaked.

"I don't feel good."

Raina's eyes flew open. Abby never used those words. Illuminators were taught not to speak ill of themselves, pun intended. Instead they'd use phrases like feeling dim, having low light, or becoming germy from unshielded contact with an unsanctioned. She turned over to find Abby shivering so much her teeth chattered. She felt her forehead. Even though her sister had chills, her forehead was as warm as it had been three weeks ago. Raina eased out of the sleeping bag, careful to keep the morning chill off of Abby's body, slipped into the thick knitted booties she'd pulled off during the night, and scurried into the tent beside her to tell her parents about Abby. Ken brushed it off as no big deal, but Jennifer was concerned enough to rouse one of the specialists. The woman took Abby's temperature and pulse, checked her tongue, ears, and fingernails, squeezed her limbs, and read her body with a light meter. The diagnosis was that Abby had probably come into contact with the bacteria of an unsanctioned. The recommendation was lots of water and vitamin juice and limited outside activity.

Abby hadn't been happy about not being able to play outdoors, and she slept the entire way home, but once there she bounced back to her usual self. Abby's discomfort abated. That night at dinner, Raina's ramped up.

"We have an issue that needs addressing," Ken said, spooning a healthy serving of roasted vegetables onto his plate before passing Abby the spoon. He looked pointedly at Raina. "It involves you."

"Me? What'd I do?"

"You called your sister Shadow."

Elizabeth's face appeared on her mental

video. Raina wanted to punch her, but instead of getting angry, Raina tried to keep it light. "Father," she said with a chuckle. "I've only been doing it since she was two."

"It's a derogatory term."

Raina looked at Jennifer for reinforcement. She sometimes called Abby Shadow, too. They locked eyes for a second. Raina saw the wheels turning. But any opinion Jennifer had on the matter stayed inside.

"I take the blame for this developing on my watch," Ken continued. "Honestly, I'd never given it much thought. I've heard Raina using that term before, but I thought it was something shared rarely, and only at home. When the Council brought it to my attention —"

"The Council?" Jennifer asked.

"Yes, honey."

Jennifer cut her steak into bitable pieces. "I thought it was just you and Graham who talked."

Raina's fork stilled in midair. Dennis's father, Mr. Patterson? Had her indignation toward Elizabeth been misplaced?

"He approached me initially, but later, while sitting around the campfire, the discussion continued with several members of the Council there."

"Oh." Jennifer's expression changed.

Raina could guess why. Her father's promotion. Being raised to the level of Supreme Master Seer was a huge deal, one of the greatest that could happen among elders. There were less than five hundred in the entire religion's membership, which, according to the Illumination website, was between four and five million strong.

"I'm sorry, Father. I was using it as a different meaning, the kind that is cast off by the sun and follows us everywhere."

"I know. I understand. Because of the impending announcement, however, this is a critical time. As I stated before, and thought I had made clear, there cannot be a spot or blemish on me or my family. From now on, that word is forbidden."

Raina was crushed. She told herself it was just a word, that her sister's real name was Abby, so nothing had been lost. Technically, that was true. So why did her heart feel empty?

Still, she shook it off. The new year arrived. Her second and final high school semester started. Soon, she was consumed with a slew of new classes, and psyched about the project she was doing with Monica and Jackie. Their assignment was to analyze a piece of classical literature and adapt it to modern times for a theatrical performance. Raina had always considered herself more a math and science girl, but she was stoked.

The euphoria lasted for two days, until Wednesday night's Light meeting and a run-in with Dennis.

"Hello, bright Vessel."

"Elder." Yes, she humored him.

"I saw you earlier today. You seemed to be having too much fun with the unsanctioned."

"You mean my friends, Jackie and Monica?"

He frowned. "There are no friends outside the faith."

"Give it a rest, Dennis. I've known those girls for half my life. I like them. We're working on a class project together. It's only civil to be nice. Besides, as Vessels we are called to spread our light everywhere."

An Illumination Best quotation in your face. *Pow!*

"We are also called to set ourselves apart, a light on a hill. We are not meant to socialize with the unenlightened."

Raina wasn't going to argue with a walking Illumination study guide. Instead, she waved Roslyn over, hoping she'd provide a proper distraction.

Didn't work. What she'd thought was a

spark happening between Dennis and Roslyn was more like a firecracker without the fuse. Roslyn was clearly interested. Dennis, not so much.

"Would you like to sit with me at Saturday services?" he asked, as Roslyn walked away.

"Thanks, Dennis, but no. We've had that conversation. I'm not interested in coupling or being claimed. For the next four years I plan to focus on school. After that, we'll see."

"I already saw."

Weird bait, but Raina didn't bite.

"I saw you, Raina. One day last month, coming out of the gym."

Oh, snap. Ish just got real.

"You were dressed quite inappropriately."

"I don't know what you're talking about." Instead of falling on the sword, Raina chose to lie and deny.

"Yes, you do. You were heading toward the alley behind the school."

She pulled Shaggy from her mother's soundtrack. "Wasn't me."

"You had on black jeans and a shawl around your neck. The big sunglasses were a nice try to hide your identity. But it was you. I'm sure of it."

"Do you have proof? A photo? Video?"

She pulled on every ounce of courage

available in Chippewa, borrowed more from the rest of the state, squared her shoulders, lifted her chin and looked him straight in the eye.

"I have what I need to make your life difficult."

"Are you threatening me?" Raina paused, took a breath. Now was not the time to go off. "I probably don't have to tell you this, but Roslyn is very impressed with all you've accomplished. She told me you were attending advanced elder classes this year. She'll be in Tulsa this summer, too, becoming a Vessel-In-Waiting."

Dennis acted as though he hadn't heard her. "It would be to your benefit to reconsider my offer."

"We've known each other forever, Dennis. You're a good guy who'll go far in the ministry. But we are not a match."

"Is that your final answer?"

"Keep shining," she whispered, before turning around and walking away. She hoped indeed it was a bluff that she'd called and he had no solid evidence of her treachery. Because if her sneaking off with an unsanctioned cost her father his promotion, there would be hell to pay.

CHAPTER 7

When confronted by Dennis, Raina played it cool. But his threat had spooked her, left her paranoid. It wasn't enough for her to abandon her normal life, but she became much more covert. The week of their confrontation she didn't change clothes or go over to Jackie's house. Instead they met in the library, as she'd told her dad they would. She saw Bryce, but only from a distance, as he pulled into the circular drive to pick up Jackie or one of his friends while on a delivery route. That's not to say they were not communicative. They did their share of flexting — flirty texting — from morning to night. Raina loved the word play and hated to delete them. But she did. Every night. Faithfully. She kept her other life on the low for almost a month, until the chance of a lifetime fell into her lap.

Like most young, urban men between the ages of ten and twenty-something, Bryce was a member of the hip-hop community and when he wasn't driving around Chippewa or neighboring towns delivering orders, dabbled in rap. He was actually pretty good, had produced a couple beats used by regional talent. His friend since childhood, Kaleb Clark, no relation to Bryce Clark, had taken the art more seriously and now, at the ripe old age of twenty-two, had established a solid regional following in the Midwest. Using the name KCK, the initials of where he was born, Kaleb touched a nerve among millennials with sometimes fun, sometimes poignant, but always creative ditties about growing up poor, chasing one's dreams, holding it down for the neighborhood, and breathing while Black. On this particular Friday KCK was shooting a video two hours away, in Kansas City, Missouri, and he'd pulled in two of the nation's most popular artists to be featured on the track — Sniper and Shanghai. A huge rap artist in the early 2000s, Sniper was a perfect mixture of street and style, known for wearing suits and Italian loafers to spit his rhymes on stage at a time his cohorts were rocking low-riding jeans, boots, and bad attitudes. Raina had only been seven years old when he scored his biggest hit, the one that would place him in the annals of time, but she clearly remembered when everybody in the world was chanting, "booyah, do-yah, woo-sah!" Shanghai was only seventeen, but the interracial phenom had been making waves in the industry for the past two years by breathing a nouveau kind of life into old-school R & B. She was, hands down, Raina's favorite contemporary artist. So when Jackie asked if she wanted to skip school to go to KC and be in the video, there was only one answer that Raina could give them. Yes.

It took full-scale strategizing and every aspect had to be carefully planned, but when Raina snuck off school grounds that cool morning on the last Friday in January, she felt she'd dotted every *i* and crossed every *t*. Instead of skipping school straight out and risking a phone call home to her mom, she'd faked a note from Jennifer requesting that Raina be excused for the day. The vice principal accepted the note and approved the absence with no questions asked. Raina was one of their top students, a good, religious girl, even if in most outsiders' eyes the religion was whack. She'd never skipped school or lied to her teachers. Excused from classes. Check!

With Dennis aware of her gym route exit, Raina didn't chance meeting the gang in the alley. Instead, when Jennifer dropped her off that morning, she walked into the school and straight out the back door next to the cafeteria. With the hood of a new parka pulled tight around her face and a scarf covering the entire lower portion, she hung a quick right and, partially hidden by a large row of pine trees, hugged the building until reaching the corner. There she crossed the street and hurried into Joe's Groceries. If anyone had watched her quick exit and followed her strange moves, they would have seen that her final destination was to grab a snack before class. What she hoped was that they wouldn't have time to notice that she didn't exit from the door she'd entered. After a quick wave to the guy at the meat counter, the older brother of a student athlete she tutored online, she was led down a short hall to the store's back door and let out. A familiar shiny car idled less than half a block down. A clean school getaway. Check! Bryce must have been watching for her because as soon as she began walking toward the car, it inched along the street to meet her. She hurriedly opened the door and slid into the back seat, rubbing her hands together, her voice husky with nervous excitement.

"Hey, everybody!"

"Hey, girl," Jackie greeted, from the far

side of the car.

"Morning," Larry said, his attention on the cell phone cradled between his hands.

Monica shifted her body to provide more room. "Hi, Raina. Glad you made it."

"What's up, Rainbow?" Bryce drawled, with a quick glance over his shoulder. He chuckled.

Raina slunk down in the seat — parka hood still low, scarf still securely wrapped. She pulled out her phone to complete the last portion of her coverup. "What's funny?"

"You, girl." Bryce shook his head, still laughing as he pulled away from the curb and headed toward Main Street and the highway entrance on the edge of town. "Back there all slouched down with your face hidden, looking like you're about to do a drive-by."

Larry pulled down the visor and looked at Raina from the attached mirror. "Ha! Stop acting like a plantation runaway. You'se free now," he continued in a falsetto voice.

"Almost to the highway," Bryce added.

"I am running, in a way," Raina countered. "And we're not on the highway yet."

Jackie turned toward Raina. "You ended up not writing out the excuse in your mother's name?"

"I did, but since it's fake, I technically

skipped school."

"See, getting technical." Bryce tapped the stereo screen. "That's your problem."

"Be quiet! I'm texting my mom."

"Like she can hear us," Jackie mumbled.

Mother, forgot to remind you about working on the English project after school. I have a ride home. Will be there around four.

A raw, hip-hop beat filled the car.

Raina's phone pinged.

Will be riding home with whom?

Roslyn. Raina typed in without hesitation, having already nailed down this part of the script. Roslyn was headed to visit an ailing grandmother in Texas. Around four o'clock she'd be at a cruising altitude of thirty thousand feet, impossible to reach. Mentioning her wouldn't raise suspicions because the two Vessel-friends often hung out.

Okay, honey. Light day to you.

Love you, Mother. Keep shining.

Raina flopped against the back seat and finally exhaled. As Bryce eased the Mustang onto the highway entrance ramp, she unwrapped the scarf from her face and pulled back the coat's hood. End of school day and ride home confirmed. Check! The perfect alibi. The entire day covered. Getting a once-in-a-lifetime chance to act like a rock star without her parents' knowing. Check!

91

Check! Check!

"All right, boys and girls," Jackie cooed, moving her body to the beat that was swirling around her while reaching for the purse at her feet. "Let's get this party started!"

Raina watched as Jackie pulled a satin pouch from her purse. She reached inside and took out a shiny pink pen, added a clear attachment, and lifted the pen to her lips.

"You're getting ready to smoke your pen?" Raina teased.

Bryce and Larry looked at each other and laughed as though the joke was on her.

"Do not tell me that you've never seen a vape before."

"A vape?" Raina asked.

Jackie gave her the side-eye. "Girl, quit playing."

"What?"

"Stop acting like you've never seen an electronic cigarette."

"Cigarette?" Raina was genuinely alarmed. "Jackie! I didn't know you smoked!"

"Well, now you do."

Jackie took a long drag from the device, then reached across Raina to give it to Monica. In the front seat, Bryce and Larry were engaged in a similar act.

"Wait a minute. All of you smoke? Don't you know that tobacco kills?"

"Yeah, we're aware of that," Larry said, blowing out a puff of smoke. "That's why this is weed."

Raina's jaw dropped. "Weed as in marijuana?"

"Girl, chill!" Jackie said.

"I will not chill. You're breaking the law."

"Keep messing with my high and I'm going to break your jaw!" The car cracked up. Raina saw nothing funny.

"It's really okay, Raina. This isn't really weed, it's a liquid that feels like weed. Plus, it's legal in a lot of places, including Kansas City."

That medical — not recreational — use was legal, and the law was strictly enforced, was something Monica chose not to add.

They were still in Kansas, where what they were doing was most definitely illegal. No one pointed that out either.

"Look," Bryce said, setting the cruise control and settling into the seat. "It's really no big deal, like having a glass of wine."

"At eight in the morning?" Raina huffed, clearly unhappy. "If I'd known this was part of the deal I wouldn't have come along."

"Well, we're too far away to take you back, so unless you want me to drop you off in the next city and give you money for an Uber, relax. Consider this preparation for

93

being on the set."

"For real, though," Larry added. "Snipe smokes enough weed to cover half of Kansas, along with the rest of his crew." He looked back at Raina. "And his will probably be a joint, not a vape."

"Maybe you should try it," Monica suggested, having waved her hand to more participation after a couple puffs.

"No. Thank. You."

"Come on, Rainbow," Bryce said, his voice cajoling, and kind. "It's something that a lot of people who work in or listen to hip-hop do. KCK does it. A lot of his boys imbibe. You want to meet Sniper and Shanghai, right, get to be in what will probably be the dopest video produced all year?"

A lengthy pause before Raina responded, "Yes."

"Cool. Then don't go all Amish in the city on us, okay? Have the folk in KC thinking your family drives a buggy and you churn your own butter."

The comment lightened the mood in the car a bit. Even Raina smiled.

"Speaking of, Jackie patted Raina's heavy wool skirt. "I hope you brought your cute clothes."

Raina had forgotten all about her needed transformation. She removed the skirt and finished the makeover. By the time they reached Kansas City, she was dressed in her hip-hop best and the party mood was back in full force. Bryce had blasted the artists they'd work with the entire way. Raina was beyond excited to meet her favorite R & B artist, and knew she'd be starstruck with Sniper, too. She hadn't heard KCK's music until this trip, but already had the hook to the song they'd be shooting stuck in her head.

I'm all about the be about it. Be about the flow how the money go. Whoa!

They reached a large, ancient-looking warehouse in a part of Kansas City called the Bottoms, a nondescript yet historical area once known for its successful stock-yards and mafia activity. Bryce navigated the parking lot and pulled up next to a tricked-out Jeep Wrangler.

Larry whistled as the car rolled to a stop. "It's cold as a mother out here, but that car is smokin' hot."

"That's K's ride," Bryce explained, shortening his cousin-the-rapper's KCK moniker to one letter.

They exited the Mustang and noticed several luxury vehicles amid the regular cars and trucks. "What's that?" Monica asked as they passed a sleek silver number that reminded her of something from outer space.

"Ferrari," Bryce said, eyeing the car appreciatively. "Snipe's probably rocking that."

"No doubt," Larry said. "I need to start rapping," he added. "Make a brothah feel bad about the whip he's driving."

"You're in an '85 Thunderbird," Bryce deadpanned, an obvious dis to driving the old beat-up clunker. "Shouldn't have taken you looking at that car to feel bad."

"Don't knock it, partner. Gets me from A to B."

"I see," Jackie said with emphasis. The group howled.

They entered the building, still laughing. Those milling around the large hallway turned around. Several women in various stages of tight clothes, long weaves, and exposed skin stared at Larry and Bryce, as though to figure out if they were famous or not. Bryce especially received several admiring glances. Raina had never considered herself jealous, but was now glad for the gold-colored suede leggings she'd matched with a pair of Monica's black thigh-high boots. The white button-up worn with the wool skirt had been removed to reveal a tight V-neck sweater. The band had been pulled from her hair just outside of Chippewa. The curly afro Jackie had expertly created with a throwback pick was easily the biggest and most standout hair in the building. Completing the look were a pair of big gold hoops and an armful of bangles. Raina felt a bit intimidated by the gorgeous women drooling over her man. But not much. Especially when Bryce threw an arm around her, letting the men whose gaze washed over her tight body know that she was not available. They passed through the hall to the end and a set of elevators. A burly guy looking like the Rock dipped in dark chocolate stood in front of the elevator's operating buttons. He looked properly menacing in his all-black attire and wraparound shades. When he saw Bryce, however, he flashed a grill.

"What up, B?"

"What up, Pook?"

"Here to rock it with cuzzo, huh?"

"A little bit."

Looking beyond Bryce's shoulder, the Rock asked, "This your posse?"

"Yes, this is my crew." Bryce introduced everyone.

The Rock punched a button. An elevator door opened. "Have fun, everybody."

Raina had never had so much fun in her life! After being introduced to KCK, she met Sniper, who seemed immediately smitten. He was complimentary yet respectful. Her look was a hit. He suggested she be placed behind him during his rap, a prime spot, wearing big shades, heavy makeup, and tons of attitude. Shanghai was a sweetheart, who also loved the 70s look. Raina was stoked to meet her and pleased that she didn't act stuck-up or holier-than-thou as she'd read about regarding other artists. Making a video, Raina learned, was hard work. She had no idea the number of times it took to get the right shot, how many times the singers, dancers, and actors were put through their paces to get whatever look the director desired. Time flew. Raina felt she blinked and it was one o'clock, with the shoot and recording far from being over. All too aware of the two-hour drive back to Chippewa, she went in search of the studio where Bryce was laying a line over KCK's hook. She found it, motioned to get his attention. He came out after a couple more takes.

"We need to leave," she told him.

"What time is it?"

"A little past one."

"Chill out, baby. I know what time you have to be back. We'll make it."

"I don't want to wait until the last minute,

Bryce. Anything can happen."

"But anything won't." He leaned over and kissed her. "Don't let worrying interrupt your good time. You're having fun, right?"

"The best time of my life."

Bryce leaned over and kissed her again. "Then relax and enjoy it. We'll leave in an hour."

"Okay."

Forty-five minutes later the group headed to the elevator. The shoot wasn't finished, but it was time to go home. Raina was high, floating above the ground. It had nothing to do with drugs and everything to do with the day she'd just had, one that she never could have imagined. She'd hung out with stars and danced in a video. A teenager's dream come true! Monica had asked if she was worried about Jennifer seeing it. In that moment she was appreciative of the church's insular tendencies and avoidance of the secular world. She doubted that a member would see the video and even if they did, figured her look in it was so far from the subdued girl they were used to seeing that the thought it could be her or anyone they knew wouldn't cross their mind. She'd taken a once-in-a-lifetime chance to have that very kind of experience. It was a memory she'd never forget. Once they arrived back home, she'd go back to her regular life and never try something so daring again.

They reached the double doors leading outside. As they neared the glass panes letting in the outside world, Raina's heart dropped. Snow was falling, and from the looks of it had been for most of the day. Fluffy white flakes dropped on top of the five or six or so inches already on the ground. Raina had checked the weather report. Obviously, the website that forecasted a chance of light precipitation got it wrong. Or the report had changed. Once inside the warehouse, Raina had never thought to double-check the weather, and since the windows had been covered for the production, no one knew what was happening outside. Raina had just over two hours to make it back to Chippewa. They'd be lucky to hit the city limits in three.

Raina tried to hold on to her ecstatic feelings from the shoot, tried to be a part of the upbeat atmosphere her friends created on the drive back. But on top of the inclement weather it was also rush hour, with a series of accidents causing further delays. What was normally a fifteen-minute drive getting past the metropolitan area today took forty-five. They cleared the last accident at just past four o'clock, the time Raina should have been heading home. Five minutes later her mom called. She let it go to voicemail. What could Raina tell her that wouldn't have Jennifer on her way to the school? A text came in, followed by another call. No doubt she'd called Roslyn and gotten voicemail, too. Raina panicked and turned off the phone. Bryce was a good driver. The highways were wet but clear. They had just under a hundred miles to go. The Mustang could do one-sixty. If they didn't get stopped for speeding, Raina figured they'd be back in Chippewa no later than five thirty. An hour and a half late. Given she'd lied to her mom and the school and the church, she probably shouldn't have called on the heavenly stars, but she did. Asked that whatever reason she came up with for being so late would be accepted. That Ken would be at the Center and Jennifer wouldn't be too mad. She petitioned the heavenlies, and almost believed that this teenage tomfoolery could still be pulled off. That was, until they left the metro area where steady traffic had kept the highways fairly clear, and reached the lesser traveled, snow-covered lanes. Bryce could barely do sixty, let alone one-six-oh. There were slick spots, making him go slower still. Night fell, adding to the treacherous driving conditions. Bryce was careful but drove as fast as he could. He had no way of knowing about the patch of ice on the other side of a curve that he took at fifty-five miles an hour.

"Damn!" Bryce cried as the car spun out.

"Hold on," Larry said, gripping the dash. Jackie cursed. Monica screamed. Raina held on to Jackie's arm and the door handle, too afraid to make a sound. What felt like an eternity was over in a matter of seconds. The car had done a three-sixty and come to rest in a field.

"Everybody all right?" Bryce asked, once he could talk again.

Except for the fear that had probably shaved moments off of each of their lives, everyone was fine. Thankfully there'd been no other cars around or there would have surely been a collision. As it was there were four very scared, extremely thankful kids and a car that wouldn't budge, no matter what they did to try and get it unstuck. As Raina's spirit continued to drop along with the temperature, Jackie remembered that she was on her mother's car insurance plan, which came with roadside assistance. A beam of sunshine burst through Raina's dark night. It only lasted until the end of Jackie's phone call to the company. The unexpectedly heavy snow had produced a plethora of accidents. It would take anywhere from two to four hours for help to be on the way. In that moment Raina knew that her plan had failed. An hour late could be explained away. Maybe even two. But four or more? No. Raina looked up at the brightly glittering stars and mumbled, "Never mind." Whatever time she arrived back in Lucent Rising, she'd have some explaining to do.

CHAPTER 8

They reached the outskirts of Lucent Rising at just past ten. With each passing mile, Raina's thoughts of her parents' reaction to what she'd done had gone from mild fear to sheer terror. She was in caca deep enough to start a sewage plant. She didn't bother asking Bryce to drop her off in the park. By now her dad and sub-division security had probably scoured every inch of the town. Illumination security had undoubtedly been notified and every available security camera had probably been rolling since four o'clock, when the first of several calls from her family was ignored.

"You going to be all right?" Bryce asked.

"Define all right," Raina said, trying to make a joke when there wasn't a darn thing funny. She zipped her coat over the modest clothes that hid the fly girl and opened the door.

Jackie placed a hand on her arm. "Give

me a call later, okay?"

"If I can."

"What does that mean?" Monica asked.

The porch light turned on. Raina swallowed her answer. Time to face the firing squad. She got out of the car without saying goodbye, took a deep breath, and walked up the sidewalk. The door opened when she was still three feet away.

It was Jennifer, resembling a thundercloud, her straight, shoulder-length black hair twisted and wrapped into a conservative bun, a drawn expression marring her pretty, oval-shaped face. Instead of the smile that often split her face there was a line straight enough to test a potential DUI.

"Where on earth have you been!" Raina reached the front door. Jennifer did not step aside. Her eyes slid from the car from which Raina had exited to the shamed face of her daughter.

Raina shifted nervously from one foot to the other. "I was with some friends and their car broke down."

"The car that just dropped you off?"

"Yes. Something with the battery. He had to call —"

"He?!?"

Raina froze. Had she really used that pronoun? When she, they, even it, was avail-

105

able, she had to put the shovel in the dirt with *he* and start digging her grave?

"Who were you with, Raina? Never mind, we'll get to that. Where is your phone?"

"Um, it died." Raina's religion didn't believe in hell, but as easily as that lie rolled out, Raina thought that for her they might make an exception. "Sorry, Mom."

Jennifer finally shifted so that Raina could enter the house. "Your dad is furious," she hissed into Raina's ear as she passed her. "He's in his study. Get up there. Now."

That last command was issued in a near bear growl. Had she turned around and seen her mom's eyes blazing red, Raina would not have been surprised.

She stopped at the bottom of the stairway. "Where's Shadow?" In her state of dread, she needed a lifeline. The nickname that she'd used for so long slipped out without a thought.

Jennifer's eyes narrowed. "Stay away from Abigail Denise. You are the shadow." A stabbing forefinger emphasized the point. "Your level of contamination is probably through the roof. The entire block has been shielded."

"Mother, I —"

"Save your lies and your stories for someone who might believe them. Your father

106

and I deserve the truth. And you're going to give it to us. Now get upstairs. I'll be there shortly, as soon as I call the Center and let them know the search party can be called off." Search party? Leave it to her parents to call out the cavalry.

Raina wished her mom were joking, but given the circumstances, she knew it was totally true. When it came to members, the Nation was overprotective. She'd been right about her dad and company scouring the streets. That's how they rolled.

She reached the closed door to her dad's study and knocked. Twice. Nothing. While debating whether to knock a third time or simply open the door, it opened. Her father's gray eyes were the color of rain. The kind that comes down in droves during a hurricane, Category 5. They were filled with emotions, but she couldn't guess which. Anger, for sure, but what were the others? Disappointment? Compassion? Frustration? Relief?

He said nothing, just left the door open and walked back to the chair behind his massive desk. She was already terrified. Being interrogated in his masculine office, with its antique furniture, plank cedar desk, and oppressive dark paneling, made it even more so. To twist the knife there was another set of eyes staring down a hawk nose at her from a museum-sized picture, that of the church founder, Daniel Best. She could almost hear his tinny condemnation. *You have kept company with the unsanctioned, broken our laws. Obscure!*

Her dad took his seat. She sat in one of two chairs in front of the desk. He didn't look at her but went back to reading from the *Book of Light*. Damn. She knew a sermon was coming, but had he prepared scripture and verse? Was he going to pass the offering plate and ask her to sing a selection? The thought almost brought a smile to her face, *almost* being the operative word. Right now fear had her so paralyzed that moving her mouth at all would be a huge win. She bowed her head, clasped her shaking hands together, and repeated the Ode of Enlightenment until she heard the door open and smelled her mother's cologne.

Jennifer took the seat beside her. Ken looked up. " 'An obedient child is like a diamond,' " he began, indeed quoting from the book as she figured he would. " 'A precious crystal, of great value and worth. A disobedient child is like a lump of coal. Hard, destructive, disastrous. Better to have one, tiny diamond, than a million lumps of coal.' "

He paused, to let those words sink in. They did, and with every consonant and vowel, pulled her heart to her toes.

"Where were you, Raina?" Jennifer had regained her composure. Her voice was calm; her question, direct.

Oh. Snap. Maybe her mother had gone to the school after all and what she'd thought a secret wasn't anymore.

"At the library." Last week.

Jennifer and Ken exchanged a look. "With whom?"

Now it gets tricky. How much truth should she tell? How much did her parents know and when did they know it?

"Jackie McFadden and Monica Wilson."

"Monica Wilson?" Jennifer asked coolly.

"Yes," Raina answered, understanding the chill.

"She is unsanctioned," Jennifer said. "You were told to stop interacting with her."

"With anyone not of the Light," Ken said.

Most of her classmates fit that title, as did everybody who wasn't a member of the Illumination. Raina thought the reason Jennifer didn't want her hanging around Monica specifically had less to do with their present than her and her mother's past.

"We're working on the English project together, remember?"

"How long were you at the library?" Ken asked. Raina didn't answer. Now it wasn't a matter of whether or not her stepfather knew anything. The question was how much.

"Because you weren't there when your mother went by the school."

Thunk.

"Raina?"

"Huh? I mean, sir?"

"I asked a question."

"I don't know," was her noncommittal answer.

Belatedly, Raina realized she should not have assumed their ignorance and just told the truth. It felt that way now and later she'd be sure of it. But on the slightest chance that he was fishing without provable bait, she continued down the road of deception.

"Why did you leave the school with them?" Jennifer asked.

"I didn't think it would be a problem."

"Didn't think it would be a problem?" Ken asked, his voice rising. Anger in a deep shade of red crept from her father's neck to his face. His jaw clenched, as Raina imagined he worked to calm his nerves. "After I explicitly told you that a road trip with them was out of the question?"

"We weren't supposed to be gone long."

Translated: *long enough for you to find out I skipped school and rode to the city.* Blasted snow! Were it not for the change in weather they'd have returned by four, Raina would have been home on time, and no one in Chippewa would have been the wiser about her great adventure.

Jennifer made a sound of incredulous disgust. "You weren't supposed to be gone at all!"

"I'm sorry," Raina said. An afterthought that even to her ears sounded like too little, too late.

"I'm not familiar with these Vessels helping you with this school project," Ken said. "They must be from the Center because I'm sure that there are no other girls you'd feel it remotely not a problem to get in a vehicle with, except a group of your own kind."

"Jackie is not a Vessel, either," Jennifer explained. "There was at least one he," she added.

Ken's expression didn't change. Not even a whisker moved. No one touched the dimmer, but Raina could have sworn the lighting changed.

"Who was this boy?" he asked.

"Jackie's cousin. It was his car."

111

"Where did you go?" Jennifer asked.

Two sets of eyes bore down on her, waiting.

"Answer your mother," Ken all but growled.

Jennifer shifted in the chair to eye Raina more fully. "You're working on a school project, why did you leave school?"

Raina hesitated. The problem with lying is that when you told one, you usually had to tell two. Then you had to keep them straight. Then tell another. And another . . .

"Just . . . for a ride."

"A ride to where?" Jennifer demanded.

"Over to . . . Clinton," Raina said, writing a story as fake as the one for English class. "To the . . . theater."

She felt horrible lying to her parents but felt a little better that this bag of perjury popcorn held small kernels of truth. As unauthorized as movie-going was, she also thought it a preferred offense to being in a rap video.

"I didn't know that's where we are going. I thought that . . ."

Ken's movement stilled her words. He reached for a manila folder lying next to the *Book of Light*. Inside were photos, blown-up eight-by-tens. Silently, he placed them before her. Black and white, a bit grainy, but with unmistakable time-stamped images of a trip that began just before eight that morning.

Raina exiting from a back door at Chippewa High. A figure bundled in a faux-fur-trimmed parka running toward a black Mustang.

Raina climbing in the back seat of the car.

A black Mustang on Main Street, heading toward the edge of town and the interstate entrance beyond it.

"You did not attend any of your classes today," Ken said. "And while you were given every opportunity just now to tell the truth, you didn't do that either."

"We emphasized what a crucial time this is," Jennifer said. "How careful we had to be in following every tenet of the Illumination."

"Mother, Father, I can explain."

"You could have, but you didn't."

"I'm sorry," she said again.

"It's too late for that," Ken said. "This could not be contained within the household. Everyone knows, including the Council."

"Especially the Council," Jennifer reiterated.

What was bad just got worse.

"We were frantic when you weren't at

school," Jennifer said.

"And we couldn't reach you," Ken added.

"All. Day. Long." Jennifer lost her cool as she leaped from the chair. "What were you thinking?"

"I wasn't. I'm so sorry," Raina cried, fighting back tears. The weight of her treachery slumped her shoulders, the mistake in thinking she could leave town and get away with it all too clear. She waited for the consequence to be meted out. It didn't come immediately. Instead, silence screamed throughout the room, almost taunting in its completeness. Raina was already stressed to the nth, she didn't want to wait another second to hear her fate.

"I will pay for the classes," she offered. "I was planning to get a summer job anyway. I'll get one now and pay back every dime."

"Are you serious?" Ken, who until now had been almost too calm, began to lose the grip on his measured restraint. "Do you think this egregious act can be mollified with a series of classes? Going deep?" He shook his head. "No. Your actions disrupted this entire community. Did I mention that everyone knows what you did?"

"Why did you tell them?" It wasn't a fair question, but she was not thinking straight.

"What did you expect us to do? We

couldn't find you," Jennifer said, sitting down once again to get in Raina's face. "None of the member classmates had seen you or knew where you were, especially Roslyn whom I finally reached, by the way."

"Dennis organized a search party," Ken continued. "And instead of being claimed by an upstanding, honorable man like him, you're cavorting with those outside of the Light. Men who drive black Mustangs," he sneered, stabbing the picture of Bryce's car with his middle finger.

Dennis. For a second, Raina's fear turned to fury as she remembered that he'd seen her leave the gym that day, dressed inappropriately, and imagined he may have been the one to suggest she'd done it again. The diverted blame was short-lived. The only way she could see the reason she was in the hot seat was to get up and look in the mirror.

Ken's anger grew. "Who is this guy? I should . . ."

"Honey." Jennifer's voice was soothing. "What if in addition to DEEP classes, I become a Vessel-in-Training?"

It's the very last thing on earth Raina wanted to do, but the feeling gathering in the pit of her stomach suggested that unless she could convince her parents of how

115

much she regretted her actions, and how committed she was to the Light, the night was not going to end well.

"None of that is an option, Raina Lynn," her mother said. "Been there, done that. It's clearly not working."

"It is. My last infraction was almost a year ago. The classes are how I shined brighter." Her parents were looking at her intently, both of their expressions otherwise unreadable.

"If not through classes, how do I begin the process of reillumination?"

Ken took a deep breath and steepled his fingers. "By leaving our home."

"What?" The word came out on the whoosh of breath that had just been taken away.

"Your actions are those of someone determined to do what they want to do," Ken continued. "To live like a grown person, be on their own. Tonight, we will oblige you."

"I don't understand," Raina said, honestly confused.

"The Council has recommended that you be obscured."

"No!"

"It's not final yet, Raina," Jennifer said, her voice softening slightly. "Your membership has been suspended until their investigation is completed. While that is happening though, you can't be here."

As the severity of this new reality dawned, fear seized her. Suddenly Raina was very much just barely eighteen, not at all ready for the grown-up life.

"You have thirty minutes to get your things," Ken said before Jennifer could answer. "And five more to get out."

The situation had gotten much further out of control than Raina imagined. This had to be some sort of dream, some twisted form of punishment meted out to get the kid's attention before laying out exactly what she needed to do to reenter the Light. Her stepfather hadn't just told her to leave home, right? Had she just heard the words, *get out*? Yes, said the devils on both of her shoulders. And she was pretty sure he wasn't referencing the Jordan Peele film.

CHAPTER 9

Raina and her parents looked around as Abby entered the office. Her braid was fuzzy, her eyes squinted as though just waking from sleep.

"I heard a scream," she said, rubbing eyes fixed on Raina. "It woke me up." She stopped in front of her sister. "Are you okay?"

Jennifer stood and took Abby's hand. "Let's go back to your room."

"Let her stay," Ken said. "Abby needs to learn what happens when one is disobedient."

It was clear Abby had been kept in the dark about what was happening with Raina. In controlled environments, such as the one the Nation cultivated, it wasn't hard to do.

"What did you do, sister?"

"I took a ride from an unsanctioned, and left school without asking."

Abby slowly shook her head. "You're going to have to go deep for a very long time."

"She is not going deep, Abby. Raina is going away."

"You mean it? You're really kicking me out? Now? Tonight?" Raina tried to keep it together but was heading straight into pre-freak-out mode.

"Yes," Ken said.

"Where will I go?" She hated the high-pitched girly tone her anxiety created, almost as much as the knot that found its way to her stomach. Crossing the room, she stood in front of Jennifer.

"Mother? Do I have to leave?"

Jennifer looked at Ken. Her eyes pleaded briefly, but she said nothing, before her expression became resigned.

"Where am I supposed to go?" Raina repeated. Since the Council had spoken, she knew no one in the community would take her into their home.

"Figure it out." He shrugged. "It's what grown folk do."

"Kenneth —"

"Silence, wife." Ken raised his voice for the first time all night.

Raina watched Jennifer swallow a mouthful of words. Her mother's fear morphed into Raina's own as the weight of Ken's words crashed into her conscience.

"Her actions have placed her outside of the orb of illumination," Ken explained to Jennifer, as if she were new to the faith. "She has broken covenant. Stepped into uncertainty. Defied our instruction in a way that impacted our entire community and the church. That has placed my promotion in jeopardy and stained our family. Until she goes before the Council, admits her transgressions and recommits to the Illumination exercises they demand, she will be treated as though already obscured."

"No, Father!" Abby cried.

"Please, Father. You're a Grand Seer. They listen to you. If you explain that this won't ever happen again, they'll reconsider."

"What I say will have no impact. It's above me, now."

Everyone in the Illumination knew what obscured meant — pretty much put out of her family's lives. The Amish were shunned. The FLDS were kicked out. Catholics were ex-communicated. Baptists were given the left foot of fellowship. The Illuminated were obscured, the most severe rebuke a member could face. Raina had never fully embraced the religion, but for the past eight years it had been a huge part of her life. But none of the members would help her now. She had little money, not enough for a hotel.

And even if she did, what good would that do? She'd get a room and then what? Suddenly the society she longed to be a part of seemed scary and huge. Except for her time at school, and stolen moments like those that had led her here, she hadn't navigated the outside world unchaperoned by an Illuminated Vessel, Beam, or Elder since she was ten years old. Suddenly, that very much mattered. On the precipice of being separated from her family, especially Abby, Raina found herself clinging to the very faith she'd rejected.

"Contact the Council as soon as possible," Jennifer said. "Perhaps they'll have mercy on you and allow you to return home while you are rehabilitated, if you are not obscured."

It was the smallest of lifelines, but Raina grabbed on with both hands. Her mind whirled with thoughts of how to get through these next hours. She willed herself calm, and focused. It was late, past ten o'clock. But if the Council could be reached tonight, she might get an appointment as early as tomorrow. Jackie had asked to be contacted. Could that be where she spent the night? Going to the home of an unsanctioned wasn't the best of moves for reillumination, but right now it was the only choice she had. One night. Less than twenty-four hours and she'd be back home. It would be her first time away from her family. But she could do it.

"Come on, Sha— Abby," she said to her little sister, speaking with a confidence she didn't feel. "I've got to go. You can help me pack."

She reached out her hand. Abby grabbed it without hesitation. They turned to leave.

"Abigail."

Ken's stern, raised voice caused Raina to flinch. She stopped and turned.

"Stay. Right. There," he continued, speaking to Abby, looking at Raina.

Abby's hazel eyes shone with unshed tears as she looked at the sister she obviously adored. The fear and uncertainty Raina saw there broke her heart and had her hand itching to punch Ken in the throat. Anger shot up and over the fear she'd felt just seconds before. With every year that passed, Ken became more of a bully in her eyes, and with each promotion in the Nation, more controlling of their family. Her mother had changed so much since marrying Ken. Abby was the one good thing that had come from his presence in their lives. Raina would be "dimmed" if he tore them apart.

"Why can't she come with me?" Raina

asked, almost as a dare. "Doesn't she have enough light within her to chance a few moments with one almost obscured?"

The truth of the matter was that in that moment Raina needed her sister much more than the other way around. She was currently in shock, but even so knew that pure panic was just around the corner, followed by beyond terrified. Abby would give her the calmness she needed to get through the next few minutes.

Abby looked at her father. His lips didn't move, but *no* was all over his face.

"Please, Father," Abby pleaded.

"They won't be long," Jennifer said.

Ken looked at his watch. "You're right. Raina's already wasted five minutes. Your thirty-minute timeframe to pack is now twenty-five."

Raina turned her eyes to Jennifer, her mother's face blurred by an onslaught of tears. "Mom? I'm sorry. Can't I . . ."

"Shh," Jennifer said quietly. "The Grand Seer has spoken." Her voice was soft, yet firm. Still, love infused what she said next.

"Speak to the Council. I believe you indeed are sorry, Raina. Your actions have jeopardized our family, but I believe you can be restored with the power of Light."

Jennifer looked to Ken as she finished, her

expression a question.

"You have dimmed to the point of being ghosted," Ken said. "Reillumination is possible. Whether or not it is allowed is what only time will tell." Ken looked at his watch. "Twenty minutes."

Raina nodded, resigned to her fate. She was leaving her family, but there was a way back. Jennifer would also work behind the scenes, speaking to the elders' wives, championing her case with the influential Sun Vessels. Raina was sure of it.

"Father, may I help her pack?" Abby asked, even as she reached for Raina's hand.

Ken nodded. Raina gave in to an indescribable urge and went over to hug Ken. Perhaps it was for the mercy she hoped he'd show later. Perhaps for the hint of grace he showed now.

"Thank you, Father," she said sincerely. "Thank you, Mother."

She hugged Jennifer and then hurried to her room. Abby, her shadow, was hot on her heels.

Once in her room, a full-on boohoo threatened. But with Abby watching her every move, Raina stayed strong. She walked into her messy closet and pulled out a suitcase, then on second thought reached for the carry-on instead. She would call the Council

124

tomorrow, set up a meeting ASAP. If she convinced the members that her regret was sincere, perhaps she could work on her re-illumination from home. She gave Abby a wink, then pulled a few items from their hangers and tossed them in the luggage. She crossed to the chest of drawers and pulled out underwear, covertly slid in a couple of cute options, then crossed over to the bathroom she and Abby shared and gathered her toiletries. Abby, like always, was two steps behind her.

"Where will you go?" she whispered.

"To a friend's house," Raina said, again thinking of Jackie. She stopped packing, reached for her phone, and sent her a text.

Plz come to park NOW. 911. Will explain. PLZ!!!

"Who is this friend? One of us?" Abby pressed.

"No, Shadow. I'm suspended from the family. No one in the Rising can take me in."

"So . . . your friend isn't Illuminated?"

"No, but she's nice." Raina walked into the closet, pulled out a pair of sneakers to go with her boots.

Jackie was the only person Raina knew well enough to ask for such a big favor. Monica would also be willing, but if Jennifer found out she was visiting the Wilsons, friends from their old life, she would not be pleased. That both were unsanctioned was only one of two worries, but Raina's packing time was down to ten minutes. She couldn't think about that now.

Abby's eyes became misty. "Sister, I'm scared."

Raina tossed the shoes into the suitcase and knelt before Abby. "I know, Shadow. I am, too. But you heard Father and Mother. There is no choice. I'm going to call the Council first thing tomorrow. I'll apologize and do whatever they ask me, to once again be a purified vessel, just like you."

"Why did you go off with them, and get yourself dirty?" Abby asked.

Gurlllll . . . Raina almost laughed out loud as the sound of Jackie's voice invaded her ear. It was the first light moment she'd had since Jennifer appeared in the doorway. Raina had no doubt that being with the girls was bad enough, but learning that a boy was involved was probably why the Council became involved. They needn't have worried about that. Aside from flirting, kissing, and a little touchy-feeling, nothing had happened between her and Bryce. But Raina had gone off with outsiders and spent time alone with an unsanctioned male. And worse than that, she'd liked it.

"I wasn't thinking," Raina patiently said. "I showed you what not to do."

Abby wasn't happy. "And now you're going to hang around them again!"

"Yes, but hopefully only overnight."

"Raina, I hate this. I'm going to miss you. We've never spent more than a few hours apart."

"Consider this practice for when I leave for college. And remember, you're my shadow. Not even distance can keep us apart."

Abby nodded, then looked toward the closed door. She stepped close and whispered in Raina's ear. "Can we sing the shadow song?"

Raina smiled. She'd made up the ditty a couple years ago, on a sad night when the family cat died and Abby learned that nothing lasted forever. It was forbidden, of course, and hadn't been sung often. The last time was months ago.

"If I move to the right," Raina began softly, taking a step.

"You've got a shadow," Abby said, mimicking her movement.

"To the left, cross step." Raina crossed the other way, then spun around.

"Shadows all around." Abby took over the

lead. "When I move you move."

Raina nodded, "Just like a shadow."

"When I groove you groove."

"Your forever shadow now."

Raina pulled Abby in for a hug. "Do you still feel good? You don't usually take naps."

"I didn't sleep well last night."

"Well, that explains it."

Ken called out. "Raina!"

It was time to go. She reached for her tablet and placed it in a backpack. She wished for a private moment with her mother, but Jennifer had gone downstairs. By Ken's orders, Raina assumed. Her heart rent just a bit. Raina ignored it. She took one final look around and headed toward the door.

"Raina, wait." Abby walked over to the nightstand and picked up Raina's personalized *Book of Light,* the organization's bible that Ken had given her when she turned thirteen. "Here."

"Thank you, Abby." Raina slipped it into the backpack and fastened the lock. "Give me a hug."

"Raina?"

Jennifer's voice floated up the stairs. Raina hugged Abby tighter. "Can you keep a secret?" she whispered.

She felt Abby's enthusiastic nod against

her shoulder.

"Between you and me, you will always be my shadow."

After a kiss on the cheek she grabbed her coat and walked out of the room. Her cell phone pinged. She stopped and checked it. Jackie was on the way and would meet her behind the park. Raina hoisted the backpack. Abby reached for the carry-on's handle and followed Raina downstairs. Her parents were solemn as she passed them. She took in the disappointment in her mother's eyes.

"Sorry, Mother," she mumbled.

"Me too," Jennifer said.

"I'll be okay."

"I hope so. I pray the Light covers and protects you."

"I'll call the Council tomorrow."

Jennifer nodded.

Raina hugged her, whispered a hasty *I love you,* and walked into the frigid night.

CHAPTER 10

She welcomed the cold. If tears fell, they'd freeze. Not wanting her exile to be watched by security via the community cameras, she cut around the side of the house and followed the walking trail behind their block to the back side of the park. She pulled a knit cap and matching mittens from her coat pockets, jammed them on as she neared the loose plank near the end of the fence. It was dark. The moon was full. With a quick look around her she moved the wood aside, ran across the short park lawn, and up to the black idling Mustang.

"What the hell?" was Jackie's greeting, as she noted Raina's bag. "What's going on?"

"I got kicked out."

"Word?"

"Yep."

Jackie put the car in gear and eased out of the park. Just as they reached the corner, a light flashed from across the street.

"Security," Raina mumbled. Wouldn't be long before the tags were run and her father would know where she was, or at least the registrant of the car that had picked her up. Which probably meant he'd know about Bryce.

"They know about the video?"

"No, thank the stars. Told them we went to a movie and on the way back the car broke down."

"And they kicked you out for that?"

"No, that happened because I lied."

"A pretty harsh consequence for something everyone does at one time or another." Jackie shook her head. "You and that crazy religion."

"Not crazy, just different," Raina snapped.

"I guess it looks that way if you're in it. But I didn't mean to offend you. Sorry."

"No, it's me." To say she was on edge was putting it lightly. "Looking back, I should have answered my phone. They thought I'd gone missing, had the whole community out looking for me. Everyone knows what I did. My dad is an elder. It makes him look bad. My whole family is affected. I've screwed up."

The weight of her mistake began sinking in. Raina's throat constricted. Tears pushed against her lids.

"I wish I hadn't told you about the video shoot."

"It's not your fault. When you asked if I wanted to be in it, which meant skipping school, leaving town, and lying to my parents, I could have said no."

"And pass up what looked like the chance of a lifetime with a fool-proof plan? Don't be so hard on yourself. If we hadn't had car trouble they wouldn't know anything."

"Maybe, maybe not. The Illumination has eyes everywhere, including the police force." Jackie glanced over. "I'm almost sure that's how he had the pictures to prove I lied."

"Pictures? Of what?"

"Us leaving school. Me getting into the car. The Mustang leaving town. Dad pulled them out after I said I'd been in the library."

"Girlllll . . . no. What did you do?"

"Almost died."

"I'd be dead, too. Are you sure your heart is beating? You'd better check."

Raina managed a slight smile. "Thanks for coming to get me."

"We were all worried. I'm glad I could use Bryce's car." They reached a red light. "What are you going to do? Where am I taking you?"

"I was hoping your house?" Raina tentatively asked.

"We can try," Jackie responded, shaking her head. "Just remember Mama's a prosecutor. Get ready for a cross-examination."

The light turned green.

"So . . . what happened when you went into the house?"

She shook her head as tears fell. The question took Raina back into her father's study. She remembered his eyes when he looked at her and was now sure that disappointment was one of the emotions he felt. Shame was another.

"That's all right. I wouldn't want to relive it either."

Conversation faded. Jackie turned up the radio. Raina stared out the window. As they rode down the streets of Chippewa, she once again marveled how a community minutes outside of a town could look and feel like a whole world away. Last month, in Lucent Rising, a subdivision owned by the church and where more than seventy-five percent of its seven hundred and fifty residents were church members, there had been no hint of yuletide cheer, not even a peppermint candy. Yet within city limits, Santa Clauses and Christmas lights had been replaced by Cupid shooting hearts with his bow and arrow. There would be no Valentine decorations where Raina lived.

And for now it seemed, not much love for her in the Reed household either.

Jackie pulled into the McFaddens' two-car driveway, and despite Raina having been temporarily obscured, seeing the house, with its warm brick façade, big picture windows, and majestic elm trees swaying against the expansive sky, it felt tonight as it had in the past — made the night feel less sad.

Jackie turned off the engine and reached for her purse.

"What should we tell your mom?" Raina asked.

"The truth, most likely. She's got a radar that can pick up 'your ass is lying' from two hundred yards away."

Raina tried not to be nervous, but Jackie's mom was a prosecutor and Raina felt very much on trial. And though lying had cost her being at home tonight, telling the truth and nothing but the truth was a tall order.

"Leave your stuff here," Jackie said, placing the carry-on against the wall and walking toward the hallway on the opposite side. "Let's let Mama know you're here."

The two girls walked down the hall side by side. Jackie peeked into Valarie's home office. It was empty. They continued on to the master suite where the sounds of soft jazz floated from beneath the closed door.

Jackie knocked softly before opening the door a crack. "Mom?"

Valarie looked up from where she was sitting against the bed's headboard flipping through a magazine. "Hey."

"Raina's here. She wants to know if she can spend the night."

"What's going on?"

Jackie opened the door wider so that she and Raina could enter the room.

"Hello, Miss Valarie."

"Hi, Raina. Why are you here instead of home with your family?"

"I kind of got kicked out," Raina said.

"How does one kind of get kicked out?"

"My parents found out I was hanging out with —"

"Boys?" Valarie interrupted, assuming the answer. "Figures."

"Not just boys," Jackie said.

Valarie crossed her arms. Ignoring her daughter, she stared at Raina. "What's his name?"

"Bryce." Raina's voice was soft, barely above a whisper.

"Did you say Bryce?"

"Yes, ma'am."

"As in my nephew, Bryce Clark? The nephew who's staying here right now, who sleeps two doors down from Jackie? Oh, hell no, honey. You can't stay here. Ain't no baby-making happening on my watch."

"It's not like that, Mama," Jackie said. "Raina's a good girl. She's still a virgin."

"Yeah, so was Mary when she had Jesus." Valarie's eyes narrowed. "Do I know your folk?"

"No," Raina said.

"Oh, that's right. Y'all are a part of that weird-ass cult just outside of town who don't like to associate with regular folk. You're one of their children and you want to stay here?" Valarie's eyes returned to the magazine. "Hell to the double no, child."

"Mama!"

The rejection was as unexpected as Raina's sudden tears.

"Ah, baby," Valarie said softly, looking up and catching Raina's forlorn expression. "I'm just kidding. Kind of, sort of. You know everybody in town who doesn't attend there thinks y'all are cray-cray. Keeping yourselves holed up out there behind those high-ass fences. Not interacting with people when you come into town. It's not normal."

Raina's countenance remained downcast.

"How old are you?"

"I just turned eighteen."

"And they kicked you out for socializing with someone of the opposite sex?"

"More like someone of the wrong religion. Outside of school, I'm supposed to only be in contact with others in the organization." Valarie looked at Jackie. "Did I mention they were weird?"

"Mama, that's not nice."

"Honest, though." She turned back to Raina. "Since you got kicked out for being with heathens, what are you doing here?"

"Because I didn't only get kicked out of my house, but kind of out of my family, and since everyone in the organization is considered family, no one else can take me in until I see the Council."

"Well that's some inhospitable bullshit," Valarie said.

"It should only be for tonight. I'm calling the Council tomorrow to get this all straightened out."

"In that case, yes, you can stay but . . . Bryce's room is off-limits, whether I'm here or not. Try and sneak in there if you want to. Trust me, I'll find out."

"She's got this placed bugged," Jackie said.

"It's called Mama radar," Valarie said. "Plus, I was once your age. And give me your parents' phone number. I'm not going to call them," she added, following the look of horror on Raina's face. "But in case of an emergency, I need the number of someone to call."

"I'll send it to Jackie," Raina said. "Then she can send it to you."

Valarie reached for her phone. "Send it to me directly. I need to have your number, too. What is it?"

Raina rattled it off. "Thank you, Miss Valarie."

"You're welcome, baby," Valarie said, her attention returning once more to the magazine.

"Did you get a chance to eat?" Jackie asked Raina.

"No, but I'm not that hungry."

"If the last time you ate was while shooting the video, you need to eat something. Come on."

Jackie turned and headed down the hall. Raina gladly followed behind her, feeling a palpable sense of relief at not being grilled by the lawyer.

Valarie's voice trailed after them. "Bryce is on his way home so be sure and leave some for him."

"He's not here?" Raina asked.

Jackie shook her head. "Larry needed his help with something so Bryce stayed with him and let me drive his car home."

Raina was happy to hear that Bryce wasn't home. To be honest, a little sad, too, though she chided herself for that. He wasn't to blame for her being attracted to him, curious about love and willing to go against her parents' wishes to experience more of life than their religion allowed. Even though the consequences had left her temporarily obscured from the community, she wasn't sure that, given the option, she wouldn't make the exact same choices all over again. As she'd told Abby, the McFaddens were nice people. She didn't regret spending time in their home. She didn't regret going against the Illumination's stupid rules, and when she decided to cross that bridge and give up her virginity, she hoped it would be to a guy like Bryce Clark.

After fixing plates and grabbing glasses of soda, they headed down to Jackie's big and perpetually messy room. Jackie kicked aside a stack of fashion magazines and closed the door. She crawled on her bed, Raina beside her, truly relaxing for the first time all night. While eating, they watched YouTube, browsed social media, and talked about the fun they had shooting the video. Jackie clicked on a music channel, then pulled an air mattress out of her closet and insisted on making up the bed for her guest. Raina thumbed through a fashion magazine. She looked at clothes she'd love to be able to wear all the time but couldn't, fashions too tight, colorful, or revealing for a Vessel like her. A song came on that sampled a beat from the 90s. Raina immediately recognized the hook from a popular girl's group. Hearing it made her sad for disappointing her mother and brought back memories of another life, the one before Ken. How she and Jennifer used to make popcorn and nachos, then plop in front of the TV and watch her favorites, like *Glee* and *Veronica Mars,* or her mom's reality preferences like *The Amazing Race.* For the most part she tried to repress those memories beneath the *Book of Light* and the Illumination. Beneath new friends and new rules, and a new place to belong. But then she'd met effervescent, carefree Jackie, and the old Raina, the genuine one, had resurfaced, bringing back a longing for normalcy and a longing for those old times. She'd met Bryce, as athletic and gorgeous as he was unsanctioned, and discovered a Raina that was different still.

"All right," Jackie said, bouncing back onto the bed and bringing Raina out of her revelry. She opened a box and pulled out a deck of colorful cards. "You're all set for dreamland. Before we say goodnight, though, let's do a reading with you and see what's really going on."

"Jackie . . ."

"I know, y'all don't believe in angels. Y'all talk to stars." She stopped shuffling the cards and looked at Raina. "What's Venus telling you now?"

Raina didn't answer.

"I thought so," Jackie said with a smile, and resumed mixing the angel card tarot deck. "Messages come from any and everywhere. Just be open."

Raina watched Jackie handle the angel cards with a mix of fear and intrigue. Any religion outside of the Illumination was considered occult, the study of which could dim you forever. But Raina needed answers and the stars were silent. So she performed a subtle shielding, a series of intricate movements with her hands while reciting a mantra, then sat back to hear what the angels had to say.

CHAPTER 11

Bryce didn't come home. The next day he texted her, said that at Valarie's strong suggestion he was spending the weekend at Larry's apartment. Later that afternoon, he called as the guys headed to Kansas City to lay down more tracks with the rapper KCK. Wouldn't be back until late Sunday, he told her. It was probably for the best. She hoped to be home by then. Already in a world of trouble, Raina could imagine the ways Bryce might try and comfort her and didn't know if she'd have the willpower to resist.

Raina's Saturday call to the Council went to voicemail, not totally surprising as that was the church's Sabbath and there were services all day. Her calls home and to Jennifer's cell phone went unanswered, too. It's what she expected but being ignored cut deeply. At one time, Jennifer had been her best friend. Now Ken was her mother's bestie, and obviously in charge. When

142

Sunday came and still no one had called her, she forced away worry, told herself to enjoy the freedom. If the Council allowed her to go back home, she'd probably never be trusted again.

On Monday, without Raina hearing from the church or her parents, Valarie dropped her and Jackie off at Chippewa High just after seven. With the message from Jackie's Friday night angel card reading etched on her mind, Raina opened the door for them to enter the building and pulled out her phone.

"See you later."

"Where are you going?" Jackie asked.

"To call the Council," Raina said.

"Good luck," Jackie told her, "or whatever it is you use," she added, under her breath.

"I heard that!"

"Ha! Good!"

The hallways were fairly empty. Classes didn't start until eight. Raina walked toward the library and the seating area just outside of it. Clicking on images, she pulled up the pictures she'd taken last night of the angel cards Jackie had pulled, and the messages they'd delivered after forming three specific questions in her mind.

The first answer was from the angel card named Desiree, in response to her question about Bryce. *Conditions aren't favorable right now,* the card read. *Wait . . . and ask the angels to help, guide, and comfort you.* She could use their help and comfort, but pretty much knew the deal. It didn't take a rocket scientist to figure out that while trying to get back under her parents' roof, seeing Bryce wasn't a wise option. Perhaps it wasn't only the angels. It could be the stars, too. Protecting her from heartbreak. Keeping her focused. Whatever the reason, having a boyfriend should be the least of her worries right now.

The second angel card answered her concerns for Abby, and how her shadow hadn't felt good the past couple days. The answer came from Opal. *Your children on Earth and in Heaven are happy and well cared for by God and the angels.* Raina felt this answer was a bit problematic. The Illumination didn't believe in God or angels. But when she substituted Light and stars, as Jackie suggested, she felt that the message was positive, and that her sister would be all right.

The third card is why she sat cross-legged on a bright yellow couch, ready to call the council and be reilluminated. Two angels were on the card that delivered the last message. Raina wasn't surprised. Given the gravity of the situation, she could understand two beings being needed. Grace and Antoinette told her exactly what to do. To help heal this situation, they said, see the other person's point of view with compassion. Even if she didn't agree, she could acknowledge the church's position. This wasn't a Burger King moment. Now wasn't the time to try and have it her way.

With the energy of the angels around her, Raina dialed the number to the Nation's offices.

"Good morning!" a cheery voice sounded. "This is the Illumination. Step into the Light!"

"Good morning."

"How can I direct your call, please?"

"The Council's office?"

"Yes, and who shall I tell them is calling?"

"Raina. Raina Reed."

A pause. One thousand one. One thousand two. "One moment," the receptionist said, with a little less light.

The transfer to the Council went to voicemail. Again. Raina was as worried as she was relieved. She left a detailed message and hoped for the best. For the next several hours, she focused on school. At lunch she joined Jackie and Monica to discuss their English project, the reenactment of a theatrical classic to be presented in March. While she was sure word had gotten around in the Rising, she didn't want those at school to know she'd gotten kicked out. So she swore Monica to secrecy, then gave her the news.

"Oh my gosh! That is crazy! They kicked you out for real?"

"Very real," Jackie interjected. "She's at my house right now."

"Ooh, I know your parents aren't happy about that. My uncle is a member of the Illumination, attends a huge center near Dallas, Texas. I know how they roll, which is pretty much only with others who believe like them. My mom is his sister and they barely talk at all."

Raina was familiar with the Texas Center. Her family had attended a meeting there last year. During services, she felt dwarfed in the auditorium that could comfortably seat three thousand people and, once home, appreciated the coziness of their smaller membership.

"It's different. But when you're in it, most of the time it doesn't feel that way. I mean, I have friends. We hang out, just inside the Rising. We listen to music, just not what's popular on the radio. We watch movies, but only those sanctioned by the church."

"And that doesn't feel different?" Monica

asked her. "Let me give you a news flash, sistah. There's nothing normal about that life. So . . . now that you're free and don't have to rush home or to the center, what are you going to do?"

It was a good question, one Raina hadn't considered. "I was hoping to hear from the Council and meet with them. If not . . . I don't know."

"You want to come with us to BBs?" Monica asked. BBs was the nickname town teens had given to Breadbasket, a local eatery especially popular among the high school crowd. "I hear they've got a couple openings. I'm going to apply for a job."

"Sure, why not."

After school, instead of studying the Way of the Woman, a class at the Center for young women eighteen and older, Raina found herself in a noisy dining room filled with boisterous teenagers. Eating burgers, people watching, and laughing till it hurt. Teenage stuff. Normal stuff. Raina hadn't known what all she'd been missing. It would end once the council set up her deprogramming, but for now she was happy to enjoy the fun.

Monica rejoined her at the table and slid over a paper next to her basket of remaining fries.

"What's this?"

"An application," Monica replied with a shrug. "You never know."

Raina glanced at the paper before folding it and placing it in her purse. If life worked out the way she wanted, she'd be back home later today, several deprogramming sessions on the agenda, finished in time for graduation and a summer job in KC. Then again, she hadn't lined one up yet, and Breadbasket was a regional chain . . . But, no, working here would be impossible. Doing so anonymously in Kansas City was one thing, but here? Where her father was an elder second-in-command? There's no way he'd let his child serve burgers to the unsanctioned outsiders. There's no way he'd eat anything prepared by one, even if that one was his daughter.

"Well, look who's pulling in," Monica said, smiling as she looked beyond Raina's shoulder.

"Who?" She turned around just as Bryce was exiting the car, all swagger and machismo, with his cousin Larry and his best friend, Steve. Until now, she'd tried to tell herself she hadn't missed seeing him over the weekend. Her mind had known otherwise and now her body agreed. Her heart went pitter and her noni-heat went patter as the boys made a beeline for her and Monica's table.

"What's this?" Larry asked, with a raised brow. "They let the church girl out the building, I see. Is the world ending tomorrow or what?"

Bryce slid over to Raina's side of the table, threw a protective arm around her. Though the chances of a member seeing them were slim and none, Raina still felt paranoid and eased from under his embrace.

Bryce took it in stride. "Back off," he told Larry and eyed Steve, too. "My girl's going through a tough time right now. She doesn't need y'all's yada yada, you hear?"

A server came, the guys placed their orders, and soon they were knee-deep into the world of sports. Bryce had the ear of several tables, especially the ladies'. Bryce had graduated high school two years prior, had done a year and change at a Kansas City college before deciding to work full-time. Restlessness and a relationship gone south had landed him at his aunt's house trying to figure out his life. But while at Chippewa High he'd been the basketball king. Those listening hung on to his every word. Raina was more aware of the curious eyes on her. She began to second-guess her decision to come here. Kids of the Light or no, word of her being with Bryce could get back to her parents. Or the Council. She excused herself, told Jackie she was going to walk to the McFaddens', then eased out the door. He was the center of attention and in the middle of a memory, so she figured she'd be at the house before Bryce was aware she was gone.

One good thing about a small town, nothing was too far away. The McFaddens lived a couple miles from the town's center. Raina welcomed the walk in the cold late-January weather. She thought to clear her head, but thoughts of Bryce stayed with her. Store windows gave way to a neat row of houses. Raina didn't notice. In her mind a video was playing, those early days of puppy love. She walked and thought back to that first time — after all the texting and flirting — when she'd seen him away from the crowd, the closest she'd gotten to a one-on-one. Deeply engrossed in reliving those feelings, the world around her faded.

It happened the second time Raina had made the tutoring deal with the phys ed coach and snuck away from school to the home of an unsanctioned. As she sat nestled in a beanbag chair in Jackie's room, doing homework, looking at magazines and listening to the latest hip-hop jams, a current of excitement hummed through her on the waves of the musical beats. It wasn't only the thrill of being somewhere she wasn't supposed to be, but of possibly seeing Bryce. From the moment of that first encounter her sophomore year, when he'd picked up Jackie, she'd been smitten. He'd occupied many of her waking thoughts and more than a few times had invaded her dreams as well. Over the next year, while he was off attending college, they chatted via text, social media, and Skype, and her feelings for him deepened. Those rare times when she saw him, even in public surrounded by others, he became the only person there. His presence did strange things to her insides, made her tingle in places that were not to be touched, even by her, and were definitely off-limits to the opposite sex. Beyond the description that the act was strictly for married couples and created only to bring little lights into the world, there was no sex education in the Illumination. These physical reactions to Bryce confused her, even shamed her, because sometimes, most times, she enjoyed them.

An hour passed before they heard the telltale signs of Bryce coming home, his heavy sneakers making contact with the shiny hardwood floor, his voice deep and melodic, as he interacted with Valarie. His laugh causing tingles as if meant for Raina alone. She steeled her body against seeing him again. A knock at the door turned her spine to noodles. She slunk deeper into the oversized beanbag she occupied, raised the magazine she held to shield part of her face, and repeated the mantra, *unclean.*

"Come on, cuz!" Jackie yelled.

Bryce opened the door and with one look Raina swore she could find nothing dirty about him. The gravity of her situation temporarily kept her subdued, but her heart still flipped a little.

He looked at her, or rather, devoured her. His eyes, warm. His smile, easy. His body toned, but loose. He leaned against the doorjamb. "What's up, Rainbow?"

Raina giggled. "It's Raina."

"Rain causes rainbows, right?"

It became his nickname for her, the only one she had to this day.

"What are you doing here?" He looked over at Jackie. "Working on a school project?"

"What's it look like," Jackie said.

Raina said nothing. She kept her eyes glued to the magazine in front of her. One look at his face, those bedroom eyes, those juicy lips, and no way would those words come out.

"Hey, Rainbow. Why don't you come hollah at me when you finish your homework?"

Jackie let out an exasperated sigh. "You trying to get kicked out of here? You know Mama don't play that."

Bryce raised up from the doorjamb. "I guess you're right," he said, his smile still easy, as though he knew what she said was a lie. He blew her a kiss. "It's cool. There's always next time. Sweet dreams."

Needless to say, Raina got very little work done after Bryce left. A few minutes later, she decided to leave, too, get back to the center before her parents arrived for Tuesday Teachings, the words of founder Daniel R. Best. She made it back to the center before they arrived, slipped into the lecture moments before her dad walked out onto the podium and her mother took a seat in the second row of the auditorium. But had someone asked her what was discussed that night, she wouldn't have been able to tell them. She spent the evening thinking about Bryce . . . and next time.

A loud horn jerked Raina back to the present. She looked up to see a red Kia inches from her hip, and a woman glaring at her through the window.

"Sorry," she offered, as she threw up a hand to hurry out of the intersection.

"Little girl, you'd better watch where you're go — Raina?"

Raina held up her hands, a nonverbal apology. Not only had she absentmindedly walked into an intersection, but she'd almost gotten run over by someone she knew? In a section of town where the unsanctioned resided? It wouldn't matter that she'd basically been kicked out of Lucent Rising. They'd still judge her for being there, unchaperoned to boot. This. Was just. Great.

She turned around, squinted, shielded her eyes against the sun.

"It's Bev, Monica's mother."

"Oh." Relief flooded through her, as upon closer examination the face was indeed one she recognized. "Hi, Miss Bev."

"No miss. Just Bev. Get in the car. I'll give you a ride."

And discover she was staying with the McFaddens? "Um, no thank you. I'm fine."

"Yes, I saw fine. It almost got you run over. Now get in so I can take you over to Val's."

Raina's jaw dropped. At the same time she realized her fingers were frozen. She

154

hurried to the car and got in.

Raina knew Bev Wilson from Kansas City, where she and Jennifer were acquainted. She'd seen Monica's mom a few months ago, but with the black hair she remembered now platinum blond, there'd been zero recognition.

"Does everyone in town know I'm not living with my parents?"

"Only the ones you told. And me, because Monica can't hold water. She tells me everything."

Good to know.

"How's Jennifer doing, married to that robot, Ken?"

Raina chuckled. "She's fine."

"I sure hope so. She's changed so much since getting married to him. First time I saw her after moving here? I hardly recognized her."

Raina remembered that day four years ago. It was just after the Chippewa Health Center had been built and brought a bit of a boon to the town's fledging economy. She and Jennifer were shopping at the Dollar Discount when the sound of laughter from another aisle led to a strange reaction. Jennifer had put down the basket of goods she carried and headed toward the door.

"Let's go."

"Mom, wait. What —"

"Just come on. I . . . forgot about something I need to do."

Raina had hurried to catch up with her. They'd just reached the door when Raina turned around and saw someone else making a hasty move toward the exit. It was a pretty woman she'd never seen before, but who was smiling like she knew her.

"Jennifer!"

Jennifer stopped without turning. The woman caught up to them. "Girl, I can't believe it! I thought that was you. I saw you in the aisle a few minutes ago but thought no, couldn't be. Then I heard your voice. What in the heck are you doing down here? Working at the clinic, too?"

In the face of the woman's overt friendliness, Raina remembered how distant her mom had acted.

"Who's this? Your daughter?" She'd looked between them. "Raina? Is that you?"

Raina, disconcerted about how unfriendly her mother was acting, had simply nodded.

"Girl, you've grown! How old are you now?"

Jennifer had cut off the conversation, and later Raina's questions, all of which only made her curiosity grow. It wasn't until after becoming friends with Monica during her freshman year at Chippewa that she ran into the friendly lady again. That's when she learned how Bev knew Jennifer. And that her mother had a past that she wanted forgotten.

"Don't you have a sister?" Bev was asking when Raina tuned back into the present again.

"Yes, Shadow. I mean, Abby."

"Shadow's her nickname?" Raina nodded. "Why, because she follows you everywhere?"

Raina laughed. "Exactly. How did you know?"

"I have one of those, too. Her name is Wanda. How old is your little sister?"

"Eight."

"No more siblings?"

"No, just her."

"I bet she misses you not being home."

"I miss her, too. I hope she's okay."

"Why would you say that?"

"She . . . wasn't feeling well the night that I left her."

"Hmm, I see." Bev reached a yellow light. Rather than run through it she eased to a stop. "I'm a firm believer in each to his own, but no one could have told me your mother would become a part of that ill nation. Don't get me wrong. I'm not judging. It's just that the woman she is now is nothing like the cool chick I once knew."

"How is she different?" Raina asked. She had her own experience and therefore ideas, but was interested to see how Bev viewed it.

Bev glanced at her. "How is she not? Your mother was fun, fearless, the life of the party. And your father? Girlllll . . . when those two met . . ."

"You knew my dad?"

"Everybody on the Vine knew Albert. He could take that saxophone and blow your mind. It's a shame that he left you the way he did. He was so happy that you were his little girl. I know that he loved you. He probably just got out there, bright lights, big city, and got swept away. I lived in New York a couple years. You can get swallowed in those places. I know because it almost happened to me."

"Did you wait tables with Mom?"

"Shit," Bev exclaimed, drawing out the word until it sounded like a song. "I was the reason your Mama had customers to serve. I'm a singer," she continued, pulling into the McFaddens' drive. She burst into an R & B number. Perfect tempo. Perfect key.

" 'No more drama' . . . oops, my bad. You can't hear that kind of song."

"It's okay."

"I bet it is. You sneak and listen, don't you?"

Raina shyly nodded. "I knew it!" Bev said with a laugh. "You're Jennifer's daughter and that girl loves her some Mary J. Blige."

Raina checked for the spare key, then reached for the door. "Thanks for the ride, Miss . . ."

Bev gave her a look.

Raina laughed. . . . Beverly." Monica's mother reminded Raina of how hers used to be.

"Tell your mom I said hi and to not be a stranger. And bring that little girl into the clinic. There's a strain of flu that's pretty bad this year. We'll get her checked out."

Bev passed on her number to give to Jennifer. Raina took it, thanked her again, and tucked the card in her pocket as she walked up the sidewalk. She doubted her mother would reach out to Beverly, but felt too embarrassed to tell her. Jennifer only interacted with the women of Illumination. Raina would call Beverly before her mom picked up the phone.

CHAPTER 12

Another day passed without Raina hearing from the Council. Raina returned to Jackie's house, did homework and discussed the English project in Jackie's room. When Valarie came home from work and said they'd talk over dinner, Raina immediately dreaded the conversation. By the sound of Valarie's voice, it couldn't be good news.

"Have you talked with your mother?" Valarie asked, around a bite of spaghetti.

"No."

"What about that meeting with the church leaders?"

"I haven't heard back from the Council yet."

"So how does this work, this put-your-daughter-out-and-never-talk-again business? How long are you supposed to navigate life on your own?"

Raina shrugged. "Not long, I hope."

"I don't mean to talk about your parents

or make you feel bad. But what if you hadn't known Jackie, or I didn't have room? What would you have done then?"

Again, Raina didn't have an answer. The *Book of Light* said all answers were written in the stars. Too bad you had to be an elder to read them.

"I'm sorry to see you go through this, Raina. You seem like a good girl with a good head on your shoulders. But I'm headed to Chicago next week for a conference. Knowing Bryce's hardhead friends, I barely trust leaving Jackie here. The only reason I do is because when it comes to his favorite cousin, he's a bigger boyfriend police than I am. What I'm not sure of is how well he can police himself and his penis."

"Mom!" Jackie exclaimed as Raina's hand flew to her mouth.

"Please. When hormones get to raging, ain't enough church in the world . . . You're probably not as fast as Jackie," she halfway teased. "And while I know you think that nothing will happen, I can't in good conscience leave you here with Bryce as your chaperone. One minute you'll be saying no and the next Bryce will be passing out cigars in the hospital ward talking about whoop, there it is."

"Ha! That was funny, Mama."

Raina was about to be homeless. She wasn't laughing at all.

"I empathize with your situation, especially what you're dealing with the Illumination. I've represented a client who had a run-in with one of your members, and couldn't believe some of what I learned."

"Nothing would happen, Ms. McFadden," Raina pleaded. "I promise."

"I know you believe that. I did too." Valarie nodded toward Jackie. "The very night she was conceived."

"For real, Mama."

"Hey, I'm just saying . . ."

Valarie studied Raina another moment, watched her shoulders fall into a dejected slump. "Tell you what. I'm not going to leave you out on the streets. My mother lives not far from here. Have you met her?" Valarie turned to Jackie. "Has she met your grandma?"

"Once," Jackie said.

"When she brought that pound cake to the school," she continued, looking at Raina. "Remember?"

Raina nodded. "She's rather hard to forget."

"That's my mama," Valarie said, with a laugh. "She'll curse you out one minute and feed you the next, but she's a good woman

162

with a special heart for children. She'll take care of you like you're one of her own."

"Don't do it," Jackie teased, her voice playfully somber. "You think Mama's scary. Nanny's no joke! I'm playing, Raina. I love my nanny. But when she finds out you're with *those people,*" Jackie said with air quotes, "she's going to have a thing or three to say about it."

"Ooh, she's going to have a field day," Valarie added.

"Just saying," Jackie said. "You've been warned."

"Stop scaring that girl," Valarie said, suppressing a smile.

Two hours later, Raina found herself in a field of flowers, courtesy of the floral-inspired décor in Christine Clark's guest room. Every piece of fabric in the room boasted some type of blossom — roses on the bedspread and sham, exotic bouquets on the curtains and wallpaper borders, daisies on the throw rug covering a hardwood floor, and red sunflowers on the upholstered chair in front of a small desk in the corner.

"It's small but comfortable," Christine said, upon opening the door and pointing to the twin bed against the far wall.

"It's fine, Miss Christine. Thank you."

"I emptied the two top drawers in that chest for you to put your things. There's a basket in the closet for your dirty clothes, and extra towels in the hall closet. There's a plug-in on the wall beneath the desk for your computer. Showing you the rest of the house will take all of five minutes, but we can do that after eating. Speaking of, I need to check on my chicken. Are you hungry?"

"Not really," Raina said. "We had spaghetti for dinner."

"That was hours ago, while I was talking to Valarie." Christine looked her up and down. "It doesn't have to be much, but I'll fix you a plate. You could use an extra meal or two."

It didn't take Raina long to get settled into the quaint, cozy room. She emptied her suitcases, set up her tablet on the desk, and washed her hands for dinner. She reached the dining room to a table set for two and glasses of cola beside the silverware and took the seat to the left of the head of the table. Christine entered carrying a tray with two plates filled with baked chicken and rice with a side of mixed vegetables. She placed one in front of Raina and set the other one down in front of her chair at the head. She placed a small plate of rolls between them, sat down, and reached a hand toward Raina, who stared at her blindly.

"Let's bless the food, child," Christine said. When Raina didn't reach up to grab her hand, she continued. "What? You've never prayed before?"

"I'm . . . no."

Christine's eyes narrowed. "You ain't one of those Lucifers are you?"

"I'm part of the Illumination," Raina explained.

Christine shrieked. "The blood of Jesus!"

Raina jumped. Christine guffawed. "I'm messing with you, child. Valarie warned me that you were one of those. Don't bother me none. I prepared for your arrival with a whole bottle of blessed oil. I ain't afraid of that slew-footed devil. Satan ain't no match for God. Now, let's pray."

"We don't . . . do that."

"Well, I'm a Christian, and we do," Christine explained. "So as long as you're living under my roof and eating at my table, you're going to have to oblige me."

"Oh, okay." Raina reached up tentatively and took Christine's hand, then watched with wide, curious eyes as Christine spoke to an unseen Father as if they were best buds, and included Raina.

"Father, we come thanking you for this

food that we're about to receive for the nourishment of our bodies. We ask that you bless the hands that planted, the ones that prepared, and the ones that partake. I am especially grateful for my house guest, Miss Raina, and ask that you be with her during this time of estrangement from her family. Protect her, Father. Help the family, Lord. Help them heal and move past any misunderstandings that keep them apart. You are not the author of confusion, Lord. So help them see the way clear to come back together. In Jesus's name."

Christine prepared to release Raina's hand, but she held on tightly. Miss Christine had spoken to whoever it was as though she fully expected an answer.

"I have a little sister whom I call Shadow. Could you ask him to bless her, too?"

"Now that I can do."

Christine petitioned her God again and asked for protection for Shadow and direction for her parents. She asked that Raina be given peace about the situation and, when prompted, that Shadow be healed. She ended the prayer with a hearty amen, then reached for her fork and began eating. She was several bites in before realizing that Raina was rearranging the food from one part of the plate to the other, but eating very little of it.

"Come on, now. That's one leg of chicken. I don't have food to waste."

Raina speared a small piece of the fork-tender meat, along with the spicy rice. "It's good," she said, and when Christine kept staring, took a bite of the vegetables as well.

Christine nodded. "One of Jackie's favorite meals."

Christine got down to business then, devouring the chicken as though it might jump up and run off her plate. She chattered through half the plate's contents, then took a long swig of the cola. Reaching for a napkin, she sat back and studied Raina. "Your spirit seems troubled, child."

"I guess, a little."

"Mama kick me out the house I guess I'd be troubled, too. It was your mama, right? Or was it that cold-looking white man she's married to?"

At her look of shock, Christine continued. "This town is too small for secrets. Plus, I know Bev, Jason and Monica's mom. We all go to Chippewa Baptist. But you probably knew that already."

"How do you know my stepdad?"

"Don't know him. Just seen him a time or two. I checked out one of your meetings on that local cable channel. Just long enough for me to know y'all's church was not for me. Your mama looks like she's from good Baptist stock. How'd she get hooked up with that devil? God forgive me, he's your father. I shouldn't have said that. How'd she meet that man?"

"Back in Kansas City, they worked together."

"He looks to be quite a bit older than her. Was he her boss? None of my business," Christine added. "Just asking."

"Yes, ma'am."

"He got money?"

Raina's face warmed. "I guess."

"I imagine you're right," Christine continued calmly. "That Lucifer Ridge neighborhood sure is fancy."

"It's Lucent Rising."

"He ain't getting up, but whatever. Money ain't no good when it's burning, and from what I can see, that church is a cult."

Again, Raina found herself getting defensive for the organization that she herself had come to question more every year.

"My mother would disagree with you. Only Unsanc— those who are not members, call it that."

"She didn't know it was a cult when she joined it?"

"She knew what my stepdad told her, and

168

also knew that because of him we were living a better life."

"Uh-huh. This your better life right here? Why you're sitting at my dinner table, on the out with your folk, worry creasing up that pretty face? I'm trying not to judge you. But the people who belong to y'all's church never seemed to have it together quite right."

"What does that mean?"

"I'm just saying there's some strange goings-on. I've watched it since the first family moved here twenty years ago. Home-schooling their children. Forced to keep to themselves. Locking up the residents behind what looks like a fifty-foot fence. The first time I saw it, I couldn't believe it. Asked Valarie if that was a new neighborhood, or a prison?"

Christine laughed at her own joke, and polished off her cola. "How is it that you're going to public school?"

"My grandma, mostly," Raina said, smiling at the memory of Jennifer's spry mom. "After my mother married Ken, I began being homeschooled. Grandma heard about it and had a fit. Said I should be around kids my own age. It took a little for Dad to agree, but he finally said okay. The private high school won't be finished for another three years. So far, the organization here only has grade school."

"Your little sister goes to the church's school. Old ladies know everything," she continued, given Raina's surprised expression. "It's what we do."

Raina shrugged, her spirit sagging under the weight of missing her shadow. "I guess she likes it well enough. It's the only one she's known."

"Bev told me she's a bit under the weather. Said you told her that the other day when she picked you up. Is that what has you troubled, you're worried about her?"

Raina thought about what Beverly had said about her daughter not holding water and realized that the apple hadn't fallen far from the tree.

"It was just a fever," Raina said. "She's probably better now."

"Probably so, but have your mama take her in to that clinic. She doesn't want no parts of that flu."

Miss Christine was as comfortable as a favorite sweater. Raina found herself sharing more than she'd intended. "We don't believe in doctors or taking medication."

"What in the world? Are you kidding me? You don't believe in doctors or Jesus either?

Lord, anything happen to that poor baby and she won't stand a chance." Christine thought for a moment. "When's the last time you saw your sister?"

"A couple days ago."

"Can you call her?"

"I can try, but my parents are probably monitoring the phone."

"So?"

Raina didn't want to explain the whole obscure, getting-ghosted situation. "I can't talk to her while on punishment," she finally said.

"What about school? Can you go see her? It'll reassure you and probably make her feel better."

It was a great idea, but unlikely to happen, Raina thought. By now everyone in the Nation would know that she'd been obscured.

"It's a private school," Raina told her. "I probably couldn't get in."

"What do you mean, can't get in? That's your sister, private or not."

"Being on punishment means being separated from your whole family. You can't see or talk to them during that time. That's why I'm here."

Christine gave her a look, the kind that made Raina think she could see through to

171

the soul. "Punishment, that's what you're calling it? Baby, I watch TV. I know about those Polly Annies and how they treat their children. You're not on punishment. You've been shunned!"

Said with such force and a sense of derision that Raina laughed out loud. "We don't use that term. We say obscured."

"You can say OB-GYN and it won't change nothing. Your bedroom across town will still be empty while you're sitting at my house."

That truth took away some of the humor. That and thoughts of Abby, staying on that side of the second floor for the first time by herself.

"I'm sorry, baby. Didn't mean to make you sad. But what they're doing is a shame. You don't cut off your child no matter what they've done. Or be made not to see a little sister who probably misses you, too. Hold on a moment. I have an idea." Christine got up from the table.

"Should I come with you?"

"No, stay there. I'll be right back."

She returned minutes later, swinging an auburn-colored wig. She held it out to Raina.

"Here."

Raina looked dubious. "What's that for?"

"It's for you to get in to that private school to see your sister."

Raina felt showing up to the facility looking like Carrot Top's cousin just might make them lock the doors faster. Still, she appreciated Christine's support, and with no bright ideas of her own, decided to play along.

"You think my wearing that will make a difference?"

"With all this hair it'll probably be wearing you, but if you're quick and can think on your feet it might get you inside long enough to see your sister. Think you can pull it off?"

"I can try. Thank you, Miss Christine."

"Think nothing of it. Hopefully knowing that she's okay will make you feel better."

Later that night, Raina called Jackie and told her the plan. "I told you Nanny was crazy," was her honest reply. It was the kind of insanity Raina could handle. The next day she skipped the class before phys ed and just before two in the afternoon, after being dropped off by a taxi, stood across from Lucent Rising Elementary Institute wearing black slacks, Jackie's oversized down coat, a black scarf, black gloves and the red wig. The streets were deserted, not another human in sight. As in the subdivision, Raina knew there were cameras at the school. She'd hoped to get there closer to the end of the day when there might be more people coming and going. But she knew that one of her parents would arrive to pick up Abby. She couldn't take the chance on missing her, getting caught, or not having the chance again. After taking a deep breath she covered the lower part of her face with the scarf Christine had given her, put her head down and crossed the street. Her heart pounded as she forced herself to not race up the concrete steps. She prayed the doors were unlocked. They were. The stars aligned! Just as she began to pull the handle someone came toward her.

It was Mrs. Brigham, her mother's good friend and the wife of an elder. The last type of Nation member she needed to see. Knowing it would be rude to totally ignore her, Raina issued a quick, "Light day to you, sister," and hurried down the hallway. She felt Mrs. Brigham's eyes on her and dared not turn around. She hoped the always helpful woman wouldn't come back to assist Raina, who with the wig and the oversized coat probably looked like a bum. Fortunately, Raina was familiar with the school's layout and knew Abby's classroom location. After taking a quick scan of her surroundings, she walked up to the open door and peeked inside. Her eyes quickly scanned the room. Then her heart fell. The chair where Abby usually sat was empty. Where was her sister?

"Excuse me."

Raina started at the sound of a voice right behind her and almost literally flipped her wig. She turned to see the familiar uniform of a healer, dressed in white. Behind her was Abby, looking tepid and pale. Raina's heart pounded with joy and trepidation. Joy that she'd seen Abby. Sadness that she was still with a healer and fear that she'd look up, call out, and blow Raina's cover.

"I'm sorry," Raina said, keeping her eyes downcast and purposely muffling her voice beneath the scarf. "I'm looking for Abby Reed. The Grand Seer sent me to pick her up."

Abby looked up then, her eyes widening, her mouth slowly opening. Raina quickly shook her head, cutting her eyes toward the healer. Abby got the message. Raina exhaled.

"And you are?"

"Moon Vessel Mavis Stanford, from the thirty-third chapter in Tulsa, Oklahoma."

Upon hearing the name of one of the organization's central locations, the woman nodded. "Light day to you, sister."

"Keep shining."

She held Abby's hand and waited until
the healer began walking away, then went in
the opposite direction, toward the girls'
bathroom. Once inside she quickly checked
for occupants. The stalls were empty. She
pulled Abby into the last one, dropped to
her knees and gave her a hug.

"Hey, Shadow," she whispered, her eyes
brimming with tears.

"What are you doing here? What's with
the wig?" Raina felt Abby's weak embrace
end abruptly. "I'm not supposed to talk to
you."

"I know, Shadow, and I won't stay."

"Don't call me that. Dad says it's like a
bad word."

She'd been gone less than a week, but the
weight of the dogma was telling. There was
distance between her and her sister that
hadn't been there before. No time to get
into all of that now, though. She'd told the
healer she was picking up Abby and just
now realized her dilemma. No car and no
Jackie. Just that morning she'd left for the
airport. Miss Christine no longer drove.
Monica? No. She'd gotten the job and was
working at BBs. Maybe Bryce? Just as
quickly that idea flew out the mental win-

dow. Abby telling Ken she'd ridden home with an unsanctioned male and her renegade sis? Ken would blow a gasket.

"I've been worried about you." She reached up and felt Abby's forehead. "You're still very warm, Sha . . . Abby."

"The healer says it's the Light shining, healing me from within."

"I say it's a fever," Raina mumbled. Then to Abby, "Are you still tired all the time?"

Abby nodded. "I want to go home."

"Mother or Father should be here soon."

"Do they know you're here?"

"No, and we can't tell them."

"You want me to lie?"

"Just don't say anything unless they ask you."

"Do you not want to be a part of our family anymore?"

"Why would you ask that? Of course."

"Then why haven't you called us, or met with the Council?"

"I've left messages, Shadow, at the house and for the council. No one has called back. As soon as the Council gives their recommendation, I'm sure Mom and Dad will call me. I'll talk to them then about moving back home. Okay?"

"Okay."

"Hey, being there by yourself can't be all

bad. You've got that whole big bathroom to yourself."

"I don't need that much room."

Raina hugged Abby again, squeezed even tighter. This time Abby hugged her back. "Am I going to get germs because I hugged you?"

"No, just shield yourself." Raina heard heels clicking against the tile. "I'd better go," she whispered. "Count to sixty, then go to the circle. Mom or Dad should be there by now. Can you do that?"

Abby nodded.

"Love you, Shadow."

Abby's bittersweet smile broke Raina's heart. She unlocked the door, eased it open and looked right into the faces of the healer she'd lied to, Mrs. Brigham, and Abby's teacher, Lucy Stone.

Lucy Stone's face was a mask of righteous indignation. "I thought it was your voice I heard outside of my classroom. Raina Reed, what are you doing here?"

CHAPTER 13

They hadn't returned her calls for days, but an hour after getting busted at Abby's school, Raina sat in front of a hastily gathered Council. It was not the meeting she'd intended, but one quickly arranged once Lucy Stone's hunch was proven right and the Moon Vessel from Oklahoma was actually Abby's soon-to-be-obscured sis. Raina had offered to leave the school, and quite hastily at that, but she was forcibly discouraged from doing so by Lucent Rising security. After a valiant struggle proved she might have been a match for one or two guards but couldn't handle four, she stopped fighting and allowed herself to be led to the office, where she'd sat until summoned to the church, driven in a security van. Now she sat in front of what felt like a firing squad, with a broken fingernail, scratches, and a bruise forming on her upper left arm. The scarf was gone and there was only one glove. She had no idea where the wig went.

She knew most all of the elders before her quite well, from the time the family arrived in Chippewa. Franklin Tessler was like a crusty old uncle, gruff, unflappable, very by-the-book. He and his wife, Mary, had been to the Reeds' home several times. Now, he looked through her as though he didn't know her at all. There was Graham Patterson and his brother Otis, Elder Montgomery, who'd performed one of her levels of light initiations, and a new member, Mr. West she thought was his name. No women were present. They were not allowed to sit on the council. One chair remained empty, and as much as she hoped it was reserved for her mom, Raina knew that was a pipe dream. She would have liked to think otherwise, but Raina knew that it wasn't being held for her mom. Jennifer was probably still angry, furious even. But Raina missed her mom immensely and would give anything to see her. Before this thought was finished, the mystery was solved. The empty chair was for the elder second-highest in command, her stepfather, Ken Reed. Just peachy.

Ken greeted the other members of the council. He did not look at her before taking his seat. Otis Patterson stood and formally announced, "This meeting is now called to order."

Mr. Tessler twirled the handle of his gray mustache. "The business at hand deals with misconduct of the highest order, a series of erroneous actions that, considering the person being charged with these violations, has the Council deeply concerned."

Raina glanced at Ken, noticed the nervous tic just above his right eye, the set of his jaw. She felt worse than horrible. Wanted the floor to open up and swallow her whole.

Otis pulled out a folder and read from what appeared to be several papers inside. "Ms. Raina Reed, vessel of our own the esteemed and noble Ken Reed, you are charged with a series of serious transgressions included but not limited to the following: egregious and continual deception, fraud, concealing identity, breaching security —"

"Breaching security?" Raina repeated, unable to help herself. "At the school? I think that statement is a bit misleading. I walked through an unlocked door."

"Providing false identification," Otis continued without pause.

Raina sat back in the seat. She couldn't deny the whole moon vessel thing.

". . . and the attempted kidnapping of —"

In less than a nanosecond, Raina was on her feet. "No way!"

The same security guards she'd "met" at the school, once again surrounded her. She looked at Ken. His face was stone. She sat down, but wouldn't be silent.

"Father! It's not true. I was concerned about Abby and only wanted to see her. I miss my sister!"

Otis Patterson held up his hand. "Be quiet, Ms. Reed. You are not to address anyone unless a question is asked. Is that understood?"

"Yes, Grand Seer," Raina said softly.

Otis eyed her with a hint of compassion. "As for missing your sister, that is because of your actions. You should have thought about that before going outside the light."

"I didn't try and kidnap Abby."

"Silence!"

Graham Patterson spoke instead of Otis, his brother. The bass in the older man's voice reverberated in Raina's empty stomach.

"You will not speak out of order again."

Order or the lack of it, didn't matter. No one asked questions, not what happened or why. Not whether she felt remorse for her actions or what she was willing to do to make amends. They handed down judgment based on one-sided opinions, not only about Raina trespassing at Abby's school, but about lying to her parents, being in the extended company of the unsanctioned, and putting the entire church through endless worry by failing to come home when expected or calling to say she'd be late. They weren't counting, but Raina was pretty sure she'd broken the record for single-incident infractions, a number that would undoubtedly double if they knew about Kansas City and the video. Her father reprimanded her, followed by Elder Montgomery, and finally Otis Patterson, a Grand Seer.

"Daughter, you have presented us with a most unique situation that involves not one or two but several points of error against the church. As such, it is not a decision that can be made within minutes, except to obscure you immediately . . ."

Raina held her breath.

". . . which I, as Grand Seer, do not recommend."

She exhaled.

"I ask if the council can abide in chambers until this matter is settled, or tabled, for another day."

He looked around. "Is there anyone who can't stay for" — he looked at his watch —

"say, an hour or two?"

No one objected.

"Fine. Then this meeting is adjourned for further private discussion. Vessel Raina, you will be informed by your father of our decision. Until then, I suggest you remove yourself from others and focus solely on the *Book of Light*. It is the sole means for your redemption, and reillumination. Though currently in darkness, try and find a ray of light."

As she'd not been given permission to speak, Raina simply nodded. She wanted to speak with her father, seek his forgiveness, ask about Mom. But he left with the others with no further acknowledgment, left her to be guided out of the church by security, and driven away from Lucent Rising to await the outcome. When asked where she wanted to be dropped off, she suggested a corner near BBs.

It was a short ride, and a silent one. On the way to town, Raina thought about the meeting, and how unfair it felt that she had not gotten the chance to speak. It was as though her side didn't matter, her point of view didn't count. If they would have asked if she was sorry, she would have said, "Yes, absolutely!" Had she had it to do over again, she would have never gotten into the Mustang that day. Never met Sniper or Shanghai, never seen a video, much less appeared in one. The best thing that could happen to her would be that the footage ended up on the cutting-room floor and never saw the light of day. Right now, she had only one desire — to remain in the church that not long ago she couldn't wait to leave. She'd do whatever it took, say whatever the council wanted to hear. As oppressive as her home sometimes felt, she had no idea how much she would miss it.

After being dropped off on the corner, she walked to BBs at the end of the block. She'd texted Monica en route and knew she was working, and Jackie, who'd agreed to give her a ride home. She didn't say much to her friends about the meeting. Until the Council issued a verdict, there wasn't much to talk about.

The call came while Raina was still at the restaurant. She recognized Ken's number and walked outside. Temperatures had dropped with the setting sun, but Raina didn't notice. All of her attention was focused on the voice coming through her phone.

"Hello, Father."

"Raina."

She closed her eyes, gripped the phone,

and waited for the inevitable.

"You have not been obscured."

Her relief was so immense tears sprang to her eyes. "Thank you, Father!"

"You being my daughter is the only reason the vote fell shy of permanent removal from the faith. As it stands, you have a tough road ahead, with stringent rules to follow. One slip, Raina, big or small, and you're out of the faith and the family."

Raina swallowed the panic that had bloomed in her throat. She knew what it meant to be obscured, or ghosted. Being ghosted was the member's dismissal from the ministry with no chance of ever rejoining the church. This permanent separation was not only from the church, but from the member's family. Their names were erased from the membership records. Numbers were changed. In some cases, addresses, too. If seen, the family member wasn't acknowledged, as though they didn't exist. Raina considered herself fairly independent with a mind of her own. But never speaking to her mother again? Never seeing Abby? Raina could imagine many things . . . but not that.

Ken provided a quick rundown of the council's requirements for her to remain in the Light.

Several months of extensive deprogramming followed by a summer spent at the center in Tulsa, Oklahoma. Instead of working a cool job in Kansas City, she'd be given a mentor and taught how to be the perfect Vessel-wife. She was to end all friendships with unsanctioned classmates and have no unchaperoned contact with any outsider, anyone not sanctioned by the Illumination. No contact. No access. No exceptions. People would be watching, he warned her. Any reports to the contrary and she'd be pulled from Chippewa and homeschooled for the remainder of the year.

"Do you understand?" he finished.

"Yes, Father. I understand."

"Do you agree to abide by everything the Council has demanded?"

"Yes, Father. I agree."

What else could she say? According to the rules of the church, her punishment more than fit the crime, especially the ones the council hadn't uncovered. Like participating in a hip-hop video, being around marijuana, not disclosing about the accident that could have gotten her killed.

"The home where you're residing. What is the name of the outsider?"

"Christine Clark."

"Who?"

Raina cleared her throat and repeated the name. Despite the frigid weather, her heart warmed. "Does this mean I get to come home?"

"Yes," Ken replied, with a warmth that Raina noticed for the first time all night. "Is that where you are now?"

"No, I'm in a restaurant, the Breadbasket."

"Your mother will come and pick you up, then drive you to the residence to pick up your things. After that, you are not to have any contact with this" — he looked down at the sheet — "Ms. Clark. Ever. Again. Is that understood?"

"Yes."

"Do you have any questions?"

It was the first time she'd been asked to speak. Questions? She had a ton. But she didn't want to ask the wrong thing, make the wrong statement.

"No, sir. I understand."

"See that you do. You are a beautiful girl, an intelligent vessel, someone who could be beneficial to the organization and a grand support to an equally loyal beam. There are several in our church," he continued, a bit less stridently. "Some live on our block. If you are diligent with your studies and committed to being reilluminated, we can put this incident behind us and welcome you back into the light."

Raina ended the call and raced into the restaurant, freezing. She called Jackie, hoping she'd not yet left home.

"I'm still waiting on Mama," was her greeting.

"Good," Raina replied. "Dad called me."

"Good news or bad?"

"Good mostly. I get to go home."

"I guess I'm happy for you."

"Gee, thanks."

"Hey, I didn't grow up with a sister. It was nice having you around."

"Thanks. I had fun, too."

"I know how much you miss your family. What's the bad news?"

Raina recounted the conversation with Ken. "I'll have to pull out of the English project," she finished. "And be on my best behavior. No doubt there will be a mole at the school ready to report any bad behavior back to Dad."

"Bad as in speaking to me?"

"Pretty much. Sucks, right?"

"I guess if made to choose between family and friends, I'd have to go with the fam."

"I don't want to choose. But it's just for a while. Once I graduate and head off to college, we'll be besties again."

189

"Who says I'll still want to be friends? Just kidding," Jackie continued in Raina's shocked silence. "Do what you gotta do."

They talked until Raina saw Jennifer's car pull in front of the restaurant. "Mom's here," she said, heading outside. "Love you, Jackie!"

"Love you back."

Raina rushed to the car. "Hi, Mom."

For a few seconds, Jennifer said nothing. The next thing Raina knew she was in her mother's arms.

"I missed you, Raina," Jennifer said, with tears in her eyes. She pulled back. Her hands cupped Raina's face as she looked her daughter over. "How are you?"

Now they both were crying. "Better, now."

Jennifer pulled herself together and pulled away from the curb.

"Tell me about this woman, Christine Clark."

"My friend at school, or rather, someone I go to school with, Jackie McFadden? She's her grandmother."

"How did you meet her?"

"Through Jackie's mom. She's a lawyer."

Jennifer glanced over at Raina. "How did you meet her?"

Again, Raina felt trapped by her lies. "While going against the rules and hanging out with the unsanctioned."

Jennifer didn't pry further and Raina was grateful, but far from out of the woods.

"I won't rehash the past and the almost unforgiveable shame you've brought on this family, especially your father. You knew how critical these next months were. Right before the solstice celebration we made that very clear. Obviously, it didn't matter."

"It did, Mom."

"No, it didn't, otherwise we wouldn't be having this conversation!" A minute passed, then another. Raina heard her mother take a deep breath.

"I know we don't talk much about our past life, before I met Ken and our lives were changed for the better. But I'm aware of how those years spent on the outside affected you. Continuing to attend public school hasn't helped. Mom meant well, but if given a chance to do it over again I would have pulled you out immediately, severely limited your contact with those who could influence you as those so-called friends did last week. It's why I've had such leniency with you, Raina, because I remember how it was being a kid. I do understand. But you are not in that world. You are a blessed and valuable vessel and you must rein in any impulses that take you outside of the church and its teaching."

"May I ask a question, Mother?"

"Yes, but when it comes to answering it there are no guarantees."

Jennifer offered an impish smile and that, combined with the glint in her eye and that straight, no-nonsense answer, reminded Raina of the mom she used to know. It felt good to see her.

"Do you ever miss your old life?"

"No," Jennifer answered, almost too quickly.

"Not even old friends?"

"No, Raina, I do not miss them. When Ken came into my life he filled it up, then introduced me to a whole new world filled with wonderful new people who've become more than friends. They've become family."

"What about Miss Bev?"

"Beverly who . . . Wilson?" Raina nodded, noting how her mother's fingers tightened on the wheel. "What about her?"

"When walking to . . . where I stayed . . . I ran into her. She gave me a ride."

"You've really forgotten your teachings, Raina. Why did you get in the car of an outsider? Oh, but wait. That wasn't your first time."

"I didn't think of her as an outsider! It was Miss Bev from my hometown. It was cold and snowing," Raina added.

Jennifer remained stone silent.

"She said the two of you used to be really good friends, and that you used to sing together."

"We never sang together."

"Well, not together but that —"

"If there was any aspect of my past that I wanted you to know, I would have told you."

"She knew my father."

Jennifer huffed. "She knew the man who donated the sperm that helped give you life. He's your daddy, Raina, but Al Jardin was never really a father. Kenneth Reed is the only one of those you've ever known."

The rest of the ride was made in silence. It wasn't until pulling into the driveway that Raina remembered her belongings that were still with Miss Christine.

"We forgot to pick up my stuff," she said, her voice barely above a whisper.

Jennifer pulled into the garage and exited the car without a word. Raina sat for only a few seconds before following her mother out of the car and into the house. Her father was in the kitchen. When he heard the door open, he turned and smiled.

He walked over and placed a hand on the shoulder of the daughter he'd adopted and raised as his own since the age of ten.

"Hello, Raina. Welcome home."

The sound of running footsteps sounded down the hall. "Sister!"

"Shadow!"

The name burst out of her mouth like a firecracker, even as her brain wished to chase down the syllables and vowels and stuff them back down her throat. She dared not look in her dad's direction. Gratefully, he let the slip pass.

Raina dropped to her knees. Abby ran into her arms. The awkward moment was over and in that moment Raina's world righted itself. "I missed you so much!"

"I missed you too, sister!"

"How do you feel? You look great!"

"I feel great. They brought an energy machine to the Center. I got to use it!"

The Illumination religion founder, Dr. Daniel Best, fancied himself not only a messiah of sorts, but a scientist, author, and inventor. In the late 60s, he developed a machine touted to have the ability to cure any and all diseases. It was patented as the ILLUX in 1974 and had been used in one form or another for the past forty-plus years.

Raina looked more closely at her sister, turned questioning eyes toward her mom.

Ken answered the unasked. "Smaller versions of the ILLUX are being installed at all major Centers across the country. Abby was chosen as one of the members used to test it out, make sure it worked properly."

"That's wonderful, Abby."

"It certainly is," Ken said. "The specialist instructing our members on its use said that your sister is in perfect health."

Jennifer returned to the kitchen. "Why don't you two set the table?" she said. "We're having enchiladas, Raina."

From the very first time her mother had made them when she was around eight years old, the gooey Mexican mixture of beef, beans, and rice smothered in cheese and sauce had been Raina's favorite meal. That Jennifer chose this as her welcome-home dinner made Raina misty-eyed, a silent message of the close bond they once shared in the past and what Raina hoped would again exist in the future.

At the dinner table, life for the Reeds resumed as though Raina had never been gone. No mention was made of the Council meeting, the decision, the unsanctioned, the reasons for Raina's absence or her return. They talked about upcoming events at the center and a field trip Abby's class took to the Kansas City Zoo. Jennifer shared news about the latest light. Their neighbor, Mrs. Sanchez, had her baby, a girl named Ariel.

It was regular and uneventful, just another night at the Reed house. Raina wouldn't have had it any other way.

After dinner, the girls helped Jennifer with the dishes, then went upstairs. Raina followed Abby into the younger girl's room, where they hugged again and for several seconds smiled into each other's faces.

"I really missed you, sister," Abby whispered. "I'm so glad you're back."

Raina moved a large stuffed animal from the foot of Abby's bed and climbed on it. "How was it here while I was gone?"

"Quiet," Abby said.

"Tell me about the energy machine."

From then until Jennifer announced Abby's bedtime, the two sisters chatted. Raina went to bed, too, snuggled under the covers. She'd appreciated Miss Christine's floral garden, but there was no place like home. Especially with Abby feeling better, laughing and smiling. That was the best part. Her shadow was back.

Chapter 14

The subdivision of Lucent Rising was basically self-contained. There was a quaint block of retail shops that in supporting the Illumination members did a fairly brisk business and were frequented by many of the town members as well. Anchoring one corner was a grocer that specialized in organic food, including chicken and beef. Next to it was a dessert shop with some of the best pastries and pies in the Sunflower State. There was a library in a coffee shop, an ice cream vendor, a beauty/barber shop, and a consignment boutique. Other businesses sold fabric and crafts, lawn and gardening supplies, and a two-story office building held offices where governmental business took place. Many Nation members had almost zero contact with the unsanctioned. But every now and then, stepping outside their enlightened bubble couldn't be helped. That was the case when a week after returning home, Raina unexpectedly came face-to-face with Valarie and Jackie, shopping at Dollar Discount. She was there with Roslyn, one of her new teammates for the English project, and their chaperone, Mary. The project required a certain poster board that wasn't carried in the community, so they'd headed to the store after school to pick up that and other supplies. Roslyn had gone down the electronics aisle while Raina hurried over to office supplies to get poster board and tape. She was so preoccupied with getting the items quickly that she turned the corner and hit Valarie head-on.

"Oh, sorry! I . . . oh. Hi, Miss Valarie."

Speaking to Jackie's mom was a natural reaction. She was quickly sobered by the reminder that talking with outsiders was not permitted and with her in the zero-tolerance phase of deprogramming and probation, it was something she didn't want to chance. Without another word, she hurried away.

"Raina."

She heard Valarie's partially confused, partially ticked-off sounding voice behind her. Totally ignoring it, instead she made a beeline for the materials she'd been looking for located near the end of the row. That's when Jackie entered the aisle, from her side.

"Girl, I know you are not ignoring my mama."

"I spoke to her," Raina whispered. "Probation," she hastily added, conveying more with her eyes.

Jackie rolled hers and added a tsk for good measure.

Valarie closed the distance between them. "Are you all right?" Valarie asked, her prosecutor eyes homing in on Raina's nervous behavior.

"Yes, ma'am," Raina answered, without looking at her. She studied the merchandise hanging on the wall, as if deciding what to choose. "I'm back with my family." Raina hoped the comment would help explain why she was acting looney tunes.

"Jackie told me they gave you another chance. That doesn't earn them a medal from me. You shouldn't have been kicked out in the first place."

The chaperone entered the aisle. "Raina . . ."

Raina stepped back, preparing to go around Jackie. "I've got to go."

Valarie stepped in front of Raina, face-to-face with the older woman chaperone. "I'm Valarie McFadden," she said, holding out her hand. "The mother who took care of this girl after she got tossed out in the street."

Mary did not shake Valarie's hand. She stepped back, motioned to Raina. "Come away from this darkness."

Jackie whirled on her. "Are you talking about me? I've got your darkness right here."

Raina stepped in front of her friend. "Jackie, she didn't mean it like that."

"She's talking about our blackness. I know exactly what she means!"

"Have you forgotten? I'm Black, too!"

"No, but it looks like you did."

"Raina!" Mary chided. "Not another word."

Raina brushed by Jackie to join Mary and Roslyn, rapidly approaching the cashier.

"What?" Valarie called out after her. "You can't have a conversation since you're back with them now? You can't talk with the people who kept your butt off the street in the dead of winter and made you welcome in our home?"

Raina looked back. Her expression was pleading.

Valarie seemed to make note of it. She changed her expression and tone. "Take care of yourself, Raina. Don't lose yourself in that cult!"

The trio finished their purchases and returned to Mary's car. Raina was shaken. Roslyn, quiet.

"I didn't want to talk to them," Raina cried, already imagining herself before another council, packing her bags and leaving Lucent Rising for good.

"I know," Mary said. "I heard the exchange." She reached into the glove compartment and pulled out a spritzer and a white votive candle.

"Let's cleanse ourselves, girls," she said quietly. "We don't want to take the energy of outsiders back into our homes."

Raina didn't refute her and went through the motions. But inside her heart broke at Mary's statement. When it came to the McFaddens and her, they'd been nothing but good. As she entered her home, Raina knew one thing for sure. Disconnecting from the unsanctioned, two of them her best friends for years, would prove to be a lot harder than Raina thought it would be. She knew something else. There was no way she could let what happened go unchecked. She'd seek out Jackie first thing tomorrow, and try to make it right.

She arrived at school early, hoping to catch them in the commons area in front of the library. It was one of the few places where she felt it less likely to run into a member. They usually congregated by the cafeteria on the other end of the school. Ten minutes before class, she saw them. They saw her, too, and kept walking up the hall. Raina made a quick check of the halls to spot church members. Seeing none close, she risked making amends.

"Jackie! Monica! Wait!"

She navigated through the crowded high school hallway, determined to catch them before they entered the main hallway where church members were more likely to be. She missed her friends. Mary had been straight-up rude. Her return to the Nation had left relationships strained. As determined as she was to get reilluminated and continue living with her family, she also wanted to apologize to Jackie, and try to explain her absence in friendship to them both. She sprinted in front of them, turned and blocked their progress, just before they turned the corner into the main hall.

"What's up, sistahs?" she asked, trying to recapture the camaraderie. It didn't take long for her to realize that the thrill had gone.

"We're not your sisters," Monica said, though there was a smile in her voice.

"Yeah, we're not light enough," Jackie teased.

"Come on, guys. You know I don't feel that way. Jackie, I . . ."

"We know."

"You do?"

Jackie nodded.

"You're not still angry about yesterday?"

"I'm not, but Mama is pissed. She knows that what happened isn't your fault, but for the next few, your little group would do well to stay away from her. That lady —"

"Was rude. I know. I'm sorry." Raina looked from one to the other. "For everything."

The halls continued to fill. She spotted a member on the other end heading their way.

"I've got to go," she said, before darting off in the other direction.

It was just after lunch, in their algebra class, when Raina was able to speak with Jackie again. The teacher paired up the students by row to work on a complicated equation. Because the besties sat across from each other, they were chosen to work together.

"I tried calling," Jackie said. She dragged her finger down the page of the textbook, as if discussing the problem.

"I'm on electronic lockdown," Raina

replied. "No cell phone, limited tablet time, all checked by Mom."

"Damn, not having a phone must be torture. Hey! Why don't you buy a burner?"

"That's a thought but . . . no, probably shouldn't. It would be just my luck for it to ring or fall out of my pocket or something. Hopefully I'll get mine back soon."

They began working on the math problem. "There's a pay phone near the center," Raina said. "I might be able to call you Saturday, while everyone's busy with church activities."

"You can try, but I might not be available when you call."

"Why not?"

"KCK is in concert, don't you remember?"

For all it had cost her, Raina had tried to forget everything about that unforgettable day. "I remember hearing that a concert was coming up. I didn't realize it was this soon."

"Yep, Saturday night. He'll be performing with Sniper and giving the audience a sneak peek of the video we shot."

"Ah, man."

"If you feel bad about that, then you definitely don't want to know about our backstage tickets."

"Just shoot me, okay?"

Jackie's laugh netted her an elbow in the side. "We can't look like we're having fun," Raina hissed, and could barely keep from grinning. She'd never appreciated algebra so much in her life. "Will Shanghai be there?"

"They don't know. She's shooting a movie but wants to try and work it out so she can make an appearance. Don't worry. The world premiere of the video will be on BHTV next month. You'll get to see it then."

Raina's spirit dipped as she thought about the fun they'd had making the video and all she'd miss on Saturday night. Try as she might she couldn't be like her mother and let go of regular life. It had only been a few days of freedom but the taste had been like ambrosia in her mouth. One of the Nation members looked over and frowned. Raina clammed up, her body language signaling Jackie that someone was watching. They focused on the equation until the member returned to her work. Raina relaxed, but casual chitchat was over.

"That's so whacky," Jackie said, wearing a frown of disgust.

"I'm sorry," Raina said. "It's the proba-tion —"

"I don't give a damn!" Jackie mumbled under her breath. "I know you're doing this for your family and all. I understand that. I don't want you to risk getting kicked out again. But I'm not going to sit here and pretend that it feels good to be treated like a second-class citizen, someone you have to sneak around to have a simple conversation with."

"It breaks my heart. You and Monica are as much my sisters as Abby! Things will be different once I graduate high school and move to KC."

"The Nation isn't in Kansas City?"

"Yes, but with half a million people versus our town of four thousand, we're harder to track."

"All right, guys," the teacher said. "Five minutes to wrap it up."

Raina spoke quickly. "Speaking of, though, and I know it sucks, but can you do me a favor? If you see me out, especially with someone older, it's probably a chaperone keeping tabs on me. Can you please not say anything, to them or to me? There are eagle eyes everywhere, waiting to see me mess up so that I can get obscured, or even ghosted, and get kicked out of the faith."

"Might be one of the best things that could happen," Jackie mumbled.

"No, it wouldn't, because I'd also lose my family. They'd never speak to me again."

Jackie shook her head again. "If it were anyone but you . . ."

"Oh, one more thing. Tell Bryce hi and that I miss him, okay?"

Jackie opened her mouth to say something, then simply nodded.

"What?" Raina asked.

"Never mind."

"Jackie . . ."

"Don't think Bryce is going to stay single. I told you from jump he's a ladies' man."

"I don't care. We were just friends anyway."

They finished the equation and put their desks back in the row. Raina tried to focus on what the teacher was saying about absolute value, coordinate systems, factorial numbers and whatnot. But all she could think of was Bryce, and all of the girls who'd love to be with him, of the one or two or twelve who may be keeping company with him right now. The thought made her heart ache, no matter how she fought it. She told Jackie that Bryce was just a friend. In fact, he was her first true love, who most likely would become her first love lost, as well.

"Jackie—"

CHAPTER 15

Between school and Raina's load of re-illumination classes, February passed quickly. Abby would help her do dishes after dinner, then they'd retreat to their bedrooms just to hang out together, creating masterpieces in Raina's young adult coloring books or putting together jigsaw puzzles, Abby's favorite pastime. For the most part her shadow was her usual free-spirited self, but to Raina she was too tired too often for someone her age. A couple times her fever spiked and she'd been placed on the IL-LUX machine. Whenever Raina asked, her mother told her not to worry about it. To repeat the healing mantra for her sister and to see her well. Raina wanted to see her go to a doctor's office, maybe even emergency. But after the energy machine treatments, Abby rebounded. For Raina, that's all that mattered.

In early March, Abby complained of chills

and stomach pains and didn't want dinner. Jennifer provided an herbal mixture and vitamin juice. After dinner, Raina checked on her little sister, who seemed warm, but was peacefully sleeping. She spent the next several hours cramming for a science test. Finals were looming and Raina worried that she was not prepared. She went to sleep with the SAT study guide for a pillow. The next morning she kept hitting the snooze button, waiting to hear the sound of Abby taking a shower. When the tandem bath remained quiet and there was not even a minute left to spare, Raina forced herself out of bed and stumbled into the shower. She turned on the water, then opened the door to Abby's bedroom to rouse her.

"Abby! Get up, get your uniform ready. We're going to be late."

She jumped into the shower, spun around a couple times, brushed her teeth, and was out in five minutes. She wrapped herself in a towel, then padded barefoot into Abby's room.

"Shadow," she hissed, reverting to the nickname as she often did when calling out before thinking. "We've got to get moving!"

She continued to her sister's bed, and gently shook her shoulders. "Abby, wake up." She said it a little louder this time, with a little authoritative bass in her voice. "Quit playing," she told the still prone figure. "I know you hear me. We don't sleep that soundly. We're leaving in ten minutes so if you want a ride, you'd better get up."

She whirled around, heading toward the bathroom and her room on the other side. With one foot on the tile, she turned again. "Abby, seriously, come on."

That's when the stillness hit her. Had she seen Shadow move? One second passed, and then another. Her heart skipped a beat as past memories of Abby being "dim" rushed unbidden into her mind. Her eyes narrowed as she returned to Abby's bedside, this time noting a thin sheen of sweat on her sister's brow.

"Abby," she said, shaking her sister harder this time. "Abby, wake up! Mother!"

She raced to the master suite. Ken had already left for his work at the center. She heard Jennifer in the shower. "Mother! I can't wake Abby! I'm calling 9-1-1."

"Raina!"

Raina didn't hear Jennifer. She sprinted into her room and grabbed her cell phone from the charger.

"Nine-one-one, what's your emergency?"

"My sister! She —"

The phone was snatched from her hand.

"There is no emergency," Jennifer said calmly, giving Raina an icy stare. "Sorry to have bothered you."

"Ma'am."

Jennifer ended the call on Raina's phone. "What were you thinking?" she asked, tapping the face of her own phone.

"Abby's not moving!"

"You're on zero tolerance and better hope no one shows up here."

Was she serious? Abby might be dead in the other room and her mother was worried about the Council? Her concern was for the church?

The call answered. "Good morning, you've reached Illumination. Step into the light!"

"Hello, it's Moon Vessel Jennifer, the Grand Seer Reed's wife. I need a head specialist, immediately. My daughter is . . . very dim."

"She's not breathing!" Raina yelled.

"It appears critical." As the harsh seriousness of the situation sank in, Jennifer began to show emotion. "We need help."

Raina took Jennifer's phone. "Please send everyone available. The head specialist, herbalist, healers, whoever. They need to come to the Reed home . . . now!"

Raina's authoritative tone spurred Jenni-

211

fer into action. She raced back into her daughter's room. "Abby! Abby, darling, wake up!"

And to Raina. "Call Ken."

Raina called her stepfather as she watched Jennifer go into the bathroom and wet a towel with cold water. She raced to Abby's bed and dabbed the sweat from her face. Raina felt suspended as if in a dream. The sound of incessant knocking followed by the ringing of the doorbell brought her back to the emergency at hand. She raced down the stairs and opened the door. Several members from the center were on the other side.

"She's upstairs," Raina said, turning around and heading to Abby's room without looking back. They followed, reached the room, and told Raina and Jennifer to leave so that they could do their work.

"That's my sister!" Raina yelled. "I'm not going anywhere!"

"Your best helping is elsewhere," the head specialist responded. "Your sister needs healing mantras and positive vibrations. Bring in the sun. We'll handle the healing."

Raina felt Jennifer's grip on her arm. "Come, Raina. Your sister needs light, not fear."

She allowed her mother to lead them

downstairs, to the rarely used formal living room. They'd just sat down and grabbed hands when the sound of sirens was heard in the distance. Jennifer's eyes widened, then narrowed as she looked toward the sound, then at Raina, with condemnation in her eyes. The wailing slowed, then got louder. Closer and closer the noise continued, until it along with flashing lights were directly outside their window.

Jennifer quickly rose from the couch and headed toward the door. She opened it just as Ken and another elder drove up. The ambulance had partially blocked the drive. Ken parked on the other side of the street and raced up to the front door.

"What are they doing here?" he demanded of Jennifer. "What's going on?"

"The healers are here," Jennifer said, just as one of them came up to join them.

"Who called the outsiders?" she asked.

Ken glowered at Raina.

"I couldn't wake Abby and panicked. It just happened. I didn't think —"

"You rarely do." He turned to Jennifer. "Take care of our daughter. I'll handle this."

The EMTs had retrieved their equipment and were almost to the porch.

"I'm sorry for the inconvenience," Ken said, blocking their path. "But your services

213

are not needed here."

"The operator tracked a cell phone call to this address," one of the EMTs said. "A caller was frantic on the other line. Reported someone not breathing."

"That was my daughter, who tends to be a bit dramatic. Her sister has been . . . challenged lately and was harder to awaken than usual. Everything's fine, now."

This said as one of the healers hurried down the stairs toward the kitchen.

"Who's that?" the second EMT asked, trying to peer around Ken's broad shoulders and through the wide-open front door.

"It's the people taking care of our daughter. Now, if you'll please get off of my property."

A police car pulled up, followed by a second one right behind it. Raina watched her father's subtle hand movements as he shielded the house.

"Can we see your daughter, sir, to make sure she's all right? Check her vitals to close out our report?"

"I've given you what you need to complete the task. My daughter is fine."

"But sir —"

A police officer came on the porch. "Don't waste your breath," he said to the technician, giving Ken a hard eye. "The Illumina-

214

tion doesn't believe in seeking medical treatment. They'll let someone die before getting them checked out."

"That is not true," Raina said.

Ken turned, surprised to find her behind him. "Get in the house!"

"She's the one who called 911," EMT One said to the police officer.

The officer stepped forward. "I'd like to speak with your daughter," he said.

"She's a minor and I will not allow it."

Several cars pulled up. Members from the Illumination security force stepped out and formed a line across the street.

"What the . . ." Words failed EMT Two as he observed the workings of the Nation's security on this, his first call in Lucent Rising.

"There is nothing for any of you to do here," Ken said. "This is private property. Please leave."

It wasn't immediate, but after taking one-sided reports with no input from the residents, the emergency crew and law enforcement left the Reed residence. Raina had remained in the hallway shadow, hoping for a chance to speak with the emergency responders. She wanted to relay to them Abby's symptoms, and while an outsider would not be allowed to treat her little

215

sister, hoped there was something they could tell her to do. When it became clear there was no chance of that happening, she went back upstairs, determined to get in Abby's room. The door was open when she got there. Abby was awake and sitting up. Raina sagged under the weight of relief, almost went to her knees. They allowed her in to see Abby, who appeared weak and frail against the sunflower pillowcases. So concerned were her parents for Abby's welfare, they forgot to censure her for the outsiders. Raina knew that as soon as Abby got better, her parents would deal with her for requesting their help. From the looks of things, that time wouldn't be soon. Abby's condition didn't worsen but didn't improve. In other words, her sister seemed very sick. When the next day came and Abby once again appeared to stop breathing, Raina knew that probation or no, forbidden or no, her sister needed a doctor. It was up to her to make that happen, and that's what she planned to do.

The next day, Raina waited until her free hour during phys ed class, then snuck away from the school. She'd taken every precaution, even told the phys ed teacher she was tutoring a student, just in case a fellow Nation student happened to ask. Then she went out a side door away from the security cameras that covered the front drive, down along a row of bushes and through a neighbor's backyard. From there she doubled back around to Joe's Groceries, hoping that the student she tutored was working the meat counter. The stars were on her side.

"Gregory, hey, my phone died. Can I use yours to make a call?"

Five minutes later she was in the back of a nondescript car-service Honda, speeding across town. Her stomach roiled as the Uber neared the McFaddens' home. She was relieved to see Valarie's Honda in the driveway and saddened to note there was no black Mustang parked beside it. She knew from speaking with Jackie earlier that after school she would be at a classmate's house getting her hair braided. Valarie was home alone, and hopefully had time to speak with her. She paid the driver, then quickly crossed the drive and walked up the steps before what few nerves she had left deserted her.

The door opened seconds after she'd rung the bell. "Hello, Miss Valarie."

"Hello, Raina," Valarie responded, looking past Raina to the street beyond them. "You're not supposed to be here."

217

"I know and I have less than an hour."

"Didn't you get in major trouble for being here the first time? You haven't learned your lesson yet?"

"I guess not, ma'am." Raina bowed her head and in doing so, missed Valarie's smile.

"Good girl." Valarie leaned against the doorjamb and looked at her watch. "Jackie's still at school."

"I know."

"Why aren't you there?"

"I tutor some of the athletes so the phys ed teacher sometimes lets me skip gym."

"She won't be here right after school, either. She's —"

"— getting her hair braided."

"So you know that, too." Valarie raised a brow. "Are you here to see Bryce, that boy who got you kicked out of your house?"

"Actually, Miss Valarie, if you have a few moments, I'm here to speak with you."

"Me? What about?"

"Can I come inside?"

"Of course." Valarie stepped back to let Raina enter, closing the door once she was inside. "I was about to take a break and have a cup of tea. Care to join me?"

"That sounds good. It's freezing out there."

"Yes, this Kansas weather is extremely

unpredictable. They say if you don't like the weather, wait five minutes and it will change."

They entered the living room. "Have a seat," Valarie said, pointing to the couch before continuing into the kitchen. She filled a teakettle with water and placed it on the stove. Then she reached into a set of cabinets, pulling a container of tea bags from one side and two mugs from the other. She set them on the counter next to the kettle before rejoining Raina in the living room.

"So, to what do I owe this unexpected meeting?"

"It's about my sister, Abby. But first, I want to apologize for what happened that day at Dollar Discount."

"I apologize as well. We both could have handled that situation differently." Valarie gave a dismissive wave of her hand. "Forget about that Nation nonsense. I know the real Raina. Now what about your sister?"

"I think she's sick, maybe with that severe flu that's going around."

"Has your mom taken her to the doctor?"

Raina shook her head. "The Illumination doesn't believe in using doctors or modern medicine."

"She didn't get a flu vaccination?"

219

"No."

"You either?"

"Not since I was eight years old."

Valarie was visibly taken aback. "What happens when someone gets sick?"

"We have healers who use natural resources to make members better — herbs, minerals, teas, vitamins — stuff like that."

"And if they don't work?"

"Mostly they do. But if not . . ." Raina couldn't bring herself to say what might happen.

"Are they like some of these religions who'd rather let their loved one die than get treatment?"

"No one wants to lose a loved one, but if it happens . . . it was meant to be."

Valarie chewed on those words for a moment. "Let me make sure I'm understanding this clearly. If the treatments given by your church don't work, they don't take the person to a hospital to see what more can be done?"

"It's against the rules."

"And despite Abby's condition, your mother goes along? Were it me, I'd say to hell with any rule that jeopardized the health of my child."

The teakettle whistled, as if to second that emotion. "Come choose your tea and dress it the way you'd like."

Talk of sickness and healing was tabled for the next couple minutes as the ladies prepared their teas. Back in the living room, Valarie leaned against the couch's cushy back. "I'm very sorry to hear about Abby. How do you think I can help?"

Raina sat back as well, her hands cupping the steamy mug. "I don't know. I thought that maybe, as a lawyer, you might have some advice."

"You want to know if there is something that can be done legally to force your parents to seek medical treatment for her?"

"Yes."

"That's a good question, Raina, though not my field of expertise." She tapped Raina's arm and stood. "Let's go do a little research together."

They walked into Valarie's office. "Pull a chair around," Valarie said.

Raina did as instructed and sat down beside her.

"Let's see . . ." Valarie's fingers hovered over the keyboard before she entered a variety of phrases into the search engine before settling on a page. "This one looks interesting. It's from the United Nations Convention on the Rights of the Child, CRC, a human rights treaty which sets out the civil, political, economic, social, health, and cultural rights of children."

Raina leaned forward and read a caption on the screen. " 'The right to participate in medical decision making.' "

Valarie continued. " 'Article 6 protects the child's inherent right to life and assigns responsibility for the child's development and survival to the state. Together with article 24, which confirms that children have the right to the enjoyment of the highest attainable standard of health and to facilities that promotes such a standard, article 6 ensures that children have access to medical treatments, technologies, and systems that promote their well-being.' "

Raina turned to Valarie, her face gleaming. "So Abby has rights? She has a say in whether or not she gets medical treatment?"

"Whoa, not so fast, Raina. This sounds promising, but it's one in probably thousands of papers on this subject. The parents also have rights and on top of that, theirs is based on religious conviction, thrusting us into the separation of church and state."

Valarie backspaced to the list of similar websites and documents. "This is definitely not an answer we'll get in less than an hour. But based on what you've told me, I'm concerned about Abby. So first thing tomorrow, I'll get my assistant to do some research. Is there a way that Jackie or I can get the information to you?"

"Everything on my end is being monitored. It's better if I get in touch with you."

"Give us until the end of the business day tomorrow, then give me a call. Do you still have my number?"

Raina shook her head. "My parents took my cell phone."

"My goodness. Your lockdown sounds almost as severe as some of the young men that I visit in prison."

"At least I get to sleep in my own bed," Raina said.

"I suggest your mom's meals outdo jail food, too." Valarie stood. "How did you get here?"

"Uber."

"Come on. I'll take you back to the school, or wherever you want to be dropped off."

"Thank you, Miss Valarie."

"I'm not sure I'll come up with an answer. Don't thank me yet."

Raina left Valarie's house feeling hopeful. Her joy was short-lived.

The next day at lunch, Jackie surreptitiously passed her a small padded envelope. Inside was a one-page document, typed and

223

double-spaced.

Raina, here is what my assistant found regarding your question and Kansas law: "A parent legitimately practicing religious beliefs who does not provide specified medical treatment for a child because of religious beliefs shall not for that reason be considered a negligent parent."

This Kansas statute further underscores that unfortunately, when it comes to Abby's treatment and because of the Illumination Church's recognized presence, the law is on your parents' side. It states:

Kansas Criminal Statute: Kansas defense to misdemeanor child endangerment. Nothing under the definition of "child endangerment" . . . shall be construed to mean a child is endangered for the sole reason his/her guardian, in good faith, selects and depends upon spiritual means through prayer, in accordance with the tenets and practice of a recognized church or religious denomination for the treatment or cure of disease or remedial care of such child. *Kansas Statutes §21-3608(1)(c)*

Should we come across something that counters this position, I'll let you know. The phone is little consolation, but I hope it helps. I'm praying for you. V.

The information was crushing, exactly what Raina didn't want to hear. She'd been so hopeful, had thought if anybody could help her it was Jackie's mom. That even the law seemed against her brought a cloud of sadness that hung over her for the rest of the day. What could she do now to get help for her sister? Raina was out of ideas. She spent the rest of the day unable to concentrate, and put her energy into visualizing a glowing Abby whose health crisis was behind them. Funny thing about life was that sometimes before things got better . . . they got worse.

CHAPTER 16

When Raina returned from school, there were several practitioners and healing assistants traversing the Reed home. Their presence made it easier for Raina to have a little privacy. After checking in on Abby and a brief chat with her parents, she took the prepaid phone Valarie had given her into the closet, leaving the door ajar just enough to hear someone entering her room. It had already been set up, complete with Jackie and Valarie's numbers saved in contacts. That was Miss Valarie, professional and organized. The thoughtfulness brought tears to her eyes. She tapped the phone face.

"Jackie, it's Raina," she whispered, when the call connected.

"Girl, I've been worried about you. I read the note Mom asked me to give you and am so glad you called."

"Abby's really sick. She almost died."

"Oh my God, Raina! Mom said you

226

thought she had the flu." All cynicism was gone, replaced by overt compassion and concern. "Is she okay now?"

"The healers and practitioners are working on her, but Jackie, I'm worried. She doesn't seem to be getting better. What they're doing hasn't helped! But Mother and Father won't hear of getting another type of treatment, and according to your mom the law is on their side.

"I'm Abby's only chance at getting medical help. As it stands right now, I might once again be obscured."

She relayed the story of what had happened the day before, and how for an Illuminated, calling emergency was the worst thing that she could have done.

"What if she doesn't get better?" Jackie asked. "This is Abby's life we're talking about. Y'all can't be messing around!"

"I know, and I feel so helpless! I want her checked out medically, but for my parents, no way! I'd do anything to find out why she keeps getting these fevers. And now passing out . . ." Raina choked back tears.

"Where are you?" Jackie asked.

"In the closet," Raina responded. "Literally." The answer brought lightheartedness to a heavy situation. Both girls laughed. "My house is full of the Illuminated. It was the safest place I could think of to call you. By the way, please tell your mom thank you for the phone."

"She did it for a reason. We've been thinking about your situation and came up with a way you might be able to get help for Abby, and somebody who can give her the medical examination she needs."

"Who?"

"You know her, too. Miss Bev."

Raina remembered the conversation her and Monica's mother had when giving Raina a ride, how Miss Bev had been concerned about Abby and had suggested she be checked out professionally.

"You already know the problem with that. My parents won't take her to the clinic."

"We think there may be a way around that, too. Let me check out a few things and call you back."

For the next few hours, a flurry of calls and texts were exchanged. Between Jackie, Valarie, Bev, and a few others, a plan was put into motion. It was an outrageous but doable one. Raina readily agreed. By midnight, everyone was in place and ready to do their part. It wasn't lost on Raina how the people she'd been told to lose all contact with had come to her aid, as though nothing had happened between them. Raina was nervous and excited at the same time. Afraid that her antsy behavior might make her mom suspicious, she feigned exhaustion, and went to bed early. Jennifer came into her room just after nine.

"How's Abby?"

"She's . . . okay," Jennifer responded. "The healers are still working to make her better but thank the stars that at least she hasn't . . . faded further."

Jennifer leaned on the wall near the headboard and stared at Raina for a long moment, then sat on the bed beside her with a look of chagrin mixed with compassion.

"Your father and I are extremely disappointed in you, Raina. Calling on outsiders for medical help is almost inexcusable. Yet we know how much you love your sister and understand that you acted impulsively. Because there was no breach of our residence, no stain of the outsider allowed through our doors, the Council is not going to consider this an error for consideration. You don't want to risk being obscured again, Raina. It can lead to months, even years, without the fellowship of the church or your family, or worse."

Being ghosted. Raina already knew.

"I'm really sorry, Mom." Not only for what she'd done already, but for what she

229

was about to do. Hopefully her parents would be none the wiser but either way, it couldn't be helped. Raina would do anything to try and help Abby.

Jennifer brushed the hair from Raina's face. "We know."

Raina continued to listen as Jennifer tried to explain her and Ken's position regarding Abby's healing. She assured her mother that she understood, even as she lay fully clothed beneath the covers. The conversation gave her pause but was not enough to stop her from fulfilling the plan.

At just past two a.m., Raina crept into her sister's bedroom and gently shook her.

"Shadow, wake up."

"Sister . . ."

"Shh . . . we have to be very quiet."

"Why?" Abby's voice was high-pitched and weak.

"Because we're going to play a game of hide-and-seek from Mother and Father. We have to be very careful that they don't hear us, and that we move just as quietly when we return home."

"But where are we going?"

"To meet a friend."

"Sister, I'm tired . . ."

"I know. You only have to walk outside. A friend of mine is playing the game, too, and will carry you from there to the car.

"Car? Where are we —"

"Shh! Abby, please!"

A floorboard creaked. Raina's heart seized. Her palms turned clammy. She counted to twenty, then fifty. Quiet resumed.

"You're my shadow, right?"

Abby nodded.

"Do you trust me?"

Another nod.

"Then I need you to put on your slippers and come with me. A kind woman is going to help give you light, and then we'll come back home and get you back into bed before anyone even knows that we're gone. Do you think you can play this game perfectly, get downstairs without making a sound?"

"I can try."

"That's good enough. Let me make sure the coast is clear."

Raina, dressed in all black, eased down the hall to her parents' suite. She placed an ear against the door. Jennifer slept quietly but Raina heard Ken's reassuring snore. She tip-toed back to her room just as her phone vibrated.

Where you at?

Coming! Are you at the house?

Can't. Security. I'm on foot, by the fence. Hurry.

Raina retrieved the sweatshirt she'd hidden beneath the bed and ran through the tandem bathroom to where Abby half sat, half lay on the pillow. She pulled her sister to a sitting position and pulled the black shirt over Abby's head. It dragged on the ground. Perfect. Just as Raina wanted. She took a last look around and in a second of ingenuity placed the pillow lengthwise in her sister's bed, along with a stuffed animal. She threw the blanket over both pieces. Anyone just peeking in could easily imagine Abby under the covers. Jackie said the nurse would need less than an hour to check Abby. Raina planned to have them back long before then.

She placed a finger to her mouth, took her sister's hand, and hurried through the bath and her room to the nearby staircase. They eased down them without incident, and over to the side door, which she left unlocked. Once outside, they stayed close to the houses and beyond the security lights. The sky was black and cloudy, yet a full moon lit their path. They neared the last home and crossed to where a loose board provided escape through the ten-foot security fence. Raina had discovered the break months before. At first she'd forgotten to tell someone. Later, she kept the secret deliberately. As they neared the escape point, she could tell the plank had already been pulled back. They eased through it, staying low to the ground. The sound of air pushed through lips came from the direction of a thick pine bush.

"Jackie?" Raina whispered.

A taller, leaner figure stepped from behind the bushes.

"Bryce?"

"Yeah, come on."

It had been more than a month since Raina had seen him. Even now, in the darkness, she felt more than she saw. There was no time to reconcile the mixed feelings his being here caused her. They had to go.

Holding Abby's hand tightly, Raina scurried over to where he knelt.

"Stay low," were the only words spoken as he effortlessly lifted Abby into his arms and led them back the way he'd come, staying close to trees and other objects that could hide them as they hurried through the park. Excitement coated with fear thrummed through every cell of Raina's body. Part of her felt happy and confident that someone other than a healer would finally see Abby and might be able to help her get better. The other part thought she was crazy and asked what the hell she was doing, especially

233

given how almost every inch of Lucent Rising was monitored by the organization's security force. Fortunately, because of her father's position and his tendency to speak freely with the door open when working from home, Raina knew where the cameras were and even more importantly, ways they could be avoided. Which is why they'd made their escape through Chippewa Park, which ran along the north side of Lucent Rising and was forbidden to the children of light.

They reached the park's entrance. "Where's your car?"

"Text Jackie," he said, stopping by a large oak to shift Abby from one arm to another. "Just send an X. She's waiting. You all right, baby girl?" he asked Abby.

Abby, wide-eyed, said nothing.

Raina sent the text. Almost immediately, the familiar frame of the black Mustang came into view. The usual booming stereo was radio silent. The lights were off.

Bryce snorted. "That girl watches too much TV." He set Abby down.

Raina grabbed her hand. "Come on, Shadow."

"Where are we going?" For the first time, Abby showed fear.

"To the light, to make you better," Raina explained.

"I don't know these people. They're out-siders!"

"Girl, get in this car," Jackie said. "Or I'm going to leave your behind outside."

"Jackie, shut up. Stop scaring Raina's sister." Bryce had opened the back door for Raina and Abby and then eased into the front seat.

He rolled down the window. "Y'all com-ing or what?"

Raina kneeled down to look at Abby eye-to-eye. "You trust me, right?"

"Yes."

"I won't let anything happen to you, Shadow. I'll protect you with my life."

They got into the car. Jackie hit a main street and finally turned on the headlights. Fifteen minutes later they pulled into the driveway of Lois Monroe, a member of Christine's church. The location had been carefully chosen to minimize problems for all involved. Beverly didn't want to lose her job at the clinic. Going to her house wasn't an option. Jackie was an attorney who didn't want to be disbarred. The McFadden home was out. Raina had given Christine's name and address to the council. Her father had it, too. So Raina found herself once again in the home of a stranger, an unsanctioned. She trusted everyone around her, but out of habit, shielded herself anyway.

They entered a small but warmly decorated home. The lights were dim, so Raina saw little of its interior, but the bedroom where Beverly had set up shop was colorful and brightly lit. Religious paraphernalia was everywhere. If that wasn't enough, the homeowner greeted them wearing a colorful T-shirt with a message: JESUS IS MY ROCK, THAT'S JUST HOW I ROLL.

Abby looked around but said nothing.

"Trust me," Raina mouthed, while executing shielding symbols. Soon Abby's little fingers were doing them, too, an action that seemed to relax her. Bev's personality was warm, her bedside manner comforting. She introduced herself to Abby, then asked that she sit on the bed. Pulling a stethoscope from a nearby tote, Bev began the examination. She checked her temperature, examined her skin.

"I think she has a virus," Bev concluded several minutes later. "I'm no doctor though, and she needs one. I know you feel it's not an option, but I recommend a hospital visit."

"I can't," Raina said. "My parents would kill me. If they awaken while I'm gone, I'm already dead."

Bev looked over at Abby, now lying back

on the bed and sleeping. "Tell you what. This isn't protocol, in fact it's against the rules. But I'm driven to help your sister and feel we have no time to lose." She reached into the tote and pulled out a tincture. "This is a liquid antibiotic, orange flavored to make it easy going down. I will administer one dose, and wait" — Bev looked at her watch — "for thirty minutes, maybe forty-five. See if there's any change. If not, I'm going to have to issue a report on your sister." She stepped closer, dropped her voice to a whisper. "I can't have this little girl dying on my watch."

CHAPTER 17

The antibiotics hadn't brought a change to Abby's condition. Her temperature had risen two degrees.

"Raina, this is very serious. Your sister needs immediate medical help. You're going to have to decide what's more important, your faith or your sister's physical condition. We need to take her to emergency, and we need to leave now."

"What do you want to do?" Bryce asked.

"Follow your heart," Jackie encouraged. "You already have the answer. Do the right thing."

Ten minutes later, Bev, Jackie, and Raina prepared to take Abby to emergency. Bryce had a slew of packages to deliver and left for work. Abby, who vacillated between shivering and sweating, still wore the long-sleeved black sweatshirt over a pair of sunflower pajamas and now also sported a pair of bright red smiley-face slippers.

Because of the medical dilemma and the potential legal fallout, Bev had called ahead to a doctor who was familiar with the Nation and understood the unusual nature of their arrival. He was expecting them and had a team prepared to act as quickly as possible as soon as the patient arrived. The early morning temperatures were still on the cool side. Bev suggested that both ladies grab a sweater or jacket to warm them as the hospital, especially the waiting room, tended to be cold. Lois retrieved a sweater for Jackie and a light jacket for Raina.

"Are we ready?" Bev asked.

Raina turned to Abby. "Ready, Shadow?"

Abby didn't respond, just leaned into her sister's side.

Bev observed the action. "We should go."

The three stepped outside and headed toward Bev's red Kia. Jackie entered the front seat. Raina climbed in the back next to Abby, placed a throw that Lois provided around her legs and feet. Bev started the car, quickly shifted into gear, and began backing down the drive. Suddenly, the yelp of a police siren pierced the quiet morning. The glow of red and blue lights bounced from Lois's garage door as five squad cars that seemed to come from every direction surrounded the car.

"Oh no," Bev whispered.

"I'll be damned," Jackie said with a sigh.

"Sister, what's happening?" Abby squealed.

Raina said nothing. Couldn't with a heart lodged in her throat.

Two police jumped out of their cars, guns drawn.

"The blood of Jesus!" Lois cried, loud enough to be heard from inside her front door.

The officer quickly swiveled and trained his gun on the door. "Don't move! Stay inside!"

"Out of the car!" the other officer demanded.

A third police car pulled up, siren blasting, lights blazing.

The women opened their doors and exited the car.

"Get your hands up!" the female officer yelled. "All of you. Do it now!"

"Hands up!" cried the baby-faced officer who'd just arrived.

"Don't move!" the first cop warned again.

Each of them walked up to a woman, spun them around and threw on the handcuffs. Lois hadn't stayed inside as the officer commanded. Once the handcuffs came out, she did, too, and witnessed it all.

"What are you doing?" Jackie demanded. "We didn't do nothing, Officer. Why are you arresting us?"

"Are you Raina Reed?" he demanded.

"I'm Raina," she said, relief flooding through her. Obviously, since he knew her name, her parents had let them know that the two were sisters and would take them back to the house. She'd probably be obscured again, but that was the least of her worries. Especially when she heard Beverly pleading on her sister's behalf, and then Abby's anguished crying, coming through the window.

"Seriously, Officer, we have a very sick child inside that car. She needs to get to emergency. We were just on our way there."

"And you are?"

"Beverly Wilson, a nurse and friend of the family."

"I want Mother," Abby wailed. "I want to go home!"

"You're Raina Reed?" the officer asked again.

"Yes! I need to help my sister!" She tried to pull away. The officer's grip was a vise. "It's okay, Abby! Please," she said to the officer. "My sister is sick. Can you please get her to the hospital?"

"We'll see to your sister. But you're under arrest."

"For what?"

"First degree kidnapping, among other things."

"No, there's got to be some kind of mistake. Abby's my sister. We're taking her to the doctor."

"If you're Raina Reed, this is no mistake. You're being arrested for kidnapping. You have the right to remain silent . . ."

"No!" Raina struggled against the officer as he led her away. "Abby! Don't be scared. I love you, Shadow!"

The Miranda rights continued as he walked-slash-dragged Raina to his squad car. She was numb, spent, the moment felt surreal. She watched as Bev was marched to another car and saw the female officer place Jackie in the car she'd driven to the scene. The officer started the car, whipped a U-turn as good as or better than any male driver, and headed down the street. Raina's head fell back against the seat. Of all the scenarios she'd played about how the night might turn out, going to jail hadn't been one of them. Prison bars hadn't entered her mind.

Later, she wouldn't remember the ride to the courthouse. Everything went by in a tearstained blur. When had her parents awakened and discovered Abby missing? How had they found her? *Security.* The word floated into her mind like a whisper. In her heart, she believed the church watchmen were how they'd tracked her down. One of them must have noticed Bryce's car, became suspicious and followed him. She wished she could speak with Bryce, ask if he'd noticed lights trailing them. She'd been too concerned about Abby to think of much else. Beyond the cameras all over Lucent Rising, they existed along the streets of Chippewa, too. There were members of the Nation on law enforcement's payroll. If they wanted to find someone, obviously, they could.

Raina thought about her mom and felt bad. They'd had a good conversation just hours before. The police had taken her purse, but the burner phone Valarie had given her was tucked into her clothing. Handcuffs prevented her from being able to reach it. Even if it were possible, it probably wouldn't matter. She doubted her parents would take her call and was pretty sure this true act of kidnapping more than crossed the Council's zero-tolerance line. Raina dropped her head against the back seat of the police car. What had she done?

They reached the courthouse. A few curious onlookers, those who worked nights in and around the courthouse and a few officers entering or leaving the jail, stopped to watch as she was led out of the police car and into the building. A part of Raina left her body to preserve the part that remained. She went through the booking process on autopilot. Her basic information was recorded before she was fingerprinted and photographed. They removed all of her personal items and placed them in a numbered bag. Because she was being taken to a holding cell rather than the actual jail, she was patted down rather than strip searched and allowed to wear her own clothes. The female corrections officer found her phone, made her remove the shoestrings from her tennis shoes, and took the band from her hair. By the time they were finished Raina was totally and completely humiliated. She wasn't an animal. Why did they have to treat her like one?

"All right, Reed," the woman said. "Let's go."

They walked away from the desk area. As they entered the hall, the officer's hold became softer, as did her voice. "Kidnapping your sister, huh?"

"She's sick. I was trying to take her to the

hospital because my parents wouldn't."

"The Nation?"

Raina turned to look at her. "You know about us?"

"I'm familiar." They reached the end of the hall where there was a pay phone. The officer stopped. "Got anybody to call?"

"I can use the phone?" Raina asked. The officer nodded. "I don't have any money," Raina said.

The officer reached into her pocket and pulled out some change.

"Thank you." Still handcuffed, Raina deposited coins into the slot and called the number she memorized during the flurry of calls earlier that evening.

"McFadden."

"Miss Valarie . . ."

"Raina? Thank God. Where are you?"

"Clinton Correctional. Where's Abby?"

"Right, they couldn't keep you in Chippewa. Their facility isn't set up to house a mixed population. So you were actually arrested. Have you been booked?"

"Yes, but I don't care about that. Where's my sister?"

"With Child Protective Services most likely."

"Not the hospital where we were headed, as I told the police?"

"Honestly, I don't know."

"Abby has never been alone with an outsider," Raina said, panic causing her voice to rise. "You've got to find her, please, Miss Valarie. She's probably terrified!"

"Being with the state might work to your advantage, as a medical evaluation is part of the intake process. If any illness is suspected, they'd definitely take her to be checked out. If she's back home with your parents, then their authority rules. They couldn't be forced to seek help for her."

Raina groaned. "This is awful. All of the planning and getting arrested . . . and for what?"

"I know this is difficult, honey, but you've got to stay calm. I'll make some calls, find out what I can as quickly as possible. Now listen carefully. We may not have a long time to talk, okay?"

"Okay."

"Don't say anything to anyone about what happened tonight, especially to law enforcement. Even if asked casually, tell them you have an attorney who will answer all questions. It's too late for anything to happen now, so you've got to be strong and tough it out for the night. I'll go before the judge first thing in the morning to try and get you released on your own recognizance. That means without posting bail."

"I can't believe I'm in here."

"This is definitely the worst-case scenario I hoped wouldn't happen. But you've never been arrested, have no criminal history, and other than this stunt your parents pulled, have no criminal charges."

"My parents are the ones who called the police?" Considering how adverse the Nation was to outside enforcement, Raina found it hard to believe. "Are you sure?"

"They woke up to find both you and your sister missing. I'm sorry Raina but yes, it was them."

The officer stepped forward. "Wrap it up," she said.

"I've got to go," Raina said to Valarie.

"I heard her. I'll get to the courthouse first thing in the morning. In the meantime, try and go to sleep. Time will pass faster that way."

They reached the holding cell. Two women were inside, one curled up on the floor, the other stretched out on the hard, metal bench. The officer took off the cuffs and walked out of the cell. Raina jumped as the heavy metal door banged and clanged shut behind her. Raina rubbed her wrists as she looked around. The surroundings were as dismal as her mood, dull gray cement painted with antiseptic spray. The harsh lighting was not strong enough to dissipate the darkness, and Raina could no longer hold back the tears. She slid down a wall, propped her head on the arms wrapped around her knees and cried silently for sleep, and for Abby.

Several hours later, a weary, hungry, thirsty Raina was led to a small room. There were two long metal tables on either side of the rectangular space and chairs bolted to the floor. Standing between the tables, looking like sunshine and rainbows rolled into one was her savior, Valarie. After the handcuffs were removed and the officer left the room, Raina walked into Valarie's arms.

"Now, now," Valarie cooed, after giving Raina several minutes to release pent-up emotions. "Cry all of your tears out now, on my shoulder. After this, you've got to be strong."

Raina shuddered, but after several more seconds pulled back and wiped her eyes. Valarie reached into her briefcase and pulled out a package of tissues. She sat and motioned for Raina to take a seat on the other side.

"How are you?"

"Still breathing, so okay, I guess."

"Were you alone in the holding cell?"

"No, there were other women in there. They left me alone. I kept waiting for Jackie and the other ladies. Where were they taken?"

"They were questioned and released."

Raina's relief was audible. "I'm so glad they didn't get into trouble. They were only trying to help. What about me? Did you talk to the judge?"

"I did."

Raina watched as Valarie's mood changed. It was slight, but definite, and didn't feel like good news.

"Your parents have asked that charges be filed against you. The judge has decided to move forward with your case."

"No way. Miss Valarie . . ."

"It's hard, I know, but these are the facts. You need to be aware of them, of everything you're facing and what you're up against. It might be difficult but I'm going to try and get a meeting with your parents. See if there is something that can be done to work this out without going to such an extreme action. I'm also going to file a separate motion to have the charges dropped or at the very least reduced, on their face. The first and most important thing to do, however, is try and get you out of here. To do that, we need ten thousand dollars. Do you know where we could get that kind of money?"

"No one other than my parents, who will probably never want to see or speak to me again."

"I'll keep trying to get your bail reduced. Until then, you're going to have to stay here. It's not what either of us want and will hopefully only be a couple days, but you'll be given a prison jumpsuit and moved to the general population. You can do this, Raina," she continued, when Raina's face melted in despair. "You've got to, for Abby. This fight to get your sister help isn't over. It has just begun."

CHAPTER 18

Raina stayed with Valarie as long as she could. When the officer returned, Raina was not taken to the holding cell but processed for the county jail's general population, as Valarie had warned, armed with several candy bars and bags of chips that Valarie bought her. Jackie's mom had been the first friendly face she'd seen since getting arrested. She still couldn't believe it. She was in jail! She'd never considered being in one, had no idea what they looked like. Secular television was largely off-limits. She'd never even seen an episode of *Orange Is the New Black*. The guard guided her to her cell, opened the door, and released the cuffs before she went inside. She surveyed the layout, bunk beds and toilet. She closed her eyes against the harsh lighting, the sound of doors clanging, women on edge, and fought to keep the tears from returning. Valarie was correct in what she said. Raina had to be strong. Not knowing anybody with ten thousand dollars who would use it to bail her out, meant that she might be there a while.

Raina climbed on the top bunk, her back against the concrete wall. She moved her fingers back and forth, working to get the feeling back after being handcuffed. The black skinny jeans and turtleneck pulled on for Abby's treatment — instead of kidnapping, as her parents called it — had been replaced by a nondescript gray jumpsuit, a shade darker than the walls and floor. She lay in bed wearing socks and shoes. The jail was freezing. Every piece of clothing helped. The scratchy wool blanket at the bottom of the bed was disgusting. Just looking at it made her skin itch. Yet she placed it over her thighs for warmth. She tried to disappear into the land of dreams. But sleep was long in coming. The events of the past twelve hours played on loop in her head, especially what had happened since arriving in county. She'd done nothing wrong and wasn't a criminal. But law enforcement treated her like one.

Raina flopped on her back and reached for one of the candy bars. Until now, fear had taken away her appetite. If that hadn't done it, the gruel they served and called breakfast that morning would have surely done the job. The bread looked stale, the coffee watery, and what they dared called applesauce looked like the last inmate's puke.

Your parents have asked that charges be filed against you. The message Valarie delivered kept echoing in her head. By parents, Raina knew she meant Ken. No matter how devoted Jennifer was to the Illumination, she couldn't see her mother making the suggestion that her daughter be put in jail. She wasn't totally surprised that her stepdad would do it. If the council found out about this latest situation, they'd almost surely withdraw his promotion to Supreme Master Seer, something that was over two decades in the making. Raina felt bad about that. Ken loved the ministry more than life. But not more than she loved Abby. Raina knew that for a fact.

The judge has decided to move forward with your case. What did that mean, besides going to trial? What would that look like? Valarie didn't want to get into those particulars, would rather Raina try and stay positive and focus on being released. The range of a prison sentence for a kidnapping conviction was wide, anywhere from one to twenty years. If Raina went to prison, who'd look after Abby? While locked up, who'd look after Raina?

The sound of clanging steel shook Raina from her thoughts. Close footsteps made her eyes fly open. Someone was being put in her cell. No! She slowly sat up and met a pair of eyes glaring at her. She maintained a cool expression and direct eye contact with the newcomer before turning her attention to slowly unwrapping the candy bar.

Raina was glad she'd already claimed the top bunk, a suggestion from the girl who shared the holding cell last night. She was in on a drug charge and pretty much a regular when it came to the Clinton County Jail. She shared what she could, verbally showed her the ropes. Said basically to be polite to the guards, quiet to the other inmates, to not talk shit but not to back down either. She'd been right in saying the food would suck and time would crawl. The one error she'd made was also the most critical. She'd doubted Raina would have anyone sharing her cell.

The guard finished removing the prisoner's handcuffs and backed out of the cell.

"Behave yourself, Banks," she gruffly implored. "You know we don't mind adding time."

"Yeah, whatever," Banks said, still eyeing

Raina. "What's up?"

"Hey," Raina replied, without looking up. For a moment she continued to feel the inmate's stare, then felt the bed shift slightly when the woman made use of the lower bunk. Raina pushed a portion of the dark chocolate and almond jail delicacy past the wrapper and took a bite.

"What you in for?"

At the thought of saying "kidnapping," Raina almost laughed out loud. "Stupid stuff," she said instead. Because her parents charging her for trying to help her sister was totally bonkers.

"What's your name?"

Raina sighed. She really wasn't up for a conversation and didn't plan to be in there long enough to need friends. Plus, the less people who knew she was in there, the less likely it would be for the Illumination to learn about it. Then again, given that it was her father who'd filed the charges, the community probably already knew about it. The Council might have been the ones who made the suggestion.

"I really don't want to talk," she honestly replied.

The woman jumped up and moved closer to Raina. "Who gives a shit what you want? If I ask you something, you need to answer.

255

Or it's going to get wrong in here real fast."

While nerves jumped on the inside, Raina slowly, calmly raised her head. Her eyes narrowed as she took in the woman in front of her — the round face, slanted eyes, big nose, and uneven lips. Her mind did a rewind, going back almost ten years. It stopped on a memory, hazy at first, and then . . .

"Ann. Banks."

It was Banks's turn to squint as her tone turned suspect. "How in the hell do you know me?"

"Because you haven't changed." Raina straightened her back with confidence. "You're still the same bully I met just after moving to Chippewa. You made those early days in my new town a miserable experience."

"How am I supposed to know you? I bullied a lot of people."

"I don't care if you remember me from all those years ago. But here's the deal. I want to get the green light from my lawyer and leave here as quickly as I can. I don't want any trouble, but my days of running from it are over. So whether it goes wrong or right in here is totally up to you."

Later, Raina would wonder just where in the heck that bravado came from. Part of it was her worry about what had happened to Abby, and that Valarie didn't know whether she'd been taken to the hospital, a state agency, or back home to Jennifer and Ken. That all of what everyone had gone through had been for nothing was something she didn't want to consider. If that was the case, she'd be ready to fight ten Ann Bankses, and whup them all. She'd be just that ticked off.

"Get up, Reed. You have a visitor."

Mother?

Raina felt a surge of happiness. Her mom had finally come to her senses and come to get her child. Raina hopped down from the top bunk, then turned to be handcuffed. Hopefully it would be for the very last time!

"You out of here, Reed?"

"I hope so, Banks."

Cell mates make strange bedfellows. After calling Ann's bluff, her cellie did a one-eighty. She actually talked like a normal person, no posturing, no threats. Raina learned that Ann had grown up in foster care, adopted by an elderly woman when she was nine. The woman died when she was twelve, around the time that Raina moved to Chippewa. She was taken in by the woman's daughter and abused by the

257

live-in boyfriend. In hearing her story, Raina understood why Ann walked around hating everybody. She'd never learned to love herself. In the years since those bullying days, not much had changed. After being forced to abort the boyfriend's baby at the age of fourteen, Ann was kicked out of the daughter's house and lived on the streets. One of the ways she supported herself was by a variety of criminal enterprises, including stealing, the reason she was now in county. She was just two years older than Raina but had lived a lifetime more, with the rap sheet, battle scars, and two kids to prove it.

"Take care of yourself, Reed."

"You, too, Banks. When you get out this time, stay out."

The guard opened the door to the visitors' room. Raina stopped short. Instead of Jennifer, Raina saw Christine Clark, smiling, dressed like she was heading to a Baptist church.

"Are you my visitor?" Raina asked.

"Child, right now I'm your salvation. Valarie is outside taking care of the paperwork. You need to send up some praise to Jesus. Some of my church sisters put our money together and just bailed you out."

Raina was floored. She forgot all about

the no touching rule and threw herself into Christine's arms. She was indeed getting out but not in the way she'd imagined. Why hadn't her parents tried to contact her? Where was Abby?

"Miss Christine, do you know anything about my little sister? We were taking her to the hospital when I got arrested."

"I know Valarie has been working to find out what's going on with Abby. I'll let her tell you what she's found out."

Just like that, less than forty-eight hours after the nightmare began, Raina was out of jail. The charges were still there and had to be worked out, but when they left the visitors' room Raina headed toward the exit, not back to the cell. She thanked Christine profusely, and Valarie as well. Once in the car she only had one question.

"Is Abby okay?"

"We don't know," Valarie replied. "I called your mom, tried to get answers."

"You did?"

"I had the number from that first night you stayed at my house, remember?"

Raina did, vaguely.

"I called and introduced myself as your attorney, and the person who'd housed you when you were kicked out. Thought that might win me some brownie points."

"Did it?"

"Not a one."

"Just as I began to inquire of your sister, I heard a male voice in the background. Your mother told me to talk to their attorney and not to call her house again. Then she hung up."

"So we don't know about Abby?"

"Sorry, Raina, but no. You're probably starving. Do you want something to eat?"

"No thank you, Miss Valarie. You've already done way more than I can ever pay back. You, too, Miss Christine, and all of your friends. I don't know how I'll ever get enough money to pay you back, but I promise, one day I will."

Christine tilted her head toward the back seat. "Don't worry about that right now, baby. You've got enough on your plate right now."

The short ride to Chippewa was mostly quiet. Everything in Raina's world had changed. She couldn't imagine what to expect when seeing her parents. But she knew she had to try and see Abby. She leaned forward, toward Valarie.

"You're taking me home, right?"

"Right now, Raina, that definition is a bit vague."

Valarie explained how Raina had been

remanded to Miss Christine's custody and as such had to reside in her home until the next court date. "Do you think your parents will see you?"

"I don't know, but I want to find out."

"I understand that." Valarie reached the Chippewa city limits, then continued on to Lucent Rising. They took the exit and shortly afterwards entered the confines of the well-maintained, planned community.

Raina got out of the car. "If you need to run an errand, you can pick me up later."

"No," Valarie replied, "something is telling me to wait right here."

That something was right. Raina rang the doorbell but no one answered. Without even checking she knew Jennifer's car was in the garage. But she checked anyway. It was there. She pulled out her key, placed it into the lock and turned. Nothing. The locks had been changed. Raina went around to the back. That door was locked, too. She returned to the front of the house in time to see Lucent Rising security pulling up in their stark white vehicles. A guy wearing shades and a baseball cap with the Lucent Rising logo, got out of the car and walked toward her.

Raina couldn't believe it. She marched down the drive to meet him.

"Dennis?" Given the circumstances, Raina wasn't particularly happy to see her neighbor but was glad it was someone she knew. "You work security now?"

"You are trespassing on private property. The owner has asked that you be removed."

"Stop it, seriously. I get it, okay? Obviously, you think you know what happened." She swung her arms around herself. "It's Abby, Dennis. She's really sick."

At that word, his eyes widened. "Very dim," she corrected. "She almost died."

Dennis repeated the standard line as instructed and finished, "The owner has asked that you be removed." He leaned forward and whispered, "You have disgraced your family and cost your dad a promotion. Do you care so little about your little sister that you now want to shame her, too?"

Raina's hand whipped around and slapped his face before she knew it had moved. The security team moved forward as one to grab her. She turned, and with tears blurring her vision, jumped in Valarie's car.

Valarie locked the door and reached for a weapon. She was licensed to carry and ready to defend her charge.

Christine welcomed Raina back into the car with a tissue and some wisdom. "Anything worth having is worth fighting for. We won't stop trying to get help for your sister. Your old family might not want to help you. But your new family will."

CHAPTER 19

A week after it happened, Raina's arrest was still the talk of the town. It hadn't yet been published in the county newspaper, but the moment she entered Chippewa High, she knew that everybody else knew, too. Most of the kids stared and whispered from a distance, but a few were bold (or tasteless) enough to comment as she passed by.

"Hey, Raina, where are your handcuffs?"

"There goes the jailbird!"

"What picture are you putting in the yearbook . . . your mugshot?"

That one almost made her forget Valarie's rule about ignoring the haters and respond.

Jackie beat her to it. "No, your mama," she said, turning around and stopping.

"Come on," Raina said, pulling on Jackie's coat sleeve. Jackie defending her the same way as when they were kids made her smile. "I'm not ten anymore."

Students who were church members totally ignored her, looked through her as though she wasn't even there. If she was on one side of the hall they'd cross to the other and shield themselves. That stung. Some of them had been Raina's friends for years. She'd almost made it through the school day when the principal's assistant came and delivered a written message to her classroom. Raina opened it, half expecting, half hoping it was from her mom. Instead there was the name and phone number of an attorney's office with a message to call as soon as possible. What was this about? Abby? Her parents? One of Valarie's contacts? Curiosity at what the attorney wanted made it hard for her to focus on the subject. Halfway through she asked to be excused. She went to a quiet area by the library, pulled out her phone, and dialed the number.

"Browder Law Offices."

"Hi, this is Raina Reed. I got a message to call a . . . Sean Browder."

"Yes, one moment."

Raina took a seat on the sofa. Sean came right to the phone. "Hello, Raina."

"Hi."

"My name is Sean Browder, one of the team of attorneys representing your parents, Ken and Jennifer Reed. How are you doing?"

"I've been better." How was the man working with the people who'd put her in jail sounding as if this was a social call?

"I understand. During this process, I'll be acting as the liaison between you and your parents, or I can deal with your attorney if you'd like."

"What do you want?"

"Your parents are open to dropping the kidnapping charges if you will sign off on a list of demands. I'd like to email them to you and, if you agree, you can sign the form and return it to me, by either scan or fax. All of the necessary information will be on the correspondence I send you. Any questions?"

"Not yet," Raina said. "If I do, my lawyer will contact you."

She'd thrown in that last line to try and sound tough, but the call left her shaken. Still, the thought of getting out of the judicial system, maybe even reuniting at some point with her family, gave a modicum of hope. As soon as the email indicator pinged and showed an attachment, she downloaded what had been sent and opened it. There were two pages. The first was a letter reiterating what Sean had said on the phone. The second was the list of stipulations by which her parents would drop the

266

charges against her. She skimmed past the paragraph filled with legal mumbo-jumbo and went straight to the bullet points:

- Admit that Abigail Reed was being taken against her will for unnecessary treatment at the hands of those outside the faith,
- Admit that these actions were without the approval of Abigail Reed's parents, and were in direct opposition to voiced directives regarding the above-named,
- Refrain from speaking of the above-named with any and all persons outside the faith,
- Agree to cease and desist from all attempts at obtaining medical treatment outside of the Illumination faith regarding the above-named,
- Agree to have no further contact of any kind with the above-named unless and/or until express permission is given in writing.

By the time she read the last bullet point, Raina was in tears. She couldn't figure out whether more from sadness or anger. Did they think her freedom meant more than the health of her sister? That she'd ever agree to sit by and do nothing, or never see

Abby again? After school she rode home with Jackie and showed the letter to Valarie, who downloaded it to her computer and printed it out.

"Are you open to any of this?" Valarie asked.

"There's no way I'd ever agree to not see Abby, or stop trying to help her get well."

"I didn't think so, but one should never assume. I'll respond formally to inform them you've turned down their offer," she said. "And request that all future contact be directed to me."

"Do you think we can counter, like suggest some things I would be willing to do?"

"Such as?"

Raina thought for a moment. "Letting Abby be checked out by a medical professional. Just one visit, for the doctors to say she's okay. If that happens, I'll shut up about everything."

"And agree not to see Abby without your parents' permission, which could mean not until your sister turns eighteen?"

"I would never agree to that." Raina thought for a moment. "The fact that they sent this has to mean something, doesn't it? That at least they're open to dropping the charges? This is Mom's doing. I know it! There's no way she'll take the chance that

I'll actually get charged and have to spend time in jail."

"You mean, like how you did a week ago? Remember, it was my mother and her church friends who bailed you out. Not your mom, and not the Nation. Your parents are a piece of work," Valarie continued. "I know you love them, but their actions are ridiculous. There's no reason in the world, religious or otherwise, that would justify the decision they made."

"You say that because you've only seen my side of the story. They have one, too. I've caused them a lot of pain and most likely cost my father a major promotion in the church."

"You were trying to get help for your sister, who as far as you know is still sick, correct?"

"For as much as me and my parents disagree, I know they love Abby as much as I do."

"You're right, of course. I've got to hand it to you. The optimism is impressive. I must tell you, however, that even if they agree to it and decide to drop the charges, the state may still decide to prosecute."

Raina's eyes widened. Valarie held up her hand.

"It's not a given that they will, but this is

269

a religious, conservative state filled with prosecutors and judges who like to see people who look like us locked up. At some point, I'd like to speak with your parents. I know that since I'm an outsider that is probably not an option. But sooner or later, if this case goes to trial, people outside of your faith will be getting all in their business and that of the church. I'll write a letter stating that this and other reasons are why dropping the charges without your agreeing to their demands may be worthy of consideration. I believe Abby's health is an appropriate extenuating circumstance for the uncharacteristic and irresponsible actions taken that night, and the public will certainly be interested in the state of her health."

That week, the Justice Bureau, a nonprofit legal organization founded by Valarie and four partners, officially took on Raina's case. Valarie responded to the letter, with Raina's counter demand. On her parents' behalf, Sean responded immediately. Their demands were nonnegotiable and would be handled by Sean Broward. Raina's parents had no desire for a meeting with Valarie or with her. Raina didn't have to receive a letter from the lawyer to know what that meant. She'd been cut off from the family and the church.

"They'll have to face us eventually," was Valarie's reaction. "Don't worry. We'll see them in court."

Raina was ghosted. Perhaps even obscured. Either way, when it came to blood relatives, she was alone. Any doubt of that was erased when Valarie received a message from Sean and later met him to pick up the belongings her parents had packed up. A new set of suitcases contained most of her clothes, a few pairs of shoes and underwear. Another duffel-style bag held books and other knickknacks that had been stacked on her dresser and chest of drawers. A large tote contained her bath items. When she saw the matching tote to the set, her heart raced. All of her contraband clothes were stuffed inside — leggings, crop tops, miniskirts. She could only imagine Jennifer's face if the tote had been opened. At least the clothes hadn't been thrown away. These items were brought into Christine's floral-garden guest bedroom, which would become Raina's sanctuary. That day, with most of her worldly possessions scattered around her, reality hit her with a force that snatched her breath. She fell on the bed, buried her head, and sobbed like a baby. She cried for a while, probably ten minutes straight.

Valarie's words pulled her back from the brink. *Be strong.* Raina wiped her eyes, blew her nose, and vowed to never cry again.

CHAPTER 20

Raina tried to adjust to a new normal. She missed Abby more than a fish missed water, but she went on as best she could. Bryce had stepped out of the bushes and back into her life. Despite being almost desperate to know details, she refrained from asking about his dating life, what he'd done in the weeks they'd not interacted. Rumor had it that he was dating an older woman named Sandy, who operated a dry-cleaning business. Raina wasn't happy about it, but she didn't own him. She would always hold a special place for Bryce in her heart. He'd stuck his neck out and tried to help her with Abby. Since then, he'd been surprisingly supportive, not as a guy trying to play with her emotions, but as a true friend.

With graduation approaching, college plans in flux, owing Christine and her band of sisters ten thousand dollars, and legal restrictions putting her plans for a summer job in Kansas City on hold, Raina finally filled out the application that Monica had passed her when filling out her own application at Breadbasket. The assistant manager who'd taken her application had said to give it a week before receiving an answer. The manager and owner were out of town, reportedly on the same vacation. Small-town gossip. Raina didn't care. Most residents knew each other's business or thought so. Not hard, with so little to do.

Jackie's dad lived in Vegas and had recently celebrated a birthday. Jackie had attended the party and returned with money she'd won on the penny slots. She shared it with Raina.

"Three hundred dollars?" Raina exclaimed. "I can't take this money. What's it for?"

"Whatever you need," Jackie told her. "Get your nails done, enjoy a massage, buy a present for Abby. They can't keep you from her for the rest of your life."

"I don't know, Jackie . . ."

"Well, I do. I'm not asking, I'm telling. We're going to the spa. Come on!"

"Why?"

"We're about to be about it! The video debuts tonight."

"We're about to be about it," Raina sang.

"Oh my gosh, I can't wait to see it."

"Bryce and Larry said we all made the final cut. They're having a watch party, which means you're about to attend your first unsanctioned jam. To do that you've got to have your look on point. Let's go!"

A short time later, Raina was in a spa chair enjoying her first mani-pedi. They left there and went to Monica's house. Raina shopped her closet like a boutique, leaving with an oversized angora sweater to wear over knit leopard leggings and the thigh-high boots she'd worn in the video. They stopped by Christine's, then went over to Jackie's to dress for the party. They put on KCK's latest album to get into the mood. Raina had a ball playing with Jackie's makeup and loved it when Jackie suggested she pick Raina's hair into an afro. When she looked in the full-length mirror on Jackie's bedroom door, she couldn't believe the transformation. It was like a tiger who'd been kept in a cage had been freed, as though the image on the outside finally matched the girl within. She loved it! When they reached Larry's apartment the party was in full swing. Bryce gave her an appreciative once-over, and a hug that lasted a beat or two past casual friendship. Raina waited to meet someone named Sandy. She wasn't there.

Rather than focus on figuring out Bryce's love life, Raina enjoyed the freedom of hanging out with friends. Everyone laughed, danced, and munched on a slew of pizzas, chips, and drinks. The video "Be About It" aired, the atmosphere buzzed, with loud cheers erupting every time someone was recognized. Jackie, Larry, and Monica were all in the video's party scene. Raina was primetime behind KCK, looking cool and more fly than she did tonight. When Bryce came on with his rap contribution, the room erupted. At the end everyone applauded as though the performance was live. It was the first time since being obscured that Raina felt not one hint of sadness. She made new friends, tried her first alcoholic drink, and cuddled with Bryce. She missed her family immensely, but being obscured had its advantages, too. Tonight was the best time of her life.

A week into her new life, Bryce came around almost daily. Raina called it friendship. Jackie said they were dating, the same as her and Steve officially began doing after the video party. The couples fell into a routine. They'd hang at Valarie's or Monica's house, or sometimes Larry's when his jerk of a big brother wasn't home. The two shared an apartment together and Andre meant well. But instead of being entertaining, his antics got on everyone's nerves. Raina still missed her family every day and was thankful for the outsiders, the unsanctioned, that stepped in and helped fill the void.

She heard from Breadbasket, a week to the day after faxing in her application. She paired a bright yellow T-shirt with black pants and boots and began her training. It was her first job, didn't interfere with school, and she loved it. Three to four days a week and sometimes on Saturday, Raina took orders, interacted with customers and thought of her mom. How Jennifer waited tables years ago at the club. No wonder Raina was a natural. It was in her DNA! A month into her stint and Raina had it mastered. She could recite and describe everything on the menu from memory and knew all of her regular customers by name. The unsanctioned became her family. Even Miss Christine came by the restaurant and ordered from her station. Bev had two reasons to eat there — no, actually three — Monica, Raina, and no cooking skills. Raina was appreciative of all the concern, and for a job that often kept her too busy to think, at least during working hours. Sometimes she could actually forget how she got there, why she was at Breadbasket instead of at the center with the Vessels. That her family had all but disowned her. That there was a shadow that she couldn't see.

We're still together even when we're apart.

The line had sounded good at the time, when Raina needed a rhyme for her ditty. But now she knew the truth. That words were bullshit. She and Abby were separated with no feeling of "togetherness" at all. She missed Abby terribly and had never spent this much time away from her mom. She even missed being around Ken. In short, she missed her family. She missed home.

For now, though, there was money to earn and tips to be made. She eased the tray of food from off the pickup window, carefully balancing the drinks and other contents as she maneuvered her way through the height of rush hour at the local hangout for the high school crowd.

"Chicken fingers and fries," she said, setting a red, paper-lined plastic basket in front of a freckle-faced teen, after placing the drinks on the table. "Double cheese and tots," she said to the guy sitting across from him, placing a basket down holding a burger with all of the trimmings and extra cheddar. She handed baskets holding pizza slices and side salads to the girls sitting with them.

The bells on the door jingled as it opened. Raina looked up to see a group of her friends coming through, including her favorite guy in the world.

"Let me know if I can get you anything else, okay?"

Raina waved to some and endured the curious stares of others as she walked over to where Bryce, Larry, Steve, and Jackie had just sat down. It made her uncomfortable to have people watch her so blatantly, but considering the news-making arrest and how Illuminated kids in Chippewa were all but invisible beyond school and the occasional grocery store sighting, she couldn't blame them.

"Hey, guys!"

"Hey, girl," Jackie said.

Larry said hello. Steve threw up a hand.

Bryce leaned against the booth's cushioned seat. "What's up, beautiful?"

All of that swagger made a Black girl blush. "You guys need menus?" she asked them.

"No," Jackie answered. "I know what I want. The Tuesday Tacos special."

"I'm getting a double cheese and rings," Larry said.

Raina looked at Bryce. "What about you?"

Bryce rattled off half a dozen items he

279

knew were on the menu. "Forget all that," he finished, as the table cracked up laughing. "I'll take a steak sandwich, a large fry . . . and you."

Raina gave him a look.

"What? I'm talking about you taking a break and joining us." He looked around the table. "What did y'all think I meant?"

Raina placed their orders and one of her own, taking her break once she'd served them. A short time later, after washing down a fish sandwich with a vanilla shake, Bryce left to take the crew home while Raina finished out her shift. It had been a grueling five hours and her feet hurt but leaving work through the back door and seeing the black Mustang in the parking lot picked up her spirits.

"Hey," she said, leaning over to give Bryce a quick kiss on the cheek. They'd dibbled and dabbled, but she was still a virgin.

"You want to go to a movie this weekend?"

"Like, in a theater?"

"No, a drive-in."

"Really?"

"No, fool!" Bryce laughed. "Of course, a theater. Don't tell me you've not been to one of those either."

"Not since I was nine or ten."

"Damn! In that case, we'll see two movies

and I'll get you all the concessions you want!"

"Right now I'll just take some lavender Epsom salts and a foot rub. Can you take me by Dollar Discount?"

Minutes later they pulled into the small strip mall's parking lot, anchored by a Pizza Hut on one end and Dollar Discount on the other. Raina stepped out of the car, so busy joking and flirting with Bryce that she almost didn't notice the pearl-white Infinity. Her eyes searched the surroundings.

Mom!

Racing into the Dollar Discount, Raina quietly scoured the aisles. She didn't know what kind of reception she'd get, or if Jennifer would even acknowledge her. Still, her heart burst with excitement. She was almost giddy. After more than a month, she'd see her . . .

"Mom."

Just like that, there she was, in the health and beauty aisle, Raina's destination. Jennifer looked up and for a moment, seconds really, love poured out of her eyes. It dried up though and was quickly replaced by a mask of indifference. She turned and walked in the opposite direction, without a word.

"Mom," Raina whispered, desperate for contact. "I know you can't talk to me. Just nod if Abby is getting better."

Nothing.

"I know you and Dad love her as much as I do! If she's not getting better it's because she might be really sick. I wasn't trying to kidnap Abby, Mother. I was trying to save her life."

Jennifer placed a basket half-filled with products on a near-empty shelf and continued out the door. Raina followed.

"I miss you, Mom. Not Mother — Mom! The one that I used to have, back in Kansas City. I miss us!"

Jennifer crossed the lot and reached her car.

"I've seen Miss Bev a few times, Mom."

The car door was open, but Jennifer paused.

"She's become something like family. I got a job at BBs, waiting tables. She said I had skills and must have gotten them from you."

With that statement Jennifer became unstuck. She got into the car but Raina wedged herself in the door before she could close it.

"I love you, Mother. I'm sorry for what happened. Aren't you going to say something, anything at all?"

Jennifer started the engine. She placed her

282

hand on the gearshift. Raina waited, holding her breath.

"We saw the music video," Jennifer said finally. She turned and their eyes met. "Stay away from Abby. We don't want her infected with whatever's taken over you."

The verbal one-two punch pushed all of the air out of Raina's lungs. She fell back, closed her mother's car door, then watched the taillights moving down the street until she could no longer see them.

CHAPTER 21

"I think you should call social services," Jackie said to Raina, who was sitting at Valarie's dining room table for this impromptu powwow, the weekend after Raina had seen her mom and been told to stay away from her sister. "Or call the police and ask them to do a welfare check."

"They'd likely send an officer from the Nation," Raina replied. "The church are huge contributors to the police and fire department funds and have members on both forces."

"Do we want to open them up to the government?" Beverly asked. "On the one hand it's a good idea, but on the other, it might get Abby removed from their home."

"I wish they would," Raina said, ready to risk Abby's discomfort in being with strangers. "But from what Miss Valarie has learned, that probably won't happen."

Valarie reached for a Danish on the platter in the middle of the table, then shared what she and Raina had initially found on the internet and information the firm had further uncovered regarding Kansas's laws on medical treatment and the rights of parents versus child. "The law favors the parent but exceptions exist. They're rare and came only after clear, irrefutable proof of imminent child endangerment was successfully presented to the court. That's a slippery slope to go down, especially given the variables we can't control."

"What are those?" Raina asked.

"Initially, children are often placed with someone outside of the family until a full investigation and report can be made. While most of these agencies and foster homes have the children's best interest at heart, I've heard fostering and adoption horror stories."

Raina shivered. "We can't do that." The thought of Abby being in the home of strangers was already unsettling but that they might be abusive sent chills down her back.

"I could make a few phone calls," Bev suggested. "See if I can get somebody who knows someone in the system that we can trust."

"In social services?" Raina asked.

Bev nodded.

"At least we can talk to someone to learn our options," Valarie suggested.

"Knowledge is power," Jackie said.

"I agree," Raina said with a nod. "Let's do that."

That Monday, Raina got an excuse from her classes and rode with Valarie to the social services offices located in Topeka, the state's capitol. They met with the woman Bev's contact had recommended, and filed a report detailing the past few months and outlining her concern for Abby's welfare. Dana Kirksey was the perfect mix of compassion and professionalism who put both Valarie and Raina at ease.

"What happens now?" Valarie asked, once all of the questions had been asked, answered, and documented.

"We'll send someone over to meet with Abby and your parents," Dana explained. "They'll document their findings and make a recommendation based on the visit. I'll contact you personally with the results."

"How long will all of this take?" Raina asked.

"That depends on your parents' cooperation," Dana replied. "I've given the case urgent status, so hopefully no longer than a week or two."

Raina would read about what happened next in detailed social services reports.

Two days later, social services showed up at the Reeds', demanding to see Abby. They had documentation that was a type of search warrant, allowing them into the residence. The law was on their side, but the Reeds pushed back. Within minutes, a Nation lawyer pulled into the driveway and refused them entrance. The police were called. After a heated argument that drew ire from all sides, the social services team went away defeated. Citing religious freedom, the Reeds' attorney prevailed. The state was denied entry into the Reeds' home, but they vowed to continue fighting. According to the report, they returned to the home the very next day, accompanied by law enforcement not on the Nation's payroll. There was only one problem when the team showed up, demanding to see Abby. She wasn't there.

When she heard the news, Raina was devasted.

"Maybe they're just out for the day," Valarie offered, shortly after relaying how social services had arrived to a home where no one answered the door.

That news made Raina even more uncomfortable. "Did they go by the church?"

"No, but they visited the school. Abby wasn't in class and hadn't been for the past week. Should they have gone to the church?"

"It probably wouldn't have done any good. If my parents have taken Abby and gone into hiding, it is with the church's protection."

"Where do you think they are?" Valarie asked.

Raina thought for a moment. "Maybe Tulsa. That's our Central Center, the hub for this part of the country. There is a major healing facility there with machines we don't have locally. If Abby isn't getting better, they may have taken her there to see if they could help."

Valarie opened her tablet. "What's the name of this center? I need all of the information to pass on to social services and get the Oklahoma offices involved."

Heavy rains marked the beginning of April with no sign of the Reed family. A few days into the month, Bryce left town, too. Rapper KCK was on tour and had asked Bryce to join him. With her special friend gone and her family still missing, Raina's heart grew heavy. Still, she wasn't without strong, constant support. The Nation was influential, but their power was not absolute.

Valarie's law partners had contacts, too. Bruce was especially adept at networking. He had friends everywhere, including on the Chippewa police force. Through him, they'd conducted a regular patrol of the Reed property and had detected no movement. No cars in or out of the garage, or other signs of life. From time to time, lights had been seen going on and off, but Raina knew timers could have been responsible for that. Through another firm member who had a relative in the Nation, Raina and the team learned the family had not been seen at church. The last bit of information that they'd skipped town came as Raina finished her shift at BBs on Thursday night, from quite an unexpected source. She returned from break to see Abby's teacher and the snitch that had sent Raina to council, Lucy Stone, sitting in her station. It wasn't just their opposing points of view that made this unusual. Lucy was a member of the Nation. They didn't keep casual company with the unsanctioned, and if given the choice wouldn't dine with them. Shooting Stars was an award-winning restaurant, and one of the best steakhouses in the state. It was located in Lucent Rising. When wanting to dine out, most members ate there or at one of the three other choices. So what was

Lucy doing at the Breadbasket? Raina wondered. Especially since Raina had now been shunned. There was only one way to find out.

It took effort, but Raina managed to not roll her eyes or spit in the water she brought out with the menu. A benefit of no longer being a part of the church family was that Raina didn't have to make nice.

"Something to drink before I take your order?"

"A cherry lemonade to go," Lucy responded, evenly. "I won't be long."

Ah, here we go. Raina could only imagine what judgmental message Lucy felt so compelled to deliver that she'd come inside the shop. She wasn't going to set herself up for it, though. If Lucy had something to say to her, it wasn't going to be by open invitation.

"Okay, a cherry lemonade coming right up."

Raina turned to leave, but Lucy's next statement stopped her. "I'm here about Abby."

Concern for her little sister tossed all other feelings aside. She took a breath before facing Lucy. "Where is my sister? Is she okay?"

"I don't know." Lucy kept her eyes on the

290

menu as she spoke to Raina. "She was taken out of school and then earlier today came the news that she won't be returning."

This news was shocking to Raina. Abby loved her classmates and had thrived in the group learning model the private school practiced. "She won't be back for the rest of the year?"

Lucy nodded. "That's correct. Your parents have decided to homeschool her."

The hairs on the back of Raina's neck stood up. As much as the message bothered her, so did the messenger who'd delivered it. "I've been rejected by my family and, obviously, the church, too. Why are you here telling me this?"

Lucy finally looked up from the menu and met Raina's eyes. "I'm worried about your sister's health, Raina. I'm concerned for Abby."

Raina sat with no thought of being on the clock. That Lucy had voiced this concern out loud was rare for one of the Nation.

"How did she look the last time that you saw her?"

"Pale, weak, not the bundle of energy that usually ran into my classroom. Her health had gone up and down like that for weeks. I have every confidence in Illuminated healing and believe those days she felt better were due to Light treatment. But I haven't been able to forget how she looked the last time I saw her, that day your mom took her out of my classroom. The fear and desperation I read in her eyes. I think that's why you kidnapped her, because you'd seen it, too."

"She wasn't kidnapped!" Raina whispered, louder than intended. A few heads turned in their direction. Raina remembered to breathe. "Never mind that. Did you share how you felt with my parents?"

Lucy's expression changed, became guarded.

"I get it. In the eyes the church they're no longer my family. But your concern is valid and you're right. It equals mine. It's why I took my sister to try and get help and, yes, am now facing a kidnapping charge. But that's not what happened. A nurse from the clinic agreed to see Abby. I had every intention of going back home once my sister had been checked out. But the nurse said Abby was in critical condition so instead of going back home we went to emergency. Or tried to. Before getting out of the driveway, I was arrested. Social services got involved, to try and get Abby medical treatment. Now my parents have left town and no one knows where they are!"

Raina felt the staring. Once again, her voice had risen along with her agitation. She looked over to discover her manager, Thomas, watching her intently. Work. Right. She'd forgotten about that.

She gave him a slight nod and got up from the table. "Sorry, I shouldn't have . . . I'm just so worried about her. Be right back with your drink."

When she returned with the lemonade, Lucy was gone. But she'd left a five-dollar bill on the table. A sticky note was attached.

The Central, she'd hastily scribbled. And beneath it, *Light day to you.*

Raina immediately texted Valarie with the information. She could barely wait to get off work, was ready to drive herself to Tulsa, Oklahoma. She'd climb barbed wire and break through glass if she thought it would lead her to Abby. Were it not for Valarie's reminder that she was in the system and couldn't leave the state, Raina would have left the next day.

As it turned out, it wouldn't have done any good. It took three attorneys, two agencies, a search warrant, court order, and judge to confirm the tip Lucy had given to Raina. Abby had indeed been treated at the healing center. Privacy laws kept her medical records sealed, but the practitioners reported Abby's health as improving. Anyone wondering had to take their word for it. Because the Reeds were no longer in Tulsa and when it came to their whereabouts, no one in the Nation would disclose them.

CHAPTER 22

Valarie's living room became the de facto ground zero for Raina and the supporting cast determined to find Abby. As the days, then weeks, passed, sympathizers wanting to help continued to grow, a motley crew of misfits, professionals, friends who became Raina's family. Today, they'd met to discuss involving the media in helping to find Abby, to have the interest generated by Raina's arrest work to their advantage. By then a few media outlets in the state's larger cities — Wichita, Topeka, Kansas City — had run the story of her arrest. The general thought was that if the public knew the *why* behind the *what,* the reasons that had driven Raina to take Abby in the first place, the story could gain traction and get people talking, and looking for her sister. To Raina, any plan that could potentially help locate her shadow was one that they needed to try.

"I have a contact at *The Call,* " Drew was

saying, when Raina's focus turned back to the activity around her. "I'm pretty confident that they'd run the story."

Andrew "Drew" Langley was one of the partners who worked at the Justice Bureau along with Bruce and Valarie. His interest in Abby's safe return was personal. He had a daughter the same age. Valarie's trustworthy assistant, Marjorie, was also Team Abby. She'd volunteered to help however she could and sat taking notes of the meeting.

"That's cool," Bruce, the Bureau's youngest, hot shot attorney added. "But theirs is a small circulation. We need this story in the major papers so it can get picked up by the Associated Press."

Valarie's look was doubtful. "That's a long shot. Every story doesn't get picked up."

"If it's written right, this one will."

Other ideas were bounced around, including starting a Where's Abby or Find Abby page on various social media, like Facebook, Instagram, and Storytime, a new app driven mostly by short video posts. Lucy, who'd responded with an offer to help when Raina reached out to thank her using the school's email address, had joined the group and offered to set up pages on the two more established sites. Someone else decided to create a digital flyer. Valarie asked for a picture of Abby. Raina pulled up images on her computer and then completely without warning burst into tears.

"I'm sorry, guys," she mumbled between sniffles. "I'm just so thankful to all of you for helping me."

Christine, who'd declared herself the resident chef whenever they got together, came out from the kitchen and enveloped Raina in her arms.

"It's okay, baby," she said, rocking Raina gently. "We're not going to stop until we find your sister. Let these be happy tears."

Jackie sat on the couch next to Monica, rubbing a white crystal. "That's what the crystals and angels are saying."

Raina looked up from Christine's comforting chest and saw her friend's movements. As she walked over to sit next to her, a soft, brief smile eased through a blanket of pain. She sniffed and felt the faint smell of sage. Jackie could always be counted on to bring help from the other worlds. That's the way her soul sister rolled.

Monica's mom, Bev, held out a box of tissues as Raina passed her. "Here you go, sweetheart."

"Thank you," Raina mumbled. "Didn't mean to lose it."

Monica tsked. "Don't you dare feel bad about that. You have every right to lose it, freak out, or whatever else, and nothing to be sorry about."

"We won't give up until we find her, that's for sure," Valarie said.

Bev nodded. "I agree. That little girl is out there somewhere and she needs us, now more than ever. We've got to continue to do whatever it takes to try and find her and get her help."

Drew, who'd been seated on the love seat quietly chatting with Bruce and another man, got up and walked to the center of the room. "Valarie's right, Raina. You're such a trooper, and the best kind of big sister that a little sister could ask for. Hang in there, okay?"

"I'll try," Raina said softly.

"Don't try, do," Christine quickly countered, looking out from the kitchen, emphasizing that last word while searing Raina with a look that could transfer power and transmit strength. "Y'all may not have the answer yet but God's got it. Don't worry. I've been praying."

Bruce chuckled. "What will prayer do?"

"Son, don't make me have to come in there and hit you upside the head with this skillet. Prayer will change things."

As if on cue, the doorbell rang.

Bev looked up. "Is that Jesus?"

Bruce went to the window and peeked out. "Young white girl," he said.

Valarie was on her way to the door before he finished the description.

"Do you know her?" he asked.

Valarie checked the peephole. "No, but I'm about to." She opened the door. "May I help you?"

"Hi," the young woman said with a confidence that belied her seeming young age. "I'm looking for Raina Reed."

"And you are?"

"My name is Kris Hall, a former member of the Nation and a freelance journalist. I received a tip about what's going on with Raina and her sister, Abby. I'd like to tell their story."

"As a member of the Nation, what kind of story would you tell?"

"I'm a former member who was kicked out for marrying an outsider. I believe that background gives me an insight that other journalists don't have and the ability to tell the kind of story that editors would want to print, and the public would want to read."

Valarie gave the woman a long look. "Do you have a card?"

"No card, just conviction," she replied

without smiling. "I want to help Abby. If you put my name into a search engine, I think you'll see that I can do that."

Valarie wasn't sure about the attitude, whether to be pissed off or a bit impressed. "Hang on a second."

She closed the door, leaving the woman on the other side, and walked into the dining room. "Look up Kris Hall," she said to Lucy, who was still working on her computer.

Lucy reacted to the name. "Kris Hall? What do you want to know about her?"

"I want to know why she's on my doorstep," Valarie responded. "Saying she's a reporter wanting to do a story on Raina."

"Let her in."

"You know her?"

"Not personally but I've read her work. Fantastic writer. Courageous, too. One of her first stories looked into the rumor of financial corruption in one of the Nation's largest churches. The leaders threatened to sue but she stood by her story. I think her career may have suffered because of it. Heard she's freelancing because so far no major paper will give her a job."

"What are we waiting for?" Bruce asked with a scowl. He rushed past them to open the door.

"I don't know," Drew replied. "But given that Illumination member's reaction, I say we let her in."

Once inside, Kris, Bruce, Drew, and Valarie retreated to a quieter space. Under the attorney's watchful eyes and keenly listening ears, Kris interviewed Raina. She asked thoughtful questions and asked for a picture of Abby. The visit was short but productive and left everyone feeling one step closer to finding Raina's little sister and getting her whatever medical help was needed. Afterwards, Raina excused herself from the group and went searching for Jackie.

She tapped on the bedroom door before opening it slightly. "Can I come in?"

Jackie motioned Raina into the room. "Hold on a minute," she said, continuing a conversation through a set of ear buds.

"Oh!" Raina stopped just inside the door. "I didn't know you were on the phone."

"I'm getting off," Jackie said, before returning to the phone call. "Steve, let me call you back. I need to talk to Raina."

She pushed aside a stack of folded clothes to give Raina room on the bed. "How'd it go?"

"All right, I guess. Where's Monica?"

"Bev had to go to work. Monica left with her." Jackie picked up a set of tarot cards and idly shuffled them. "That girl was in the Nation, huh?"

Raina nodded.

"Did that make it easier to talk with her?"

"Definitely. There was a lot of stuff that I didn't have to explain. Most importantly, I felt I could trust her with my story. I know she believed me."

"What happens now?"

Raina shrugged. "I guess we'll wait and see."

Jackie continued shuffling the cards. Raina reached for a pen lying on the bed, twirling it around her fingers as she gazed out the window.

A moment later, Jackie began placing the cards in a spread. "What song is that?"

"You heard me?" Raina hadn't realized she'd been humming out loud.

"Yeah. Who is it?"

"Nobody." Raina ducked her head, embarrassed.

"Didn't sound like nobody."

"It's a song I wrote for Abby, about her being my shadow since the time she was small."

"Let me hear it."

Raina shared the song, sing/rapping both hers and Abby's part.

"Ahh . . . that's sweet," Jackie said, once

Raina had finished. "Hey, I've got an idea. You should put that on Storytime."

"My song for Shadow? Um, I don't think so."

"No, really, you should! Dedicate it to your sister. Give a little intro about why you wrote it and how it's even more special now."

Jackie slid off the bed and looked around. "Where's your phone?"

Raina's answer was a deadpan stare.

"Never mind. We'll use mine." Jackie reached for her phone on the nightstand, then continued looking around. "We need a nice background," she mused. "What about here, Raina?"

She pointed to the bed, which had a colorful picture on the wall behind it. "Those colors match your sweater. A little makeup, and fluff out your hair, and people will know it's the girl in KCK's video. We can use that as a hash tag and maybe increase views."

"I don't know, Jackie."

"Look, now is not the time to be shy. You want to find Abby, right?"

"You know the answer to that."

"Then we've got to use whatever it takes to get people talking about her, asking where she is and if she's healthy. When something goes on the web, you never know

303

who might see it. Anything could happen. It might even go viral."

Raina doubted that. But at one time she'd been sure that her mother wouldn't see the rap video. That she had was proof that Jackie was partly right. Anything could happen. Maybe it was worth a try.

"I just interviewed with Kris. Lucy is setting up pages on other social media sites. Your mom thinks that's enough. Maybe we should ask her about it."

"I don't want to do that. She could say no."

"All the more reason to ask her!"

"I've got a feeling we should do this, Raina."

Raina pointed to the cards on the bed. "Let's ask the angels."

"Okay." Jackie returned to the bed. "We want a clear, definitive answer. Let's just pull one."

She shuffled the cards several times, then asked the questions as she placed the deck on the bed. "Angels, should Raina tell her story on Storytime?"

She nodded toward the cards. "Cut the deck."

Raina did, a feeling of something akin to excitement bubbling just below the surface.

Jackie reached for the top card turned it

over and began reading the words on its face. "You know what to do." Her eyes met Raina's, then shifted back to the card. "Trust your inner knowledge and act without delay."

The feeling in Raina's gut exploded. "Let's do it," she said.

Raina decided not to wear any makeup but let Jackie fix her hair. "What do I say?" she asked, once they felt she was ready for the camera.

"Talk to the camera as though you were talking to me or Monica about Abby. Then do the song like you would if she were here. One more thing. Wait here."

Jackie left the room and returned with one of the eight by ten glossies Valarie had ordered from a photo shop. With her back against the wall and the colorful picture just above her left shoulder, Raina looked directly into the camera and began speaking.

"Hi, I'm Raina, the girl behind Sniper in KCK's Be About It." Suddenly nervous, Raina felt her heartbeat increase. Jackie motioned for her to keep talking. Raina swallowed her fear.

"That's not what this video is about though. It's about my sister, Abby. I call her Shadow because she's ten years younger than me and used to follow me around all the time like a shadow does."

The memory allowed Raina a tentative smile before it slid away. "I'm worried about her because she might be really sick, and I don't know where she is. See, my parents belong to the Illumination and don't believe in doctors or hospitals or getting treated the way others do. When I tried to sneak Shadow out of the house so a doctor could see her, my parents had me arrested for kidnapping and then basically kicked me out of the family which sucks cause . . . this is . . ."

Raina teared up as she again looked at Jackie.

"Keep talking," Jackie mouthed.

"I don't even know why I'm doing this," she continued, raising her knees to her chest and wrapping her arms around them. "Probably no one will see me and even if you do . . . it's just that I love my little sister. I miss her, and we can't find her and it's all so frustrating."

Tears fell. Raina swiped them away but didn't try to stop them. "The church has their own treatment for when someone gets sick or goes dim as they say in the Nation. I hope it's helping that Shadow, Abby, is being filled with Light. But if not, I want them to take her to a hospital. Or at least call me

306

and tell me what's going on. It's killing me not to know if she's all right.

"Kids in the Nation don't come on sites like this, but my friend Jackie said I should try and send her a message anyway, that maybe somebody somewhere will see it, and then see Abby, and alert the police or somebody so that we can find her and help her."

Raina reached for the picture. "This is Abby, my shadow. One of the last times I saw her, we sang our secret song. Me and her reciting every other line while doing a little dance. I wrote it to cheer her up after our cat died. Thinking she might hear this makes me feel a little better now. I'm not a singer or a rapper but . . ." Raina cleared her throat. "This is for Shadow, Abby Reed, wherever you are.

"When I move to the right, you are my shadow.

To the left cross-step, shadow all around.

When I move you move, just like a shadow.

When I groove you groove, my forever shadow now."

Raina felt lighter. It showed in the smile she gave while staring directly at the camera phone before a shy wave and quiet, "Okay, that's all. Thanks. Bye."

She looked at Jackie. "So . . . how did I do?"

Mimicking Raina's earlier actions Jackie shrugged and said, "I guess we'll wait and see."

Jackie added hash tags #BeAboutIt, #KCKVideo and #SavingShadow to the post, and tagged all of her friends. Minutes later, Monica called.

"Oh my gosh, Raina," she gushed, when Jackie placed the call on speaker. "You've got me crying over here!"

An hour later, Larry and Steve called. Bryce did, too. "Yo, that was cool what you did for your little sister. Had me choked up a little bit."

"Quit playing." That he'd seen it and approved made her feel good. His words made her smile. "Glad you saw it, though."

"I'm serious. I showed it to KCK. He wanted to help and shared it on his page."

"For real?" Raina's eyes widened. Jackie was excited, too.

"I gotta run," Bryce said, "But I'll be home next weekend. Whatever help you need . . . I'm there."

By the time Raina and Miss Christine went home, more than twenty of Jackie's friends had called raving about the video. Raina checked the website before going to bed. Almost seven hundred people had viewed the video. The next morning, a ringing phone woke her up before the alarm set for seven.

"What is it, Jackie?" she groggily asked.

"You're going viral!" Jackie shouted. "Already more than twenty thousand views!"

That news woke Raina up. She hopped out of bed. There was no guarantee that they'd find Abby. But she felt a few thousand more would be looking.

CHAPTER 23

The Storytime post went viral — one hundred thousand views in less than a week. But that was just the tip of the iceberg. Kris Hall's story ran in the regional paper two days later, read, it seemed, by everyone in Chippewa. When Raina went back to school, most of the students were very supportive. Some apologized for jokes made at her expense following the kidnapping charges. Others shared her posts and helped pass out flyers. The major papers in the state's three largest cities published Kris's article before it got picked up by the Associated Press. Within twenty-four hours, Raina's story, along with a recent picture of her and Abby, were featured in papers from Seattle to Maine. Raina's cry for help was genuine and raw and tugged at the nation's emotions. Most who watched it could see themselves — siblings, mothers, teachers, friends. Except for defending and supporting the

Reeds on their network, the Illumination had been silent. By week's end, however, they were forced to issue a statement to the national press. That Saturday, Raina watched as Grand Seer Otis Patterson, the man who'd been like an uncle before conducting the council that eventually voted her obscured, appeared at a press conference and provided a Nationesque spin on the Reeds' disappearance. In America, he said, families weren't required to post their vacation plans and had a right to privacy when it came to health issues and family decisions made based on their faith. He promoted Light healing, criticized the biased mainstream media and admonished those in the Nation to avoid the unsanctioned.

The story set off a national debate around the rights of parents and children, and how sometimes the line got blurred that separated church and state. Talk shows. News outlets. Men and women. Old and young. Everyone had an opinion. After the first couple days, Valarie advised Raina to stop watching the news and return to a singular focus — Abby.

They hired a publicist that Drew recommended. Felicity Moore was a quiet, experienced professional with an attention to detail. She fielded calls from every major news outlet and several television talk shows. Even Hollywood came knocking in the form of an A-list producer who thought their heartstring-tugging story was perfect for television, maybe even the big screen. Valarie, Bruce, or Drew vetted every inquiry. They were very protective of their client and concerned that Raina might be exploited. To say Team Abby, which after the viral video was renamed Team Shadow, became overwhelmed with the media frenzy was an understatement. But they were holding their own.

At the moment, Team Shadow was gathered at Valarie's house, their usual spot — Raina, Jackie, Valarie, Bruce, Drew, and Valarie's assistant, Marjorie. The back wall of the dining room where they sat had been turned into an organizational board. Potential media appearances for Raina had been scribbled on sheets of white paper, then taped to the wall so everyone could see the potential big picture, literally. ELLA, the name of the number one talk show in its time slot for over ten years, was at the center of the wall.

Valarie sat back, tapping her chin with a manicured finger. "Ella is a given. Her platform is known for helping others, and she has a special heart for kids. I think an interview with her would be thorough but compassionate and, hey, since she's always surprising her guests, she might even help us find Abby."

"Ella's big," Felicity agreed. "But I'm negotiating a booking with national news phenom Gayla Kingsley. She wants an exclusive, no other one-on-ones for thirty days before or after her show has aired. Going on Ella would take that interview off the table. I'm not sure we'd get it back."

Bruce rocked back in his chair, frowning. "In today's news cycle, thirty days is forever. Our main goal is getting the word out about Abby, as quickly as possible, to as many who will cover the story. Gayla is big, but so is Ella. I say we counter with a maybe a week on the exclusive but if Ella reaches out, we can't say no."

Felicity tapped a key on the tablet in front of her and quoted the stats on both shows, which ran on different networks. Everyone at the table concluded that the ideal would be for Abby's story to run on both.

"I could counter with a nonexclusive offer," she said, "with the incentive for Gayla to be the first national newscast to interview Raina. Hers would likely air on a morning show versus a primetime spot. Given the demographics, and Ella's lock on the afternoons, that would actually be a great situation."

They agreed on half a dozen other appearances on popular video blogs and radio stations before Valarie shifted the conversation.

"I hate to dampen the mood, but we need to discuss how to handle our opposition — FOX and other conservative outlets that have sided with the parents. Our other nemesis is obviously Illumination TV. They have a solid following and an expansive reach, and are spinning the narrative in a way that's harmful and untrue."

"It's America," Bruce said. "Everyone has the right to voice their opinions, even if they are untrue, outright lies."

"As long as they use the word 'allegedly,' " Drew added.

Bruce shook his head. "People can lie without using that word. Look at the dude in the White House. Case closed."

"Doesn't mean we can't sue them for libel," Marjorie said, her years of working at law firms paying off.

Valarie agreed. "But as long as the content isn't especially damaging, it's not worth our time and effort. Their rhetoric is a distraction, a way to sidetrack, derail us. We won't let that happen. But we need to be ready to counter whatever distractions are created with what's important, finding Abby and making sure she's okay."

The doorbell rang. Drew stood up. "I asked a buddy of mine to stop by, Valarie. He read Raina's story in the paper and thinks he can help us."

He answered the door and returned with a short, average-looking guy sporting a bald head, a slight paunch and an easy smile.

"This is a college buddy of mine, Stanton Palovich, a former computer technology geek who's quickly and quietly become one of the best private investigators in the country. He wants to help you, Raina, in any way that he can."

Even with a viral video and national talk show host interest, Raina was surprised. A private investigator? Her emotions rose to the surface. That all of these people, most of them strangers, would want to help her was overwhelming. These were outsiders, the unsanctioned, deemed off-limits by the Nation. Yet other than Lucy, Raina hadn't seen a familiar face from her former religious family. Help hadn't come without consequences, though.

Recently, the Nation's school had found and flagged the email Raina had sent to Lucy and questioned her about it. She admitted to being in contact with Raina, violating a no-contact order given by the church, and almost lost her teaching job. Raina learned this in a final text from Lucy asking not to be contacted again.

"Thank you," Raina said to Stanton, who looked to be all of eighteen but was actually thirty-two.

Stanton nodded, smiling politely as he slipped a hand in his pocket, which brought to mind a thought Raina hadn't considered.

"I appreciate you coming here and everything, but aren't private investigators expensive? I don't have any money to pay you."

"Don't worry about it," Stanton said. "I just want to help you find your sister."

"To that end," Drew continued, "he's already started trying to track your parents electronically."

"How?"

A commotion at the front door stopped conversation. Everyone turned as Bryce entered the house.

"Bryce!" Raina jumped up and ran over to hug him. "When did you guys get back?"

"Just now. I told you I'd be here." Bryce held Raina in a warm embrace, until a pointed throat-clearing from Christine cracked up the room. "Did y'all find Abby?"

Raina shook her head. "Not yet. How was

the tour?"

"Cool, starting back up in a couple weeks. KC asked about you. Said to let him know of any way he can help."

"I appreciate that."

Bryce sat down, initially listening as the others discussed how best to find Abby, and finally jumping in. "She's probably hiding out with someone in that cult. That's where you need to be looking."

Bruce gave him a look. "You really think we haven't thought of that? You sound pretty good on that KCK track. Stay in your lane."

"This is my girl," Bryce shot back. "So this is my lane."

"Calm down everyone," Valarie said, with a hand toward each man. "Bryce, the Illumination is a huge organization to crack. They have money, power, and a network that extends all over the country and out of it. The very fact that the church and Raina's parents know we're looking will make Abby very hard to find."

"We're not going to stop looking," Bryce declared.

"Absolutely not," Raina said.

With the increased media coverage, social media coverage and the Storytime viral video views still climbing, Raina's private life all but disappeared. Someone leaked her cell number. The phone began to ping so much she turned off notifications. Texts poured in from friends and strangers alike. She had to quit her job at the Breadbasket. That night she came home to find Christine and her friend Lois Monroe, one of the woman who'd helped bail her out of jail, with their heads together at Christine's dining room table, reading a national paper. Even from a few feet away, the article's title jumped out: "Saving Her Shadow." Beneath it was the picture taken at the winter solstice celebration. Memories of that moment flooded in. Raina had said something funny to Abby, who responded with one of her contagious laughs, bright eyes and a toothy grin. Raina grabbed Abby's hand while looking directly at the camera. She hadn't seen that Abby only had eyes for big sis. It was one of Raina's all-time favorite pics.

Jackie and Monica handled the social media sites — reading the comments, responding to some of the messages, and tracking the numbers of likes, shares, and views. Raina's video on Storytime grew the fastest. Two hundred thousand views. Then six hundred thousand. Felicity secured the interview with Gayla Kingsley and had been contacted by Ella. Raina appeared on the

Gayla Kingsley show, via satellite. The day her segment aired, five million people were watching. That night her video reached one million views.

Just past seven thirty on the following Monday morning, Christine's doorbell rang. It was Bryce, looking for Raina.

"Don't even think about going to school," was his greeting, after she'd shimmied into a T-shirt and a pair of jeans and met him in the living room. Had she not been so consumed with all things Abby she would have remembered to be upset and ask what he was doing there.

Instead she simply asked, "Why not?"

"Reporters are everywhere. There's at least a dozen news trucks lined up and down the block."

"You're kidding."

"I wish I were. I thought it was crazy before but the interview with Gayla has blown your story up for real."

Raina walked to the couch, plopped down, and covered her eyes. What had she done? They'd wanted attention on Abby's situation. She hadn't considered how that would look or what it might cost her.

Christine walked into the living room and sat beside Raina. "Baby, what are you going to do?"

319

"I can't deal with any of that," Raina answered, waving her hand toward the window and the news crews she imagined beyond it. "I don't want to go to school."

Christine placed a comforting arm around her. "You don't have to, sweetie. We'll call Valarie and see how we can get you excused."

"I need to make sure they'll let me make up any assignments up that I miss. This close to graduation, I don't want any problems."

"That's admirable to be focused on your education, honey. But I'm more concerned about you." Christine pointed a finger at Raina's chest. "Your welfare is what's most important right now."

"That's right," Bryce echoed, as he pulled one of Raina's hands into his own. "Can't let nothing happen to you."

Valarie picked her and Bryce up later that morning. She'd gotten Raina excused from school, spoken with the principal and guidance counselor, and arranged for the possible use of a tutor, at least until the frenzy died down. The message Raina heard a short while later when checking her voicemail, assured that wouldn't be happening soon.

"Hello, Raina, this is Shanice Gibson with

the Ella Show. We've been speaking with Felicity Moore about you and your sister. Ella saw your video and wants to speak with you directly before possibly having you booked on the show. Please return my call ASAP at 310 . . ."

She didn't wait to hear the number. "Miss Valarie! That was a message from someone named Shanice with the *Ella Show*! What should I do?"

"The obvious," Valarie calmly replied. "Call her back."

First, Raina had to calm down. When it came to talk shows, day or night, Ella De-Blanc was her hands down favorite, the comedic actress-turned-host of the biggest and best talk show on television. They pulled into the bureau parking lot. Valarie turned off the engine. Nobody moved.

She looked at Raina. "Well?"

Raina retrieved the message, dialed the number and tapped the speaker button.

"This is Shanice."

"Hi, Shanice. It's Raina."

"Hey, Raina! It's great to hear from you. Ella has heard your story and is so proud of you."

They talked a bit more, then Ella got on the line. After joking a bit, she had only one question. "Have you ever been to California?"

"No," Raina said.

"Well, start packing, baby girl. I want you on my show."

CHAPTER 24

The whirlwind continued as five days after speaking with Ella, and nine days since being interviewed by Gayla Kingsley, Raina was in the back seat of Valarie's car, headed for the airport. Conversation was light but tension hung in the air. Gayla's segment had been done by satellite, from the studios of a network affiliate. This would be Raina's first national, face-to-face appearance. Though confident that Ella's would be a sensitive, compassionate interview, they'd wanted a list of the questions that might be asked. Shanice had told Valarie that wasn't possible. Ella's conversations were spontaneous, unscripted. Valarie had watched the show and understood. But still, she was wary. Bruce, even more so. They were also concerned for their client's mental well-being. A lot had been put on her eighteen-year-old shoulders. For the most part she'd handled the pressure like a trouper, but that didn't mean she wasn't ready to blow.

Valarie tried to lighten the car's heavy atmosphere. "How do you feel about your first trip to the City of Angels?"

"So nervous that I'm about to throw up."

"Relax, Raina," Bruce said, with a wink. "You've got this."

"That's right," Valarie said. "Try not to focus on the interview. That's not until tomorrow. Today is all about oceans, palm trees, and Hollywood."

"Wow!" Raina said. "I feel better already!"

"You've never seen palm trees?" Bruce asked, as Valarie's SUV ate the distance between Chippewa and Kansas City International Airport at eighty miles an hour.

"I've seen them, in Florida. My family attended a conference in Orlando a few years ago."

"Did you go to Disney World?"

"No."

"Really?" Bruce said. "I thought everybody who visited Orlando went to Disney World."

Not members of the Illumination, Raina thought, but said nothing. To do so would bring up more that she'd have to explain and she didn't want that organization in her energy right now.

"I've been to Florida and seen the Atlantic

Ocean," he continued, "but California is my favorite coastal state hands down. Many people who visit don't like Los Angeles, but, Raina, I think that you'll like it just fine. Lots to do, the people-watching is fabulous, and the food . . . man! Some of the best I've ever had."

They boarded a stress-free flight and, three-and-a-half hours later, arrived in LA. April showers had brought May flowers. The city burst with flora of all shapes, colors, and sizes. The bird of paradise bushes that dotted the landscape took Raina's breath away. They met Shanice and quickly learned that whatever sightseeing they were going to do had better happen this evening, because tomorrow would be work without play.

Raina's nose was pressed against the window of the limousine, looking out at a view that she'd only seen in pictures, online, and on TV. She marveled at the palm trees, the crowded highway, and buildings that stretched as far as the eye could see. Beside her Valarie, in Jackie O–style shades, looked the epitome of calm, as if it were every day one got invited to the country's number-one talk show. Bruce sat on the opposite side in the oversized limo, focused on his cell phone. Raina wished she'd been able to share the experience with Jackie and Monica, and especially Bryce. They'd not been around each other much, and were technically not dating, but whenever she thought of boys and love, which wasn't often given the focus on Abby, his face was still the one that she saw.

"Look!" She pointed out her window. "It's the Hollywood sign!"

"It sure is," Shanice said, without looking up. She'd been on her phone, either talking or texting, since waving the gang over to where she stood near the carousel in baggage claim.

"Will we get to see it up close?"

"Not really. It used to be that you could walk right up to the letters, but not anymore."

"I want to see some of the stars' houses," Raina gushed, "and Hollywood, and Beverly Hills. And how far away is Disneyland?"

Even as she reeled off these fantasy locations, the words of her dad and the council rang in her ears. One selfie taken with Mickey Mouse and she'd be damned to eternal darkness and totally obscured. Being this close to the places she'd dreamed of gave her the courage to take her chances. She'd take her chances while she had them and then try and find her way back to the light.

"Both the hotel where you're staying and the studios are in Hollywood, so if you'd like, you and Valarie will get a chance to see some of those sights tonight. I put together an itinerary of what's in the area along with their hours of operation and ticket info. In the morning, we might be able to do a quick limo tour before heading to the airport. Other than that there's no room for sight-seeing. The schedule is pretty tight."

Raina tried unsuccessfully to hold on to her smile.

"Sorry, kid," Shanice said. "Maybe next time."

Raina all but laughed out loud. Next time? Raina knew that this trip was a once-in-a-lifetime situation.

After receiving a detailed schedule of tomorrow's taping, the SUV limo dropped them off at the Hollywood Roosevelt hotel, an iconic landmark built during the "Golden Age of Hollywood" and named after the twenty-sixth president of the United States. Located on the aptly named Hollywood Boulevard, part of the stars' Walk of Fame, Raina learned that in its heyday guests at the hotel included Marilyn Monroe and Montgomery Clift. Later, music icon Prince and actors Brad Pitt and Angelina Jolie were among the famous people who stayed there.

Once in their double deluxe room, Raina couldn't help but wonder about the other people who'd stayed in this room; celebrities whose feet may have touched the same floor. She didn't ponder for long though, because Shanice was right. The hotel was located smack dab in the middle of the Hollywood happenings. Bruce left to visit his LA pals. After freshening up and eating burgers from a restaurant in the lobby, which cost more than the dress from Ross Dress for Less that Raina wore, she and Valarie went to explore the neighborhood. Every few steps it seemed Raina found something else to snap with her cell phone camera. They took selfies in front of the Chinese Theatre, where they also saw Michael Jackson's gloved handprints. They saw more than a dozen other names they recognized on their way to the Madame Tussaud's wax museum, where they posed with everyone from Samuel L. Jackson to Halle Berry, and Will Smith's character in *Men in Black* to President Obama. Valarie had a particularly fun time schooling Raina on "old" actors she didn't know about, like Bob Hope and George Burns and directors like Alfred Hitchcock. Once out of the museum, they spent about an hour just walking the streets and found people-watching as fun an adventure as visiting the museum had been. Raina could have stayed out all night, but because Shanice said a car would pick them up tomorrow promptly at eight, the ladies called it a night in time for Valarie to catch the latest episode of her favorite show, *Queen Sugar.*

Raina was so excited she barely slept. The next morning the limo arrived early. They arrived at the studio ten minutes later. Shanice was there to greet them. She chatted with Valarie and Bruce while Raina was taken directly to hair and makeup. Afterwards, Shanice provided a rundown of the show's overall direction and what they could expect to be asked. They were also informed that there might be other guests joining them, experts perhaps with counter arguments to the position taken by Raina and backed by Valarie, who along with Bruce would be seated in the front row. They were taken to a green room. Inside was a nice layout of breakfast options and a variety of drinks. Raina watched Ella's show entrance and monologue while munching on a Danish and drinking a glass of freshly squeezed orange juice. Valarie sipped black coffee. She couldn't eat a thing. At the first commercial break, Shanice came backstage.

"You're on, guys," she said, while listening

to someone in her headphones. "Come with me."

They began walking down a hall with a curtain at the end. "It's hard to relax, especially the first time, but try not to be nervous. Just be yourself. Don't focus on the audience. Look at Ella and answer her questions naturally, as though it's just you and her in the room."

Shanice stopped them at the curtain's edge. Raina's stomach flip-flopped. She heard the familiar theme music and could feel the energy of the audience. One of her favorite TV stars was just on the other side of the curtain. And she was about to go out there and meet her. This was crazy!

"And we're back!" Raina heard Ella saying. "My next guest is kind of like the best big sister, ever. Her story came to the attention of one of the show's producers when a video about her little sister that she posted on Storytime went viral. She can tell you about it better than I can. Guys, please help me welcome Raina Reed!"

Shanice guided them out through the curtain. Raina tried not to "fan" out as she saw Ella smiling and waving, and the familiar chairs she'd watched on television every chance that she got. She reached Ella and was given a hug. The nerves went away.

Raina looked out at the audience and was struck by how much smaller it was in person than it appeared on TV.

"Welcome to the show!"

"Thanks for having me."

"As I said in the intro, you definitely get the best big sister award for bringing attention to Abby. How were the two of you separated, and why is it so important to find her?" Ella turned to the audience. "I know many of you saw her video and know the story. This is for those who've just crawled from under a rock."

The audience laughed.

"Yes, so my sister is Abby. I call her Shadow because of how she's always followed me around . . ."

Raina went on to share the story, succinctly and in a way that was heartfelt.

"Now you're her counsel," Ella said to Valarie, seated in the front row.

"Yes, that's right."

"What's your name?"

"Valarie McFadden."

"Kudos to you for helping Raina. How'd you become involved?"

"Raina is best friends with my daughter, Jackie. I'm one of four attorneys at a legal agency called the Justice Bureau that's based in Chippewa. She came to me for

331

advice on how best to help her sister. Since then, we've been working on that answer."

"I understand that the parents have gone into hiding and so far refuse to allow their daughter to get medical treatment, citing religious freedom. Isn't that like, illegal or something, if doing so endangers the child?"

"We don't know that the Reeds are hiding, just that they can't seem to be found. A parent has the right to observe the tenets of their religion or beliefs. And while some states have laws regarding medical care that err on the side of protecting the child, the state of Kansas protects the parents and their right to not choose modern medical treatment."

"Do you believe Abby's well-being may be in jeopardy?" Ella asked Raina. "I mean, you tried to kidnap her to get help, so you must have felt pretty strongly about it."

Valarie intercepted the question. "We can't talk about the kidnapping charge as it is an open and ongoing case. However, regarding Abby's health, we don't know how she's doing because we haven't seen her. Raina hasn't seen her sister in more than two months. Other than members of the church who say Abby is fine, and that they know of the Reeds' whereabouts but refuse to divulge them, we don't know anybody who has. Abby was pulled out of the private school she attended and according to them is being homeschooled. I find such behavior curious, at the very least. Raina wants to see her sister. I believe siblings have rights, too."

The audience showed their support with sustained applause.

Ella asked a few more questions. "FYI," she said into the camera, "we did invite members of the church to be on the show. A representative who was scheduled to join us today canceled at the last minute. We also reached out to the law firm representing the Reeds, with an invitation to fly the parents here with Abby in hopes that they'd want the country to see that she's fine and to hear their side. We were told that any rebuttal or information provided by the Reeds would be broadcast directly from the church's network, Illumination TV."

Once again, Ella trained her bright blue eyes on Raina. "I understand their religion doesn't watch my show." This comment produced the intended laughter and lightened a somber moment. "But if Abby were to see this and you could say something to her, what would it be? Look right over at that camera, yes, the one straight ahead, and talk to her."

Raina sat up and looked at the camera. "Hey, Shadow." Her voice broke. "I love you so much and miss you like crazy. I hope you're getting better and that whoever is treating you is able to make you well. I'm looking for you because life is empty without my shadow. And I won't stop until . . ."

The sentence faded as Raina choked up.

Ella reached over and squeezed Raina's arm. "Well, the whole country is cheering you on, big sis. And we at the station add our voices to the many calling for your parents to come out of hiding and have Abby checked out by doctors who can make sure she's okay. We're going to stay on top of this story and do whatever we can to help Raina save her shadow. We'll be right back."

The taping and trip to California was over as quickly as it had begun. Looking back on it felt like a dream. The trip was successful. They hadn't caught the fish they were looking for, but with Ella's daily audience of almost three million, they'd cast a net that had already expanded even wider still.

CHAPTER 25

In Chippewa, life after Ella was even more chaotic than before being on the show. In a small town everybody already knew almost everyone else, but now on top of being recognized, she often got stopped by locals wanting to voice their opinion or otherwise show support. There'd also been a deluge of hate mail sent from the Illuminated to the Bureau's office, calling Raina an unsanctioned and worse. Go figure. To put a sense of normalcy back into her life, Raina went back to school. The administration did what they could to keep interruptions to a minimum. Focusing was difficult, but she studied hard and kept finals at the forefront of her mind. Any downtime was spent at the McFaddens', often with Bryce by her side when he was in town. She began to think of graduation and college, moving to Kansas City and starting life on her own. A frightening prospect, but Raina knew she could do it. She'd created a whole new family who would lend their support. The only person missing was Abby, but Raina was determined that unless Abby said otherwise, somehow her sister would be a part of this new life, too.

"Hey, girl."

Raina looked over as Jackie joined her walk down the hall. "Hey!"

"Okay, that cheerful greeting tells me your ass aced the test."

"Of course! I told you how hard I studied. How'd you do?"

"Let's just say I didn't study."

"Jackie!"

"Yes?" Jackie phrased the word in a way that suggested she hoped the topic had changed.

Raina pressed the issue. "What'd you get?"

"A grade C, okay?"

"That's not so bad. It's . . ."

"Average," Monica chimed in, having heard part of the conversation on her way to join them.

"Who asked you?" Jackie asked.

"No one," Monica quipped. "No one asked me to add that it was a C-minus, either. I'm doing that on my own."

"Heifah."

"If she's going to be a cow," Raina said,

"at least be a truthful one."

The three girls descended the stairs in a fit of laughter and burst through the school doors to the outside. They were met with flashing cameras and a bevy of reporters. Raina looked beyond them to see several news trucks lining the street. The trio was quickly surrounded, but they continued to move, pushing people aside, blocking their faces from the cell phones and cameras pointed at them.

"Raina!"

"Have you seen the interview, Raina?"

"Raina, over here! Is what your parents said true?"

"Did you abuse your sister?"

The last question froze her, stopped her dead in her tracks. "What?"

"Trent Bowman, Fox News."

"Fox?" Jackie stepped in between the reporter and Raina. "Ah, hell, no!"

The reporter continued, undaunted, side-stepping Jackie and continuing to speak. "Your parents have come out strongly denying the accusations you made against them. They say you're lying."

"Just keep walking," Jackie mumbled, grabbing Raina's arm.

Raina jerked away and wheeled on the reporter. "That's not true!"

337

The rest of the reporters ran over. The three were surrounded again.

"Come on!" Jackie insisted.

"I have never abused my sister," Raina said, the insinuation sending her anger to the moon. "If anyone is being abusive it's my parents, for not letting her see a doctor. For not letting her be properly diagnosed and treated through modern medicine, like the rest of us."

"That's following the protocol of their religion," another reporter yelled out. "Correct?"

"Aren't you also a member of the Illumination?" a third one asked.

"Let's go," Jackie hissed through clenched teeth.

Just then the familiar sound of a souped-up engine and a hip-hop beat penetrated the mayhem.

"Yo, Rainbow!"

Jackie, still holding Raina's arm, steered them toward the sound of Bryce's voice. "Come on, girl. We need to get out of here."

Raina didn't fight being pulled away but wasn't finished with the media. "You can't believe everything you read," she threw over her shoulder.

"Then can we believe you?" the Fox reporter asked her. "Can we believe that you were being raised by unfit parents?"

"I never said that!" Raina screamed, once again jerking her arm from Jackie's clutches. "You need to get your story straight," she continued, a manicured finger pointing in the reporter's face. "This isn't about me. It's not about my parents. It's about my sister. She's the only one who matters right now."

By now Bryce had managed to stop the car, push through the crowd and next to Raina. He reached for one arm, Jackie grabbed the other, and together they headed toward the car.

The taunting from the opposing reporter increased, aided by Illuminated students. Raina's escape efforts doubled. But Jackie and Bryce's combined body weight of over three hundred pounds proved too much for a buck and a quarter's worth of I-ain't-the-one. With a solid grip around her waist, Bryce managed to get Raina to the car and into the back seat, wedged in between Jackie and Larry, who'd waited inside. Bryce jumped in and took off, revving the engine and honking his horn so that the looky-loos risking their lives by standing in front of a moving vehicle would move.

"Good looking out, bro," Jackie said to Bryce. "I don't know where you came from but it was right on time."

"I was going to surprise Raina, give her a ride home."

"Ha! And the surprise was on you."

Raina sat with her arms crossed, boiling. "I hate you both."

"Whatever," Jackie said out loud. "Mama told you that the media would come for you, to not say anything without her or the publicist present."

"I only told the truth," Raina said.

"So did your parents, according to them. It's not what you say, it's how they twist it. And putting your hand all up in that reporter's face like you did? Probably gave that fool just what he wanted."

Jackie's words proved prophetic. When the next issue of the county paper came out, Raina was once again above the fold. Only this time it wasn't a flattering picture of her and Abby. It was one of her looking crazed, with a finger that looked as though it was about to gouge out an eye and the caption: *Savior or psycho?* The article focused on Raina's kidnapping charge and painted her as a misguided teenager defying her parents and viewed her "lewd" participation in a "profanity-laden gangster video filled with debauchery" as further proof of her downslide since leaving the faith. Accompanying the article was a supposedly recent picture of Abby. In it she looked radiant, wearing a bright yellow dress accented with flowers and a bright smile. It wasn't a picture that Raina remembered. Could the article be telling the truth about her, that she was fine and Raina was the one who needed to seek help? She tried contacting the reporter, but he was with the Nation. No way would he talk to her. Studying the picture again, Raina was struck by something she didn't notice the first time, something that made her believe she was on the right track. Her sister's dress was just the right amount of cute, and for those who didn't know her the grin was convincing. For Raina, however, there was a problem. Her shadow's smile did not reach her eyes.

CHAPTER 26

After eight weeks, countless interviews, hundreds of false sightings, and still no sign of Abby, Bruce had a suggestion. He voiced it on an overly warm day in late April, while sitting at an outdoor café with Valarie, Drew, and Raina.

"What if we turn up the heat by filing criminal charges?"

"It's a thought," Drew replied. "Aiding and abetting. Obstruction of justice."

"All options are on the table," Valarie replied. "I want to find Abby as soon as possible, but I also try and keep Raina's feelings in mind. Whatever they've done or not done, those are still her parents and she loves them. I just hope they come to their senses and are giving that child the help she needs."

"Looks that way if that recent picture is proof. Pretty little girl."

"Unless it's somehow altered, which is

super easy to do."

"There's another option." Bruce looked at Raina before picking up a barbecued rib slathered with sauce and taking a healthy bite. "Go for custody."

"Of my sister?" Raina queried. "I can do that?"

"Interesting idea," Valarie mused. "Tricky one, though."

"No doubt."

"What made you think of it?"

"A call from a friend I hadn't seen in a while. When he was a kid, his family belonged to a religion similar to the Illumination. Very secretive, kept to themselves. Lots of rules that didn't make sense."

Bruce reached for a napkin and began methodically cleaning his fingers. "He gave me the idea based on what one of the members did to take over raising her sister's child. Getting custody isn't easy, involves court filings and orders, even more so when it's a sibling requesting as opposed to a parent."

He reached for his phone and after scrolling down a bit read from the screen "Factors on whether granting custody is in the best interest of the child include the child's wishes, mental and physical health of the parent, whether there is evidence of domestic violence, drug or alcohol abuse, or excessive discipline."

"They don't say anything about medical treatment?"

"Not on this site, Raina, but I'm sure it is a factor that applies."

Valarie digested Bruce's comment as she chomped on a fry. "What do you think of that, Raina?"

She shrugged. "I don't know. I mean, I'd love to take care of my sister, but how? I'm planning to go to school in the fall. I can't bring Abby on campus. Where would we live? Who would take care of her while I work and take classes?"

"All valid questions," Drew said. "A lot to work out, maybe more than Raina can handle given the transition she's about to make."

"You're right, Drew," Valarie said, "from a practical standpoint. But for a long-term solution, I like it."

"I do, too," Raina said.

Valarie eyed Raina keenly. "Do you really?" Raina nodded. "Then we'll start researching possibilities around that option. If it indeed turns out to be something we want to tackle, I think we should get started right away."

"I agree," Bruce said. "Not only will it

potentially smoke the Reeds out of hiding, but putting it out there that this is something we're thinking about will keep the spotlight on Abby's story and Raina saving her shadow."

"Sounds like a plan. Are we done here?" Valarie stood and placed the strap of her purse over her shoulder. "I say we head back to work and get started."

Two weeks later, Raina was once again in the news. "Sister Seeks Custody" the newspaper headline read, from a story Kris Hall had written. Valarie and Bruce handled the legal work. Felicity managed the media. The details of Abby's care should Raina indeed get to raise her were still being hashed out, but Miss Christine had promised to do what she could, even if that meant moving to Kansas City while Raina was in school. Along with a high GPA, Raina tried to manage her sanity and not get overwhelmed. "We've got you," Jackie had assured her. Raina chose to believe. Working toward getting custody of Abby was keeping hope alive.

The response was fast and furious. Sean Browder and his law firm came out swinging on the Reeds' behalf. They claimed everything contained in the court filings was false and threatened to sue the Justice

Bureau for falsifying documents and defamation of character. The fight got nasty as anonymous assassinations of Raina's character began showing up online. There wasn't much dirt to find on someone who'd been an Illuminated Vessel during most of her teen years. They milked the KCK association for all it was worth, putting her picture next to controversial ones of him, Sniper, and even Shanghai. It was daunting, overwhelming, sometimes almost too much. Valarie encouraged her to focus on her high school finals and forget everything else. That's what she did, which is why on a sultry evening in late May, Team Shadow put a pin in the legal proceedings, put on their Sunday-go-to-meeting clothes, and gathered at Chippewa High's auditorium to cheer on Raina, Jackie, and the rest of the seniors at their high school graduation.

"Can you believe it?" Jackie gushed, positioning her cap just right over thin, fresh braids. "We're about to get out of here!"

"I can't." Raina's demeanor was more subdued. Her emotions were jumbled and all over the place. When she arrived in Chippewa almost ten years ago, she never could have imagined a night like this. One where a major milestone was happening without her mom present to see it. She'd mostly tried to ignore the fact that in all the time the Reeds had been MIA, Jennifer hadn't reached out once to contact her. Not a call, a card, or letter from her, Ken, or anyone from the church. Raina had been aware of this, was technically familiar with how being obscured worked. But the definition on paper and its real-life reality were two different things and hard to reconcile. She hadn't been able to believe that Jennifer could ever totally abandon her. But tonight, as she prepared to walk across the stage, accept her diploma, and be recognized as the recipient of multiple scholarships, she had to accept the truth. The family she'd been raised with wasn't here. But there was a throng that had stepped in to replace them. As she stood at the edge of the auditorium, prepared to march in to the sounds of Pomp and Circumstance, Raina squinted her eyes, found her tribe, and decided that instead of lamenting what had been lost, she'd embrace the family she had.

CHAPTER 27

That café conversation got the ball rolling. The Justice Bureau filed for custody of Abby on Raina's behalf. The Reeds had been located, and while there was still no sign of Abby, a date had been set for their hearing in Topeka, the state capitol. Raina's days of studying for the finals had been exchanged for mock hearings with Bruce, Valarie, and Drew coaching her on how to answer the judge's questions and countering arguments that Sean Browder would undoubtedly wage against her character, maturity, and ability to properly care for a minor. Bryce had moved to Kansas City and taken a job at KCK's newly built production studio, but through phone calls, repeatedly encouraged Raina to relax and be confident.

"No matter what they throw at you," he assured her, "you're stronger."

Because of all the media attention, a case

that might have taken months to reach the judge's chambers was delivered in a matter of weeks. Shortly after the nation had celebrated its independence, Raina found herself seated between Monica and Jackie on the way to court in Topeka. It would be a closed session in the judge's chambers, but her friends had insisted on coming along for the ninety-minute ride to lend their support. Bryce couldn't be there in person but remained supportive. In between his texts of encouragement were flirty notes about their getting back on track and taking what they started to another level. Now that they'd both be in Kansas City, he'd decided, it was "time to get serious about this thing."

Details of the hearing had not been made public, but reporters had access to court dockets and had monitored them closely. The date had been leaked, a minor inconvenience, or so the Justice Center attorneys had thought before arriving at the courthouse. But a crowd that Raina guesstimated at a couple hundred was milling around the courthouse steps. Police were already on the scene, keeping the streets in the area clear. Raina's eyes widened as she looked at those gathered, some wearing T-shirts bearing Abby's likeness. She saw the back of one shirt, with the #SaveShadow hash tag made popular by the Storytime video. The bold black letters stood out against the bright yellow fabric. Could the person carrying the placard have any idea that yellow was her sister's favorite color? Raina saw glances pass between Bruce, Valarie, and Felicity, and the PR whiz kid hurriedly typed notes into her phone.

"Did you guys see that T-shirt?"

"Duly noted," Valarie replied, shooting off a text to Marjorie. "We'll have an online store up before nightfall."

"Mugs would be a good idea," Bruce added. "Maybe those rubber bracelets, too."

"Do I get a say in this?" Raina asked. "I don't want to merchandise Abby just to make a buck or two."

"It's called promotion," Felicity said.

Valarie nodded. "Awareness."

"And there's nothing wrong with money," Bruce said. "If the judge decides in your favor, trust me, you'll need it."

Raina observed that all who'd gathered were not her supporters. A group from the Nation was there as well. With their conservative clothing, the men in suits despite the hot weather, they were easily recognizable. Other Reed sympathizers were sprinkled among them. The messages carried, screamed or worn on T-shirts set one apart from the other. Some of them also carried signs, touting verses from the *Book of Light* and slogans like, "Parents First" and "Reeds Rule." Not to be outdone, there was even a hashtag: #ReedRights. Raina thought to herself, *We'll see.*

Bruce wanted to avoid the front steps melee and drove them around to a back entrance. There was a smaller group of reporters there too, but they formed a human shield around Raina and ushered her into the courthouse. Her outfit had been chosen with care, a smart yet age-appropriate navy pantsuit paired with a cream-colored knit top and bone-colored sling-backs. Her hair was parted in the middle and slicked back into a ponytail at the nape of her neck. She wore little makeup and sensible jewelry. Her stomach might have been jelly but on the outside she looked young yet capable, poised, and self-assured. The closer they got to the judge's chambers, the more frantically the butterflies in her stomach flittered. She'd be seeing her parents today. Whether or not she'd see her sister was still up in the air. How would they react when they saw her, she wondered? Would there be any sign of recognition, of friendship or love? Would Jennifer's eyes portray warmth and understanding, or would they be daggers ready to pierce her heart? These thoughts pounded in her head to the beat of her heels against the cold tile floor. The hushed tones of the massive hallway and three-story-high ceilings were in stark contrast to the noisy protestors and supporters outside. Raina kept her eyes straight ahead, buoyed by the presence of Bruce on one side of her and Valarie on the other. After handling business with the clerk, the trio reached the judge's chambers and stopped just outside his door.

Valarie turned Raina toward her with a hand on each shoulder. "Are you ready?"

Raina nodded.

"In there, you're going to have to verbalize your answers. Might as well start now."

"Yes, Miss Valarie. I'm ready for this."

"Good girl. Inhale."

Raina took in a deep breath.

"Exhale."

She blew it out.

"Now, once inside these doors, don't forget to keep breathing."

The first thing Raina noticed once inside was that her parents were not there. Instead it was Sean — whom she knew by his internet photos — a woman, and another man. Of course, this meant there was no Abby, either, causing Raina's heart to drop along with her stomach. The other thing was that the image she'd created for a judge's chamber — dark, imposing, with lots of wood and books — this one did not look like that. Judge Madeline Atwater's place reminded Raina a bit of Valarie's office. At once, she felt more at ease. Immediately after formalities were over, the judge called the room to order.

"We're here for the custody case of Reed v. Reed. All parties, or their representatives, are present. Let's get started."

Two hours later, Raina and the team left the courthouse. Valarie had acted as lead attorney and gave a clear, succinct argument for why they were there and what Raina hoped to gain by becoming her sister's custodial guardian. When asked to testify, Raina had poured her heart out in that chamber, left all she had on the table. But she was by no means confident that she'd win the case, or had even gained the judge's sympathy regarding Abby having medical care. Her parents' lawyers had laid out their case well, too. They'd cross-examined her with ruthless tenacity. She'd flinched inwardly but otherwise held her ground. Sean also presented a video testimony by her parents, through which she learned what had happened when they took Abby and fled to Tulsa.

Abby's eyes fluttered opened. She squeezed them shut and opened them again, adjusting to the dimly lit room as she took in her surroundings.

Where am I? "Mother!"

Seconds later a familiar face swam into view. "It's okay, Abby. I'm right here. Are you thirsty?"

Abby nodded. She watched Jennifer's shaky hand reach for a pitcher of water and pour her a glass.

"Where's Father?"

"He's talking with the head healer, honey. They're getting ready to put you on the IL-LUX machine. It will circulate the good energy, take out the bad, and make you feel all better. Won't that be great?"

"It will. I don't like being sick."

"That doesn't happen to the Illuminated, don't you remember? Your body is dim, that's all. The machine will help it brighten."

"Mother, where are we?"

"We're in Oklahoma."

"Is that far from Kansas?"

"Not too," Jennifer answered with a shake of her head. "Just one state over."

"Will it take a long time to . . ."

"Circulate the good energy?"

"Yes."

"I'm not sure how long the procedure is. I think it varies from person to person, depending on how much energy needs to shift. We don't care how long it takes, honey. Your dad and I are going to be right here, every step of the way."

"I'm scared, Mother."

"Shh. None of that kind of talk. There is nothing to be afraid of, absolutely nothing at all."

"But what if I don't get better? What if I die?"

Jennifer found herself giving the same pat answer that, had Ken told it to her in the car earlier, would have gotten him chopped in the throat.

"There is no life. There is no death. There is only Light."

Jennifer felt Abby's head. Her concern grew. For the past few days the fever had gone down. Abby's skin felt almost normal. But she was still lethargic and her appetite was weak. Now, she felt warm again. She looked at Abby, who yet again appeared to be sleeping. Jennifer stepped into the hallway.

"Yes," came a kind voice from behind. "Can I help you?"

"Light day to you," Jennifer said, bowing slightly.

"Keep shining. You're the mother of the young girl from Kansas, the one who will undergo the energy treatment?"

"Yes, my name is Jennifer. Jennifer Reed."

"My name is Pat Thompson. Everyone calls me Mother PT."

"Nice to meet you, Mother PT. What can you tell me about this ILLUX machine, and what makes it different from the ones we've used before?"

"Power, dear, such that allows the Light to penetrate more deeply, and the recipient to be healed more quickly. Just last month I experienced dizziness and shortness of breath. Two hours on the energy machine and voilà! Good as new. It was invented by our founder, the esteemed Supreme Master Seer Daniel Best. Being a faithful member, you already know this, of course. It was an idea inspired directly from Divine Light and holds the very essence of life within its coils."

The mother was very, well, motherly. Jennifer felt her tense shoulders loosen, the muscles relax. "How long have you been in the Nation, Mother PT?"

"Almost since the beginning," she proudly responded. "Supreme Master Best founded the Nation in 1952. I joined in '57 and have been here ever since."

"You've always been here, in Oklahoma?"

"Oh no. I've traveled all over the United States and other countries, spreading the Light. I spent time in our West Coast center, in St. Louis, trained teams of practitioners from the Atlantic to the Pacific and everywhere in between."

"It has to have been so satisfying, this work. Living your passion, doing what you were born to do."

"Living in purpose isn't easy. Every life comes with its ups and downs. The secret is to remain in the light so that no matter what comes, you can still see clearly. The path is always easy to find when following the light."

"I agree that it's not always easy," Jennifer said, thinking back to how skeptical, vulnerable, and fearful she felt just hours ago. "Following the light. I'll admit to being trepidatious about this procedure. Almost a decade into the Nation, yet there was a moment when I doubted and felt a more conventional approach might be what my daughter needs."

"Doctors only pretend to know what they're doing," Mother PT responded. "That's why they call it a practice. They practice on patients and get paid for learning. Practitioners come to earth armed with an inner knowing and we heal for free."

As they chatted a bit more, the sun began rising. Jennifer wasn't aware of how much time had passed. She bit back a yawn. Just then Ken came around the corner, accompanied by a slight, white-haired, white-bearded man with a weathered face and pale blue eyes. For a moment, Jennifer's eyes widened.

"Is that . . ."

"No, child. That is not the Master. Though there is a close connection. It's Benjamin, Dr. Daniel Best's youngest son, the one who embraces the Sun light but shuns the spotlight, if you know what I mean."

Ken nodded. "A man after my own heart. You may not remember, Dr. Best, but I met you several years ago at one of our conventions. It was just after the latest updates to the ILLUX machine. You spoke on those innovations as well as the commitment made by the Nation on creating natural pathways to optimum health."

"I do remember," Benjamin said. "It is a pleasure to see you again."

"Likewise."

Jennifer wasn't sure that Benjamin actually remembered her husband, but the smile on Ken's face was proof that it didn't matter.

Brief introductions were made, gratitude offered. Then it was time to get the procedure underway.

"Let's go take a look at our little angel," Dr. Best said, referenced as such for an honorary doctorate and not a medical degree.

They entered the room to find a sleeping Abby, who indeed looked like an angel. Jennifer noted the long, dark lashes against her gently sun-kissed skin, and thanks to her father, the blond highlights in her hair.

The doctor lifted Abby's hand and placed it in his own. He placed a finger on her wrist. "Such a cute little thing, I tell ya."

"We love her dearly," Ken said.

Jennifer nodded, her smile in place, even as she watched the doctor's thumb roll over Abby's wrist as though searching for a pulse.

The doctor cleared his throat and pulled out a pair of thick glasses. "Mother PT," he called. "Come over here, please."

"Check her heart rate, will you, while I set up these pulse points."

"Moderate or full body?" Mother PT asked, placing two fingers on Abby's wrist, and then on her throat.

"We'll go for the full treatment," the doctor replied. "Have her up and these good people on their way in no time at —"

"What is it?" Jennifer interrupted. Mother PT's movements had gone from slow and steady to fast and frantic. "What's going on, Mother PT?" she repeated, growing more frantic as well.

"Is everything all right?" Ken asked. If there was any fear in him, it wasn't showing.

Mother PT managed a brief, tight smile. "Everything is always all right in the Light. But your child? She isn't breathing."

Mother PT's smile threw her off. It was incongruent with the next words that flowed from her lips. Everything was all right but Abby wasn't . . .

Breathing?

"Abby!"

The guttural scream felt wrenched from the throat of a terrified mother. It bounced off of the gray cement walls and shattered the quiet of an overcast morning. The sound seemed to break everyone in the room out of a trancelike state when, in the seconds after the ex-nun's pronouncement, no one had seemed able to move.

"Abby!" Jennifer lunged toward her child, grabbed her by her shoulders and shook her, gently at first and then with more fervor.

"Mrs. Reed." Dr. Best spoke decisively as he stepped forward, a hand on her arm.

Jennifer shook it off.

Dr. Best looked at Ken. "Get her."

"Honey." Ken pulled Jennifer back as Mother PT pried her fingers from around Abby's shoulder. Dr. Best began rapidly placing the energy connectors on the meridian points of Abby's body. Mother PT began CPR.

"Leave the room, please." A whirring sound broke into the melee when Dr. Best turned on the ILLUX machine. Green, red, and yellow lights flashed. He adjusted dials, then clasped iron brackets onto Abby's wrists and ankles. Her entire body began shaking.

"What are you doing?" Jennifer broke away from Ken.

Dr. Best blocked Jennifer's beeline to her daughter's vibrating body. He turned and pushed toward Ken. "Get her out of here!"

"She's back with us!" Mother PT said. "We have a pulse!"

"Honey, let's go!"

Jennifer fought, but she was no match for a muscular, determined husband who ushered her out of the room just as a young woman in what looked to be white scrubs hurried by them.

"Is my daughter going to be all right?" Jennifer asked her.

"Speak to the Light!" the woman said, before opening the door, sliding inside, and just as quickly closing the door behind her.

"The Light shines forever," Jennifer mumbled, a general chant used in times of despair. Ken's deep voice joined her whispered fervor. They paced the hallway in front of where their daughter was hooked up to the ILLUX and repeated the phrase over and again. Intermittently they shielded the door and themselves, sent light to their daughter and conducted a half-hearted attempt at meditation. Both were too nervous to sit still for long. When the door to the room opened fifteen minutes later, Jennifer jumped to her feet and sprinted toward it.

Dr. Best closed it quickly. Jennifer grabbed the knob and gave the door a yank. It was locked.

"Open this door!"

"Not yet," the doctor calmly replied.

"Why can't I go in there?" Jennifer shook the knob again. "I need to see my daughter!"

"And you will, later, once she has been totally energized."

Ken walked up and placed a firm arm

around his wife. "Jennifer, stop. You need to calm down. Our daughter is okay" — he turned to Dr. Best — "isn't she?"

"She is fine," the doctor assured them. "She needs to be allowed to continue sleeping while the machine does what it was designed to do."

"Really? She's okay?"

The doctor nodded. "She's fine."

Jennifer clasped her hands together. "Yes!" She looked upward. "Thank you! Thank you for shining the light!"

As she celebrated, Mother PT slipped into the hallway.

"Doctor, what's going on with our daughter?" Ken asked.

Dr. Best turned to Mother PT, who answered, "She was severely dehydrated."

Jennifer joined the discussion. "Is that all? She has been ill for weeks, running a fever . . ."

Dr. Best put a hand on Jennifer's arm. "What's past is past. She's fine, now."

"How long before I can see her?"

The doctor looked at his watch. "Why don't you go to the restaurant and have a nice breakfast? You can see her after that."

Before leaving for Tulsa, Jennifer had been too nervous about Abby's condition to eat. Now, hearing that her daughter would be fine, a ravenous appetite returned. She and Ken walked across the pristine campus that served as Illumination Campus Central, more commonly called Central Center. Along with the health center they'd just left and an auditorium that could seat seven hundred and fifty people, there was an educational facility for grades preschool through twelve, gym, bookstore, and Light Fare, an eatery that boasted using fresh, organic, mostly plant-based ingredients, and was popular with Nation members, locals, and visitors alike. After enjoying vegetable-filled omelets and fresh, homemade biscuits, and a quick stroll through the well-stocked bookstore, the Reeds returned to the health center and straight for where they'd last seen their daughter. The door was open. Jennifer raced inside the room. It was empty. Abby was gone.

Jennifer panicked. She ran out of the room and down the hall. An attendant walked out of another room, typing on a tablet. She got blindsided by a frantic mom.

"Where is my daughter! Someone took my daughter!"

"Ma'am, please, who are you looking for?"

"Abby Reed," Ken replied, even as he yet again and for the umpteenth time calmed his wife.

"Come with me."

The three walked down another hall to an area that hadn't been open in the early morning hours of their arrival. The attendant walked up to a receptionist sitting behind a long white desk.

"We're looking for a young lady named Abby Reed."

"They just moved her," the receptionist said without hesitation. "Room 309."

They were directed to an elevator and sent to the third floor, where Jennifer quickly spotted the room number. When they walked in Abby was sitting up in bed — eyes bright, skin vibrant, her thick curly hair brushed back into a ponytail.

"Hi, Mother! Hi, Father!"

It was a joyful reunion. Jennifer wept at the profound change in her daughter. She inwardly vowed to never doubt the Illumination's healing again.

"You did good in there, baby girl," Bruce said, giving her a fatherly hug and kiss on the forehead.

"Thank you," Raina said, with a hug to Valarie. "I'm just glad it's over. What happens now?"

"We wait," Valarie said, watching a group of reporters walking toward them. "And keep making our case before judges that matter almost as much as Atwater . . . the people."

That night, Raina's court appearance was a part of headline news, further sparking the national conversation and debate regarding parental rights and the need for siblings to have rights as well. Again, her phone sang with message indicators, friends and supporters wishing her the best. She was shocked when a text came in directly from Ella, saying how proud she was of Raina, to save her number, and to call her if there was anything she could do. A somber moment, a heavy matter, yet for a second all Raina thought about was *I've got Ella's cellie number in my phone!*

With at least the first court date over, Raina turned her attention to college. She made preparations to leave Chippewa and relocate to Kansas City. Bryce had offered to let her stay at the place where he'd just signed a lease, but she declined. She wanted to have the full college experience, not to mention be able to stay focused, and since her scholarship covered it, would be housed in the dorms. She did agree to spend a weekend with him in Kansas City, to take a break from all of the hoopla and start to get a lay of the land. He took her by the studios where he worked, talked her into laying her voice down on an upcoming track.

It was simple, a hook that encouraged the crowd to "pick it up," and "pack it up." Bryce came behind her with a counter punch. "Pickin'. Packin'. Uh-huh."

"That was good, babe!" Bryce said once they'd finished, reaching out for her arm and pulling her into a tight embrace. They kissed. It quickly became clear Bryce wanted to go further. But Raina still wasn't ready for that.

She pulled away. "Let's eat. I'm hungry."

"Bryce wriggled his eyebrows, looked at her meaningfully. "Me too."

He let it go though, and soon they were in heading to downtown Kansas City in his newly purchased, tricked-out pickup truck. Clearly, KCK's tour had been successful. Raina reached for her purse and turned on the phone she'd turned off while recording. As had often been the case after a news story, the phone fairly sang with indicator pings.

"Damn, baby! Your phone is beginning to sound like KC's!"

"Reporters, mostly," she said, switching the volume to silent. "Another article on the custody case must have come out today. She tapped a search engine and was just

367

about to google her name when the phone vibrated in her hand.

"Hey, Jackie. What's up?"

"Raina! Where are you? I've been calling for an hour!"

"With your cousin, same as yesterday."

"I've been calling him, too. Never mind, listen. Y'all are in Kansas City, right?"

"Right," Raina said, the word coming out slowly as she tried to gauge Jackie's mood. "What's going on?"

"Don't freak out with what I'm about to tell you, but Abby's in the hospital."

"What?" Raina shouted, freaking all the way out. "When? Where is she? What's the number?"

"Raina, slow down. Listen, and breathe. I don't have the details, just the name and address of where she was taken."

"Taken? From where?"

"She's there, Raina, in Kansas City at . . . Children's Grace Medical Center. I'll text you the phone number and address. Get there as soon as you can."

Jackie hung up.

"What is it, babe?"

"Abby's here. In the hospital. Do you know where the one is that's called Children's Grace?"

Bryce hit his Bluetooth. "KC does."

While he waited for KC to answer, Raina's phone pinged with Jackie's text that contained the address. She tapped it into the GPS. The app showed the hospital was fifteen minutes away. Bryce made it there in seven. He pulled into the emergency circle. Raina opened the door and was out of the truck before the wheels stopped rolling. She raced inside and up to the desk.

"I'm here for Abby Reed," she gushed, filled with emotion. "My name is —"

"Raina?" One of the nurses interrupted. "We've been waiting for you. Come right this way."

CHAPTER 28

They moved quickly down the hall to an elevator and down another set of hallways. As they neared a corner suite, however, the nurse stayed Raina with a hand on her arm.

"I need you to try and stay calm in there," she said softly, compassion streaming from her cornflower-blue eyes. "I'm going to be honest. Your sister's pretty sick. She's going to need all of the strength, support, and love you can muster, okay?"

Raina's eyes filled with tears. The nurse tightened her grip on Raina's arm and shook it gently. "But . . . shh . . . but the doctors know about your shadow, Raina. They've read about Abby, and are especially determined to diagnose her condition as quickly as possible to get her on the road to recovery."

Raina calmly but firmly dislodged her arm from the nurse's grip. "I want to see my sister." She turned and softly opened the door. The first person she saw wasn't Raina, but her mother. Jennifer's face was a blessed combination of surprise and relief. She moved silently across the room and bear-hugged her daughter.

"Oh, honey," she whispered, stepping back to look in Raina's eyes while keeping her daughter tight in her arms. "I'm so sorry. I love you. I've missed you."

Raina relished the feel of her mother's arms around her, a moment she'd dreamed of since leaving Lucent Rising. The circumstances could have been better, but the hug? It was the best. She broke away and turned to look at her sister.

"Shadow," she whispered. Tears leaped into her eyes. She walked over to the small, pale form lying against the stark white sheets, her frame smaller than Raina remembered, dark circles under her eyes.

"Abby, I'm here," Raina whispered, her hand caressing Abby's cheeks and brushing back errant strands of hair from her face. "Sister's here."

She stayed there for several minutes, just staring at Abby. That she was next to her, in a hospital no less, felt totally surreal.

Finally she turned toward her mother, now seated in a chair by the bed. "What happened?"

"She passed out, like that time at the house. The ILLUX machine wasn't working. Her skin color changed. I didn't even think about it, Raina. My fingers had a mind of their own. I don't remember dialing 911."

Raina's smile was bittersweet. "I know that feeling."

"I know that you do. On the way here by ambulance, you're all I thought about. How I'd screamed at you the day you'd instinctively done the very same thing. The right thing. That's when I called you. There's so much to say. But the short of it is that I had to go against the rules and reach out to my daughter. In seeing my child pale, lifeless, her lips turning blue, a fog lifted and I remembered, Raina. I remembered someone I hadn't thought of or felt like in a very long time."

Jennifer looked up at her daughter somewhat incredulously. "Me."

Raina hugged her mom. Fresh tears pressed against her lids. She held them at bay. "How long has she been this . . . sick?"

Jennifer sighed. "After leaving Central Center, she seemed really well. Her skin was glowing. Her eyes were bright. She was back to the old Abby. But we lessened the light treatments little by little, until a month ago we were told we could stop them altogether. I don't know if her worsening condition around that time was coincidental or if whatever she has just came back . . ."

Jennifer's voice trailed off as she looked at Abby.

"Where's Dad?"

"I don't know."

Raina felt there was a whole other conversation packed into those three words. She returned her attention to Abby.

"What have the doctors said?"

"Very little, in terms of what's wrong with her. They stabilized her vitals. She was dehydrated, so the intravenous tubing is providing liquids, vitamins, and minerals to help all of the areas where she's depleted. They said it may be a few days before they have tests results back and anything to share. We just have to watch . . . and pray."

Raina's eyes widened. "Have you left the faith? And Dad?"

"No . . . I . . . right now I'm just focused on Abby getting better and will use any and everything available, including prayer, to help her heal."

Abby stirred, immediately cutting off conversation.

"Shadow?" Raina whispered.

Abby's eyes fluttered open, widened

briefly before closing again. "Sister."

"Yes, Abby. It's me. I'm here." Raina placed her face against Abby's and squeezed her shoulder. With all the contraptions and tubes it was the closest she could come to a hug.

Abby opened her eyes again. "You're really here."

Raina laughed. Tears blurred her vision. "Yes, Shadow. I'm really here."

Abby turned and saw Jennifer. "And Mother, too?"

"Yes, baby," Jennifer said.

"You're both here . . . together?"

"Together," Jennifer noted. "Raina's got her shadow back."

Over the next month, Jennifer and Raina practically lived at the hospital. She put her classes on hold for a semester and moved into the home her mother had rented. They reconnected in a way that hadn't happened since leaving the city when Raina was ten. One day, while having lunch in a spot in the city called Country Club Plaza, Jennifer received a call.

"It's the hospital," she said, already reaching for her purse and starting to rise.

Raina was right behind her. "What is it?"

"I don't know, but it was the doctor. He

wants to see us right away."

They arrived at the hospital and instead of going to Abby's room, they were directed to the doctor's office.

"Hello, ladies," he said when they arrived. "Please, come in. Have a seat."

"I don't feel like sitting," Jennifer said. "Do you have something to share about my daughter? Do you know what's wrong with Abby?"

The doctor went behind his desk and sat. Raina sat too and after a few seconds, Jennifer joined them.

"It appears your daughter is suffering from a very rare blood disorder. A type of leukemia. That's been at least one of the causes behind the symptoms you've witnessed — the near constant fatigue, shortness of breath, fevers and chills, and lately, the weight loss."

"Isn't that cancer?" Raina asked.

"A form of it, yes," the doctor replied. "But treatable."

Jennifer slumped back in her seat. "Dear God."

"We'll do everything we can to make Abby better, you have my word." He looked at Raina. "Everyone wants to save your shadow."

Abby remained in the hospital for another four weeks. Abby sat, wide-eyed and nervous, looking every bit as small as her seventy-two pounds, the hot-pink children's hospital gown contrasting sharply with the white bed linen, tables, and walls. A nurse entered the room and began chatting comfortably while checking IVs and fluid bags and monitored the machines.

"Hello, beautiful."

"Hi."

"My name is Maria. I'm going to be your nurse today. On the chart your name is listed as Abby, but I understand you also go by the name Shadow?"

"That's my sister's nickname for me. But my parents don't like her to call me that."

"Why not?"

"They say it means darkness."

"Hmm." The nurse continued working. "What do you think?"

"I kinda like it because of how my sister used it. Like our shadow created by the sun and follows us around."

"Let me guess. You're the younger sister."

Abby's smile widened. "Yes."

"I'm the oldest of three sisters and two

brothers," Maria continued, "so I have four shadows. For most younger siblings it's the perfect description and therefore a perfect nickname. May I call you Shadow?"

"Yes."

"Okay, Shadow. Let's get your temperature, make sure you're not too *caliente.*"

The nurse used an accent and rolled the *r* dramatically. Abby giggled, the desired effect. "We want you to be hot but not like a hot tamale, right?"

Abby nodded. "Right."

Abby held up her finger and watched as the nurse slid on a finger thermometer. The nurse attached another set of monitors to Abby's chest. Her look turned serious.

"What's wrong with me?"

"You have some blood cells that don't want to cooperate with each other," Maria answered. "But don't worry. A group of specialists have been assigned to your case. They've flown in from different parts of the world, just for you."

"Why?"

"Well, because you're Shadow, of course." Maria winked at Abby. Producing another giggle, the desired effect.

CHAPTER 29

At times, Raina had thought she'd never see another good mood. But the day had finally arrived. There were still a plethora of challenges ahead of them, but today she focused only on the good news — Abby had been released! Life continued to move at a frantic pace with major changes happening daily, sometimes faster. Some were glorious new beginnings, like getting a great reference from Thomas in Chippewa and enjoying her first day working at the Breadbasket's Kansas City location. Others swung the pendulum of her emotions in the opposite direction, like Ken's unexpected appearance at the hospital last week. He arrived with two senior members from the Illumination and talked Jennifer into meeting with them. Two hours later, her plans had changed. Instead of them all moving in together, she'd decided to return to Chippewa and to her marriage. What that meant for the mother and daughter's future relationship was unclear but for now, Raina was Abby's legal guardian. After Jennifer had signed her over, Valarie quickly withdrew the petition for custody from the court. The change left Raina scrambling for a place to live. Again, Valarie was her angel. Through her connections and just days ago, she'd secured a temporary residence not far from the school. It was a quaint yet beautiful restored Spanish bungalow with high ceilings, big windows, a patio, and a fenced-in backyard. It was barely furnished, and Raina had no idea how she'd be able to afford the rent, but she'd worry about that later. Christine had honored her promise and for now would help Raina look after her sister. Today, she had a place to bring Abby. For Raina, that's all that mattered in the world.

She turned to her as Christine neared their street. "We're almost home, Shadow. How are you feeling?"

"Okay." Abby's voice was weak but her eyes were bright, taking in the tree-lined street and the homes beyond them.

Christine reached over and squeezed Raina's hand. "How are you, baby?"

Raina let out a breath. "Still breathing. That's good."

"It's a big step you're taking today, and

perfectly fine to feel a bit nervous about it." She gave Raina's hand a final squeeze before returning her hand to the wheel and turning on to their block.

Raina's jaw dropped. Abby squealed with delight. As soon as Miss Christine's gold SUV turned the corner, a riot of balloons came into view. Welcome home, congratulations, and other positive messages on balloons and placards could be seen up and down the street. They were on fences and in the trees. Decorating stop signs and light poles and cars. Held by the dozens of family, friends, and supporters who now lined the street to welcome Abby to her new, temporary home, A couple news trucks were parked nearby, with cameramen beside them recording the scene. When the crowd parted to allow Miss Christine to turn into the drive, she turned up the volume on the gospel tune playing on her radio. It was an apropos message for the long journey they'd all just experienced, the one where Abby had come through victorious and healthy on the other side.

Victory is mine. Victory is mine. Victory today is mine!

The crowd descended on the car and surrounded it, dancing and clapping to the upbeat tune. Christine beamed and joined in the celebration, shaking her shoulders as her fingers danced. From somewhere came the sound of a tambourine. A young teenager, marching like a troubadour, broke out of the pack, beating the skin and kicking his heels.

"That's Julius," Raina said, recognizing the boy who'd come to visit Abby a week ago, along with other visitors and former patients who had also spent time on the children's trauma ward. "Look! Over there! It's Katie, Ramona, and Mike!"

The impromptu party was infectious. Even the nursing assistant, Becky, who'd be visiting them daily for the next couple weeks, bobbed her head in time to the music. Abby sat there wide-eyed and stunned. Finally, she turned to Raina and asked her, "All of this for me?"

"Yes, Shadow. All of this, because you chose to live!"

The crowd was boisterous but respectful. When Miss Christine exited the driver's side of the vehicle, they stepped back to give her room. Becky got out on the passenger side, then walked around to where the wheelchair was stored in the back. A determined news reporter pushed through the crowd, cameraman in tow. Raina had been about to open the passenger side for Abby, but she pushed the door shut and stood in front of it. Raina watched as Bruce once again appeared, as if by magic, along with half a dozen other burly-looking, shades-wearing men dressed in black T-shirts and black denim jeans. One directed the reporter and cameraman away. The others formed a semicircle around the car to keep the crowd away from the SUV door. Bruce walked up, gave Raina a hug, then turned to direct the crowd backward. Only then did Raina see the writing on the back of his shirt. SHADOW'S SECURITY. She laughed out loud. Perfect!

Abby was still too weak to speak with anyone, but Raina gave the young newsperson a tired smile, pausing his question with her finger. She watched as Bruce opened the door, lifted Abby into his arms, and then gently set her in the wheelchair. The crowd whooped and celebrated as though she'd run the one hundred . . . and won. Abby gave the crowd a wave, timid at first and then increasingly enthusiastic as she was wheeled up the sidewalk and into their temporary home.

Raina returned her attention to the reporter. It was largely due to media coverage that everything had turned out as well as it had. She was grateful for their interest.

"You want to know about Abby?"

"Your shadow, right?"

"Yes," Raina nodded.

"After such a public battle, how does it feel to be bringing her home?"

"It feels amazing to have my sister here with me, ready to start our new lives. I want to take this moment and thank everyone who did anything to help us — made a call, sent a card, said a prayer, whatever. It took all of us to get to this moment and I'm very grateful."

"What about your parents? How do you feel about them?"

"I love my parents and know they feel the same about Shadow, um, Abby and me. No matter the differences we've had in the past, I am sure they're happy their daughter is alive."

Raina worked to keep her smile in place. Mentioning her mom and stepdad caused drops of sadness to seep into the happy occasion. With Jennifer having returned to her husband, Raina had sent an invitation to Lucent Rising and held out hope that they'd respond, that for the day anyway the four of them could be a family. Raina swiped away the lone tear that trickled down, even as she wondered if that scenario would ever happen again. Later she'd have to come to terms with what fighting for Abby may have cost her. Now, however, was not the time for that. Today was all about celebration.

"You have legal custody of Shadow, correct?"

"Yes, that's right."

"Quite a bit of responsibility for someone so young, trying to go to college as I understand it, and having to work as well. Do you worry that all of this will become too much and you won't be able to do everything?"

"A very wise woman that I know" — Raina paused and looked at Christine — "told me that I could pray or I could worry, but I shouldn't do both. So I'm going to just keep moving forward and believe that everything will turn out all right."

A determined individual pushed through the crowd. "It's been a long and trying morning," Valarie said, stepping in between the reporter and Raina. "That's enough questions for now."

"Valarie McFadden, the attorney, right?"

"Today, I'm just a friend of the family. If you'll excuse us. We need to join Abby inside."

Inside, the well-wishes continued. Raina looked around, shocked, at the fully furnished interior that was almost empty just days ago. The living room had been transformed and looked like a toy store with stuffed animals, flowers, and baskets containing fruits, nuts, cheeses, crackers, and a variety of meats taking up every available surface. The dining room table held a multi-tiered cake decorated with stars and unicorns and a beaming picture of Abby in the center. Cards of all shapes and sizes surrounded it. Beyond the table were the patio doors. Amid a profusion of balloons out there, too, and a smattering of people, Raina could see that rectangular tables set in a U-formation held stainless steel warmers, foil-covered dishes, and a large basket of single-serving bags of chips. Smoke curled up from a row of grills, and an aluminum tub held cold cans of soda and beer. Soon the crowd descended into the backyard and the party began in earnest. At one point, after going inside to retrieve her cell phone, she stopped at the patio door and observed all of the people she loved. Old friends, and new ones. People who'd fought for her and for Abby. The medical staff who'd stabilized Abby's condition. Raina's eyes teared up as she watched Christine playing cards with the women who'd helped bail her out of jail. Near them were Valarie and Bruce, and the guys from the rest of the Justice Bureau staff. Kris, the reporter, and surprisingly, Lucy Stone. Of course her besties, Jackie and Monica, with Larry and Monica's new boyfriend, DeMarcus. Bryce was there, too. And . . .

"Shanice? Oh my God! What are you doing here?"

The producer who'd set up Raina's appearance on Ella walked toward her with arms outstretched. "You didn't think I'd miss this amazing moment did you, and a chance to meet Abby, the star of the show?"

"Not at all." They hugged again before Raina walked her over to where Abby sat taking everything in, protected by Becky and one of the self-appointed security team making sure their charge wasn't overwhelmed.

A cameraman followed, and then another. Raina almost stopped them but then remembered that Shanice was a producer for the nation's number one talk show. Of course they'd want to film her meeting Abby. It would be great for the evening news.

"Shadow, this is Miss Shanice. She's how I got on television to talk about you, a show called *Ella*."

"Hi," Abby said, shyly. "Thanks for helping my sister," she added.

Shanice knelt to be eye level with Abby. "It was my pleasure. I'm so happy to meet you and see that you're on the mend. Ella and all of the people who watch our show have been hoping for this moment. I'm sure they'd love to see you, too."

Raina touched Shanice's shoulder. "It'll be a long time before Abby can travel. But we can shoot a video."

Shanice stood, her eyes twinkling. "I think we can do better than that."

Shanice turned and took a microphone from a young man Raina hadn't noticed before. She also slowly realized that instead of chatting in their individual groups they were all gathered together, as if waiting for something. Raina looked at Jackie, who looked about to burst with excitement. Shanice was smiling broadly. What was going on?

"We have a little surprise for you, Raina," Shanice said, "And your sister Abby, too. Ella couldn't wait to meet Shadow and felt that her viewers probably felt the same so guess what. That's happening right now. You're on *Ella*, Raina." Shanice motioned toward the cameraman standing a short distance away. "Wave hello!"

Raina was stunned, not believing what she'd just heard. "I'm . . ." She looked around her, at Shanice and back at the camera. "I'm on *Ella*, now?"

"Yep. Right this moment. Look over there, at the monitor."

"Hi, Raina!" Ella said waving enthusiastically, along with the crowd.

"Oh my gosh, hello!" Raina became giddy with excitement as the reality began to sank in. She rushed over to wheel Abby to where she'd been standing. "Ella, this is my sister, Shadow."

"Hey, Shadow! It's good to see you, darling."

Abby, overwhelmed and confused, simply stared from the monitor to Raina and back.

"Say hello, Shadow."

"Hello."

"There's a lot of people who've been sending good wishes that you were getting better and would be reunited with your sister. She was so worried about you and determined to get you better. How does it feel being there with Raina?"

Abby beamed at her sister. "Good."

"Hey, Raina."

"Yes, Ella?"

"We know you're in the middle of a big celebration, but I have one more surprise before letting you go. That living arrangement you think is temporary? It's permanent, Raina, a gift from the show."

"This house?" Raina was dumbfounded.

"No. Way!"

"Yes way," Ella said, laughing. "Job well done big sister. The house is yours."

The live feed ended and the party began in earnest. Abby tuckered out early but Raina felt she could party all night. Almost every wish had been granted. Almost everyone she loved was in the backyard. The only one missing was . . .

"Raina."

Raina froze before slowly turning around. She could have sworn she just heard . . .

"Mother!"

She squealed and ran into Jennifer's arms. Abby heard the commotion and came running over. "Mother! Mother! You're here!"

"I heard somebody was having a welcome home party," Jennifer said, with glistening eyes. "I wouldn't miss it for the world."

"But, Mother. The church. You went back. I'm an outsider."

"You're also my daughter, and I love you. I was your mother before I was a member of the Illumination. There's nothing light about my world if you're not in it. That's what I told the Council, and Ken."

"What are they going to do?"

"I don't know, but now is not the time to talk about it. There's a backyard full of people that I want to meet." Jennifer turned.

"Starting with this lady. Hey, Bev."

"Jennifer. About time you came to your senses." The two ladies rocked back and forth as they enjoyed a bear hug.

"I'm still married, Bev, and still with the church. But I'm also here for my girls."

"Good." Bev came over and gave Jennifer a big hug. "I missed you, girl!"

"Me too."

Bev grabbed Jennifer's hand. "Come on. I want to see if you've still got it. Hey, Rodney! Put on some Mary J. Blige."

It was hands down the best day in Raina's life, one she couldn't have dreamed of. Every aspect of her life was what she wanted. She was going to college. Abby was getting help and getting better. And her mother, Jennifer Reed, was outside on the patio working her groove to a family affair! Indeed, it was. Who knew? Maybe one day even stepdad Ken would come around. No doubt love was the fuel that helped Raina save her shadow. And most importantly, she was able to step outside an institution that was out of step with who she really was, and save herself.

■ ■ ■ ■

READING GROUP GUIDE: SAVING HER SHADOW

LUTISHIA LOVELY

■ ■ ■ ■

ABOUT THIS GUIDE

The suggested questions are included to enhance your group's reading of Lutishia Lovely's *Saving Her Shadow.*

DISCUSSION QUESTIONS

1. Raina's life totally changed when her mother, Jennifer, met and married Ken Reed. How much of your lifestyle could you change, alter, give up in the name of love?

2. Do you know someone who belongs to a modern religion such as Scientology, Jehovah's Witnesses or FLDS? Have you been to one of their services? If so, what did you think?

3. Raina used disobedience and deception to hang out with her friends and have a "normal" life. Do you believe her behavior was justified? Why or why not?

4. While most of us never disobeyed our parents, talk about that one time you went against them and did what you wanted. Did you get away with it? If not, what were

the consequences?

5. If you have children, have they ever been defiant of the rules you've imposed? What were the consequences? Are you as strict with them as your parents were with you?

6. If you are a parent formerly raised in a strict religious environment, do you find yourself being more lenient with your child? Why or why not?

7. If going to the hospital or being treated by modern medicine went against your religion, would you comply?

8. If you identify with a religion, are there any rules or commandments that you oppose, feel are a bit too strict, or totally disagree with? Discuss.

9. What do you think of how Jennifer handled Abby's initial not feeling well? Can you empathize with her position of trying to obey her husband and be true to the faith?

10. What about Valarie, Jackie, and Miss Christine, who were not Illuminated yet

treated Raina like family?

11. Raina took dire steps to gain help for her sister. What do you think about her actions? Would you ever take a relative to court? In what situation?

12. Abby's parents took equally desperate measures to protect their daughter from a perceived injustice. What do you think about their decision(s)? Is there an instance when you'd help a loved one even if it meant going against other family members or breaking the law?

13. Social media played a large role in the outcome for Raina, Abby, and their family. Have you ever used the internet to bring attention to or settle a family matter? Would you? What do you think about how it was used here?

14. Love was a driving force in this story. Do you believe that love conquers all?

15. Throughout the story, Raina had to make hard choices between the life she'd been handed and the one she wanted. What similar choices have you had to make? Who was affected? Are you living

out someone else's expectations, or walking a path you've chosen? If not the latter . . . what are you waiting for?!?!

ABOUT THE AUTHOR

Lutishia Lovely burst onto the literary scene with *Sex in the Sanctuary* and now, more than a dozen books later, hasn't even thought about slowing down. When not writing contemporary fiction, she lends her muse to her alter-ego, Zuri Day, and writes steamy romances. But all work and no play makes Tish a dull girl, so she knows how to put down the pen and pick up a good time. Lutishia loves to hear from readers, so visit her online at LutishiaLovely.com, or on Facebook and Twitter @lutishialovely.

The employees of Thorndike Press hope you have enjoyed this Large Print book. All our Thorndike, Wheeler, and Kennebec Large Print titles are designed for easy reading, and all our books are made to last. Other Thorndike Press Large Print books are available at your library, through selected bookstores, or directly from us.

For information about titles, please call:
(800) 223-1244

or visit our website at:
gale.com/thorndike

To share your comments, please write:
Publisher
Thorndike Press
10 Water St., Suite 310
Waterville, ME 04901